A MATTER OF PEDIGREE

Books by Leslie Meier

Lucy Stone Mysteries
Mistletoe Murder
Tippy Toe Murder
Trick or Treat Murder
Back to School Murder
Valentine Murder
Christmas Cookie Murder
Turkey Day Murder
Wedding Day Murder
Birthday Party Murder
Father's Day Murder
Star Spangled Murder
New Year's Eve Murder
Bake Sale Murder
Candy Cane Murder
St. Patrick's Day Murder
Mother's Day Murder
Wicked Witch Murder
Gingerbread Cookie Murder
English Tea Murder
Chocolate Covered Murder
Easter Bunny Murder
Christmas Carol Murder
French Pastry Murder

Candy Corn Murder
British Manor Murder
Eggnog Murder
Turkey Trot Murder
Silver Anniversary Murder
Yule Log Murder
Haunted House Murder
Invitation Only Murder
Christmas Sweets
Christmas Card Murder
Irish Parade Murder
Halloween Party Murder
Easter Bonnet Murder
Irish Coffee Murder
Mother of the Bride Murder
Easter Basket Murder
Patchwork Quilt Murder
Bridal Shower Murder
Halloween Night Murder

A Carole & Poopsie Mystery
A Matter of Pedigree

Published by Kensington Publishing Corp.

A MATTER OF PEDIGREE

Leslie Meier

KENSINGTON PUBLISHING CORP.

This book is a work of fiction. Names, characters, businesses, organizations, places, events, and incidents either are the product of the author's imagination or are used fictitiously. Any resemblance to actual persons, living or dead, events, or locales is entirely coincidental.

To the extent that the image or images on the cover of this book depict a person or persons, such person or persons are merely models, and are not intended to portray any character or characters featured in the book.

KENSINGTON BOOKS are published by

Kensington Publishing Corp.
900 Third Avenue
New York, NY 10022

Copyright © 2025 by Leslie Meier

All rights reserved. No part of this book may be reproduced in any form or by any means without the prior written consent of the Publisher, excepting brief quotes used in reviews.

Without limiting the author's and publisher's exclusive rights, any unauthorized use of this publication to train generative artificial intelligence (AI) technologies is expressly prohibited.

All Kensington titles, imprints, and distributed lines are available at special quantity discounts for bulk purchases for sales promotion, premiums, fund-raising, educational, or institutional use. Special book excerpts or customized printings can also be created to fit specific needs. For details, write or phone the office of the Kensington Special Sales Manager: Attn. Special Sales Department, Kensington Publishing Corp., 900 Third Ave., New York, NY 10022. Phone: 1-800-221-2647.

KENSINGTON and the KENSINGTON COZIES teapot logo Reg. US Pat. & TM Off.

ISBN: 978-1-4967-5302-1

Printed in the United States of America

A MATTER
OF PEDIGREE

Chapter One

December 2023

"You're going to kill them," she said, making eye contact with her two companions. "You're going to blow them away."

As if providing emphasis to the tense situation, a stiff December wind kicked up, bending the bare branches of the trees and clattering the tightly curled leaves of the enormous rhododendron bushes on either side of the grim mansion's impressive and rather intimidating portal.

"Follow me," she said, charging up the steep stone steps. "Don't be nervous; you've got this," she added, crossing her fingers for luck. Real estate agent Susan Weaver had high hopes for this deal; she stood to make a killing if the owners agreed to accept Frank and Carole Capobianco's generous offer. "You've got plenty of ammo."

Frank Capobianco had reason to be optimistic. The four million he was willing to pay for the condo at prestigious Prospect Place was double the asking price. But money was no object to Frank; he was rolling in the stuff. It hadn't always been that way, of course. He'd grown up in the Italian Federal Hill section of Providence, Rhode Island, and after graduating from high school, he'd taken his place in the family business, Capobianco and Sons. He'd made a good living working in the plumbing and heating business, but it wasn't until his patent for the Bye-Bye Toilet was purchased by Wexler Industries that he began to see serious dough. Frank's invention of the low-flow fixture, which was guaranteed to work as well as traditional water-guzzling models, was seen as a genuine breakthrough by the industry. The Bye-Bye Toilet technology was quickly embraced by the green building movement, and the royalties had started pouring in. Global warming was the best thing that ever happened to Frank.

And now, his pockets stuffed with money, Frank was ready to take his rightful place in the city of his birth. He wanted to let everyone know he'd arrived, he was a success. A big deal. A very big deal. And the best way to do that was by moving out of Federal Hill and buying into Prospect Place, the absolute primo address on College Hill in the city's most exclusive neighborhood, the extremely hoitsy-toitsy East Side.

Unlike on Federal Hill, where the cramped wood tenements were jammed together in the streets around Atwells Avenue, the substantial brick and stone houses in the East Side stood in spacious gardens, rising out of professionally landscaped green lawns dotted with leafy trees and flowering shrubs. And none was grander than Prospect Place, built of sturdy ship's timbers and carved blocks of stone, its wooded acre securely walled off from its neighbors.

Erected in the eighteenth century, the edifice was a tribute to the daring and financial success of its builder, Jonathan Browne. One of the first to join the fight for independence from Great Britain, his fortune had grown along with the young nation as his ships plowed the waves of the vast Atlantic Ocean, reaping profits from the notorious Triangular Trade. Jonathan's ships brought human cargo from Africa to the West Indies, trading men, women, and children into slavery for the molasses and sugar the hungry new nation demanded. And although Jonathan lived hundreds of years before Frank, his motives for building Prospect Place were exactly the same as Frank's. From his lofty perch on the high hill overlooking the city and its bustling harbor, the massive stone structure announced to the world that Jonathan Browne was a man of wealth and importance.

Now, more than two centuries later, Frank identified with Jonathan Browne, apart from the reprehensible and disgusting human trafficking, of course. Like Jonathan, he was a man of vision who'd risen above the common mass. It was time to proclaim his ascension to the upper class, the one percent.

Carole, Frank's wife, didn't share his enthusiasm for the massive mansion, but she had dressed carefully for this interview in hopes of making a good impression. She was beginning, however, to think the taupe Ferragamos with the four-inch heels may have been a mistake. They were far and away the best shoes in her extensive collection, but she was having trouble negotiating the steps, which tilted this way and that. Nearly losing her balance, she grabbed Frank's arm. He responded by taking her elbow to steady her and then squeezing her hand, and Carole felt a sudden surge of affection for him. She hoped he wasn't in for a big disappointment.

Unlike her husband, who'd gone to work straight from high school, Carole had spent a year at Mount Holyoke College, one of the highly selective Seven Sisters. It was there that she'd had her first brush with the East Coast snobbism practiced by the daughters of the White Anglo-Saxon Protestant elite, or WASPs, as they were called by the other scholarship students. It took only a question or two for these privileged girls to identify their own kind: "Where did you prep? Where do you summer? Did you bring your horse?" If you didn't have the right answers, you were clearly not a member of the tribe and not worth knowing.

At the time, Carole had been stung by their attitude, and she'd been relieved when Frank got her pregnant during summer vacation, a vacation spent working as a waitress in one of the restaurants on Federal Hill. A hasty marriage was arranged, Carole and Frank settled into the third-floor apartment at the top of his parents' tenement, and Carole was warmly embraced as a young wife and mother by the Hill's traditional matriarchy. There was always someone to mind the kids, someone to gossip with over coffee and biscotti, someone's shoulder to cry on. Now, looking at the forbidding structure Frank was determined would be their next home, Carole was afraid they would encounter the same snobbish attitude she had faced at Mount Holyoke.

Susan rang the bell, and they huddled together on the stoop as the cold wind blew around them. They'd dressed to impress instead of for the weather, and Carole was freezing in her beautifully tailored Armani suit; she didn't like to think what the wind was doing to the hair she'd had styled that very afternoon. Frank was getting restless as they waited on the doorstep. "What's taking so long?" he fumed, rubbing his hands together.

The door was finally opened by a very slight woman with thinning, faded red hair, dressed in a pleated plaid skirt and a threadbare cashmere twin set topped with a truly fabulous string of pearls. Carole's heart sank, as she knew the look, but the woman's welcome was warm.

"Come in, come in," she urged, "we're all waiting for you. Oh, my goodness gracious, haven't I forgotten my manners? This is Susan, of course, and you are the Capobiancos, and I am Millicent Shaw." She grabbed Carole's and Frank's hands in turn. "I am so happy to finally meet you."

Somewhat reassured, Carole smiled at Frank and straightened his tie. He was built like a fire plug, there was no denying it, but in a blue oxford-cloth, button-down shirt, a conservative tie, and a Harris tweed sport coat with leather patches on the sleeves, he could pass for a college professor who enjoyed his dinner a bit too much. Carole hoped she hadn't overdone it when she chose his outfit at Brooks Brothers.

They hardly had time to take in the worn Oriental rug, the stately grandfather clock, the hand-painted antique wallpaper, and the staircase with elaborately carved mahogany balusters before Millicent opened one of the massive doors on either side of the hall and ushered them inside. They found themselves in a spacious sitting room with wood-paneled walls and long, red velvet curtains hanging on either side of the tall, paned windows. Five people were seated on the leather sofas and chairs arranged in front of the fireplace, and from the looks of them, Carole knew they were in enemy territory. She gave Frank's arm a pinch, warning him to let Susan introduce them.

"You all know me, I'm Susan Weaver from Prestige Properties, and I'm representing the vacant unit, Unit 3, which is owned by Jon Browne. Tonight, I've brought two exceptionally well-qualified buyers, Frank and Carole Capobianco." She paused. "Millicent, could you please do the honors?"

"Oh yes, oh yes," said Millicent, nodding and fluttering her hands. "Let me introduce the other owners. First, of course, is Hosea Browne." She indicated a tall, thin, elderly man seated in a massive leather wing chair. Wire-rimmed glasses were perched on his hawkish nose, his gray hair was thinning above a high forehead, and long parentheses ran from each side of his nose to his thin slit of a mouth. Like Frank, he was wearing an oxford-cloth shirt and tweed blazer, but his were soft and worn from years of wear, unlike Frank's crisp new togs. Hosea tented his hands in front of his chest and nodded.

"As you no doubt know, Prospect Place was built by Mr. Browne's ancestor, Jonathan Browne," said Susan. "It was the Browne family home until 2008, when it was converted into five luxurious units and became the premier address in Providence."

"A lot of folks took a hit in 2008 when the stock market tanked," observed Frank, with a knowing nod.

Hosea was quick to put this notion to rest. "The place was too big; there's just myself and my brother now. Made no sense for us to rattle around in here all by ourselves." Left unsaid was his rock-solid belief that failure to capitalize on a potential source of income was a sin of the highest order.

"Absolutely," agreed Millicent. "Times change, and we have to change with them." She indicated a well-dressed young couple with blond hair, seated together on one of the sofas. "This is Celerie and Mark Lonsdale; they have the charming unit on the top floor."

"The attic," said Celerie, giving a broad smile that revealed a dazzling set of very white teeth. "So nice to meet you," she said, speaking through her teeth as she extended a pale, slender hand. Carole couldn't help noticing the decidedly unimpressive diamond and slim gold wedding band on her other hand.

"Same here," agreed Mark, also rising and offering a firm but dampish hand.

Once the handshakes were completed, Millicent continued her introductions. "Last, but not least by any means, we have our lovely professors, Stuart and Angelique Poole."

Angelique, a dark-haired woman of a certain age, chicly dressed in black, remained seated beside her husband on the second sofa but offered her hand. Her nails, Carole noticed, were neatly trimmed but free of polish. "*Enchanté*," she said. Her husband, Stuart, casually dressed in a cardigan with leather buttons, rose and also shook their hands.

Introductions completed, Millicent indicated three straight-backed dining chairs with elaborately carved backs and urged them to sit. She herself perched on a hassock shoved beside Hosea's armchair. Frank and Carole sat down, but Susan remained standing.

"As you all know," she said, "the Capobiancos have put forward a very generous offer, which is actually double the asking price of two million dollars."

"That is, unfortunately, of no importance to us," said Hosea, sounding regretful. "The unit is owned by my younger brother, and none of us have any financial interest in the sale. Our concern," he said, including the other owners in a sweeping gesture, "is whether the Capobiancos will fit into our tight little community." He paused. "We want to know if they are the right sort. As Mrs. Weaver mentioned, Prospect Place will be forever associated with the Browne family name, and therefore we absolutely cannot tolerate the least hint of impropriety."

Frank shifted in his chair. Like trafficking in human lives wasn't improper, he thought, biting his lips.

A touch of color rose in Susan's cheeks. "I can assure you that Mr. and Mrs. Capobianco will be terrific neighbors. Mr. Capobianco's business is extremely successful, and they will have no problem at all assuming the financial obligations of ownership, such as maintenance fees and taxes. In addition," she added, with a nod to Celerie, "I know Mrs. Capobianco is eager to decorate the unit in the style it deserves."

"I'm certainly glad to hear that," said Celerie, nodding and tossing back her stylishly long, wavy, blond hair, hair that Carole was sure was not naturally blond. "You may know that I have a little decorating business, and I already have some ideas."

"Terrific," said Carole, more enthusiastically than she felt. She somehow doubted that Celerie's taste matched hers, but she was willing to play along.

"I think we all understand that Mr. Capobianco has been remarkably successful, thanks to his ingenuity with toilet fixtures," said Hosea, adding a sniff. "What we are interested in is the Capobiancos themselves. What are your interests?" he demanded, fixing them in his hawklike gaze.

"Thanks for asking," said Frank, placing his hands on his knees and leaning forward. "I'm a big sports fan, love the Pats and the Sox, and what about those Celtics, hey?" He looked around, but didn't get any response from the professor or Hosea and only a small nod from Mark Lonsdale. "I love fishing. I've got a boat, *Royal Flush*, I call her. It's, you know, one of them double entenders."

Millicent smiled at this, as did Angelique, but the men in the group were not amused. Hosea, especially, seemed offended and pressed his narrow lips together. Carole shifted nervously in her seat, worried that things weren't going their way.

"I'm not much of a churchgoer," continued Frank. "I get to Holy Ghost on the big holidays, Easter and Christmas, but Carole here goes regularly, and she always puts plenty in the collection plate."

The others all nodded approvingly, but Hosea's back stiffened.

"And I don't mind admitting I have a fondness for Foxwoods and Mohegan Sun," added Frank, naming two casinos located over the state line in Connecticut. "O' course my favorite is Bally's here in Little Rhody; might as well keep that money in the state, no?"

The others laughed, apparently amused at Frank's forthrightness, but Hosea remained expressionless. "And what about you, Mrs. Capobianco?"

"Well, I attended Mount Holyoke College," she began, going straight for her biggest gun. Unfortunately, it didn't have quite the bang she'd hoped. Going to a Seven Sisters school was par for the course with this crowd. "But I left to marry Frank. I've been a homemaker my whole life; we have two children, a son and a daughter. Connie is a first-year associate at Dunne and Willoughby," she said, naming one of the city's top law firms. But once again, these folks were not impressed. "And our son, Frank Junior, is a sophomore at RISD." On the Hill, admission to the Rhode Island School of Design was a feather in anyone's cap, but of this group only Celerie seemed interested. The others considered RISD as somewhat inferior to its Ivy League College Hill neighbor, Brown University.

"I'm active in the Altar Guild at Holy Ghost," continued Carole, plugging away. "I try to keep in shape at Curves. I help Frank's folks; they're getting on now and have trouble with their health insurance and driver's licenses, things like that." Carole was aware she was running out of ammunition. "And I'm always happy to bake something for a good cause; anybody who's having a bake sale only has to call," she finished.

"Very laudable, I'm sure," said Hosea, not meaning a word. "Well, would you prefer to step outside while we vote, or would you prefer to remain?"

Carole was half out of her seat when Frank grabbed her hand, restraining her. He was never one to run from a challenge. "We'll stay," he said.

"Very well," said Hosea, once again tenting his hands and surveying the room. "Does anyone feel the need for discussion?"

There was a bit of an awkward silence until Millicent spoke up. "I do. First of all, I want to thank Mr. and Mrs. Capobianco for coming tonight and for their interest in joining our little community." She smiled warmly at Frank and Carole. "I think the Capobiancos are a lovely couple and would be a terrific addition to Prospect Place."

"I agree," said Angelique, speaking in a charming French accent. "In France, you know, life is richer because people of all sorts intermingle. No one looks down on the waiter; he is a master of his craft, as is the *boulanger*, and the *boucher*, and the *artiste*. Sometimes you have all these different people in one family, gathering on Sundays for the big family dinner, along with the *avocat*, the *docteur*." She looked to her husband for confirmation, and he gave a firm nod. "I would like very much for us to open the doors to Prospect Place wide and to welcome the Capobiancos. "*Bienvenus*," she added, concluding.

Hosea turned toward Mark and Celerie, and Mark began speaking. "As for Celerie and myself, well, we also feel the Capobiancos would be a terrific addition. I mean, how often do you need a plumber, but you can't get one?" he demanded, getting a little round of laughter. "If Frank moves in, that definitely won't be a problem. And I don't know about you, but I can't remember when I last had some home-baked cookies." He took his wife's hand. "Celerie is awfully busy with her business..."

"Too busy to bake," added Celerie. "That's for sure."

"So we think it would be great to come home to decent water pressure and the smell of something delicious baking in the oven," said Mark.

"This is wonderful news," said Susan, hopping to her feet and setting her briefcase on the chair. "I happen to have a purchase and sales agreement all ready for signing, and I understand that you, Hosea, have power of attorney for your brother, Jon, who is out of the country. Is that correct?"

"It is indeed," said Hosea.

"Wonderful," said Susan, producing the paper and carrying it across the Persian rug to him. But instead of taking the proffered document, Hosea brushed it aside.

"I will not sign that."

"But I thought everyone was agreed?" said Susan, stammering a bit. "What possible objection could you have?"

"I do object," said Hosea, "and I'm sure my brother would also object. In his absence, Jon has given me his power of attorney. As is stipulated in the deeds, all sales must be approved unanimously by all the owners."

"But you're turning down an offer that is double the asking price," said Susan, unwilling to watch her commission go down the drain.

"As I mentioned, I'm acting for my younger brother,

who I must admit has never shown the least interest in the prudent management of his finances." Hosea twisted his thin, gray lips into something like a smile. "But, that aside, it's for the Capobiancos' own good," he said, in a condescending tone, as if he were talking to an errant child. "I'm sure they are wonderful people and much appreciated in their community, but I am quite sure they would not be happy here, among people like ourselves. That's all; it's nothing personal." He turned and looked at Carole, baring his yellowed teeth. "I do hope you won't take this personally."

Carole felt as if she'd been slapped across the face, but she was determined not to let it show. She swallowed hard and found her voice. "Of course..." she began, but she was interrupted by Frank.

He was on his feet, fists clenched and jaw set. "Take it personally? You bet I'm taking it personally," he shouted.

Carole jumped up and grabbed his arm, attempting to lead him out of the room. "Let's go," she urged. "We're not wanted here, and that's fine. There are plenty of other, nicer places where they won't expect you to fix the plumbing."

Frank took a deep breath. "You're right, babe." He laughed, a harsh, dismissive sound like a cough. "These people are not worth raising my blood pressure," he said, heading for the door. He paused by Susan and took her hand. "Sorry we wasted your time, honey."

"I'll be in touch," she said, folding the unsigned agreement and stuffing it in her briefcase. "Can you find your way out?"

"No problem," said Frank, wrapping his arm around Carole's waist. They stepped together into the hallway and he pulled open the massive six-panel door, carved from a single slab of mahogany over two hundred years ago, fingering the gleaming, handwrought brass knob. "I'd like to kill that, that stuck-up old fossil of a Yankee," he was heard to say, before the door closed behind them.

Chapter Two

March 2024

Carole wasn't naturally an early riser, but her little dog was. Poopsie, actually Shady Brook's Madame Pompadour, was a pedigreed Brittany, which made her one classy dog. Brittanys were bred as bird dogs; they're the smallest pointers, and they all have docked tails, elegantly feathered legs, and dazzling white coats spotted with either red, black, or liver patches. Poopsie was a redhead, her long, droopy ears covered with soft red hair that frizzed when it rained, and the patches of color spread from her ears to circle her eyes, giving her a mischievous, masked appearance. Her high energy level made her playful, but her sherry-colored, pleading eyes were all spaniel. Carole couldn't resist those eyes, even though the clock said it was barely six o'clock.

"Okay, Poopsie," she sighed, throwing back the covers and getting up, leaving Frank snoring on the other side of the king-size bed. "We'll go out."

Poopsie bounded through the living room to the front door, furiously wagging her little dishmop tail and waiting anxiously as Carole pulled on a track suit and boots and made her way through the dim apartment, pausing in the entry hall to put on her coat and leash the dog. Minutes later, they were climbing the Holden Street hill to Smith Street, headed for the spacious lawn around the state capitol.

Like all Rhode Islanders, Carole was proud of the enormous white-marble, wedding cake of a building that embodied the great spirit of the tiny state, though she sometimes wondered if the building's exceptional size was a way of compensating for Little Rhody's minuscule size. As a young child in school, she'd learned all about the building, how its dome was constructed only of marble blocks, making it the fourth-largest such dome in the world after Saint Peter's Basilica, the Minnesota State Capitol, and the Taj Mahal. The sculpture on top, newly replaced following restoration was the Independent Man. The statue recalled the state's founding by freethinker Roger Williams and its status as a colonial sanctuary for Quakers and others fleeing the restrictive and punitive Puritan government of neighboring Massachusetts.

Carole glanced at the building as she walked by on the brick sidewalk, but the thing she liked best about this morning walk was the sight of the sun rising over the East Side hills, dotted with trees and houses. It was chilly and misty, and Poopsie was tugging at the leash, practically pulling her arm off, but the sight of the gray sky giving way to rosy dawn made it all worthwhile.

As she walked down the hill and turned into the path that meandered through the large statehouse lawn, Carole counted her blessings. It was something she tried to do every day; she'd done it even before they got rich, ticking off things like health, the kids' successes, a roof over her head, food to eat, clothes to wear. It was important to be grateful, she thought, and on this early March morning, the thing she was most grateful for was that the old snob Hosea Browne had nixed their application to buy into Prospect Place. Poopsie spotted a squirrel and darted after it, yanking Carole's arm, but she hardly noticed. She was thinking about how much she loved her new apartment at the Esplanade, a derelict factory that had been rehabbed into luxurious, loft-style apartments. It was only a rental, sure, and they were still looking for property to invest in, but it was a terrific temporary home. They had one of the best and biggest apartments, high up on the top floor, with eighteen-foot ceilings and enormous windows that wrapped around three sides of the building and gave a gorgeous view of the Woonasquatucket River and the west side of the city, including Federal Hill and the red, neon Coca-Cola sign on top of the nearby bottling plant.

Carole loved that view, and she loved the fresh, clean apartment where everything was in the right place. Until now she'd always lived in older buildings. They'd started in the apartment in Mom and Big Frank's tenement; then they'd bought a tenement of their own, keeping one of the three apartments for rental income and combining the other two into a big space for their growing family. But even after the remodeling, there were never enough electric sockets, the rooms were small and cramped, and there wasn't nearly enough closet space for her constantly growing wardrobe.

None of these things were problems at the Esplanade. Their apartment was enormous, with an open floor plan that Carole loved. She could cook in the beautiful kitchen with brand-new, top-of-the-line stainless-steel appliances and Calacatta marble countertops while keeping an eye on the TV and chatting with Frank sitting in his brand-new leather recliner. There were tons of closets; one even had a washer and dryer, which meant no more climbing up and down the cellar stairs, and both bedrooms had roomy en suite bathrooms, lousy with more Calacatta marble. And not only were there plenty of electrical outlets, they also had Wi-Fi in every room.

The truth was, she told herself, as she and Poopsie made the turn around the back of the statehouse and started across the lawn toward Providence Place mall, the new apartment was much nicer than the unit Frank had been so hot to buy at Prospect Place. That apartment was dark and poky and dusty; there was only one bathroom instead of the four she had at the Esplanade, his and hers in the master suite, plus two others, and there was no parking. One of her favorite things about the Esplanade was the adjacent parking garage, which was connected to the residence by a bridge high above Edith Street. That meant you didn't ever have to hunt for a parking space and could get to your car without facing the weather or ruining your hair.

Carole and Poopsie climbed the steps leading to Francis Street, and Carole paused at the top to take one last look at the gorgeous pink sky, then headed back across the bridge over Route 95 and on toward home, keeping Poopsie on a short leash whenever they passed a pedestrian. Poopsie had been known to nip the ankles of passersby, but if Carole kept up a steady stream of soothing conversation and a tight hold on the leash, she could usually get back home without incident, as long as nobody spoke to her. Problem was, people in Providence tended to be friendly and usually gave you a nod and a "good morning" at a minimum. And Poopsie was so cute that sometimes they'd want to pet her. Not a good idea. Poopsie did not approve of strangers.

This morning, however, Carole made it back to the apartment building without any unfortunate encounters and even walked all the way around to the front entrance to pick up the morning paper. Nobody else was in the vast lobby, and she relaxed her hold on Poopsie's lead as she walked to the elevator, passing the mailboxes, the 75-foot lap pool, the community room, and a seating area with modern furniture grouped around a gas fireplace. The brick walls were hung with enormous black-and-white photos of people who once worked in the building when it was a factory: women in shirtwaists with leg-o'-mutton sleeves, men bent over lathes and presses. An odd choice of art, thought Carole, who figured that none of these people could ever have afforded to pay the current rent, even allowing for inflation. She pressed the button for the elevator and opened the paper, as she usually did, to check the headlines.

This morning's headline was a stunner: BLOODY MURDER ROCKS EAST SIDE.

The elevator arrived, the doors slid open, but Carole didn't move. She stood there, her eyes flying over the black print, and the doors closed. Poopsie yipped, expressing her displeasure at this unreasonable delay, and she pushed the button again. She could hardly believe what she was reading. Hosea Browne was dead, apparently bashed on the head, possibly with a pipe or other blunt instrument. His bloody corpse had been found at a construction site on the Woonasquatucket River, not far from the Esplanade.

This time, Carole got in when the elevator arrived, checking first to make sure it was empty. Poopsie didn't like to share her personal space. Reaching the fifth floor without encountering anyone, she hurried down the carpeted hall to the apartment. Frank was up, standing in the kitchen in his robe and slippers, pouring himself a mug of coffee.

"You won't believe this!" she declared, excitedly. "Hosea Browne is dead! Blunt injury trauma or something like that."

Frank took the news in stride. He didn't spill a drop but continued pouring until he'd filled his king-size mug, then replaced the carafe on the coffee maker. He added some cream and sugar to his mug, stirred, then took a swallow. It was only then that he spoke. "Serves the old bastard right," he said, taking the paper and shuffling over to the breakfast area in his slippers. "You didn't happen to notice, did ya, whether the Sox beat the Phillies down in Florida?"

While Frank read the sports section, Carole cooked breakfast. Frank liked three eggs, sunny-side up, bacon or sausage, and toast with lots of butter. Thank God, he was faithful about taking his Lipitor. Carole made herself a whole-wheat English muffin, lightly buttered, and accompanied it with a 80-calorie pot of yogurt. While they ate, she peppered Frank with questions.

"What was Hosea Browne doing at the Factory?" she asked, naming the construction site where his body was found. She knew that Capobianco and Sons had the plumbing contract for the huge riverfront development that was going to combine residential and commercial space in a garden setting.

"He was one of the backers," said Frank, shoveling in a forkful of egg.

"I didn't know that," said Carole, feeling a bit uneasy.

"Yeah," said Frank, his mouth full of toast. "He's a venture capitalist."

"I didn't know you had any contact with him, except for the condo," said Carole.

Frank shrugged. "He came around once or twice; it's no biggy. Business is business. I haven't had any problems with him on the job. We do good work, always have. What's he gonna say, anyway?" Frank finished off his coffee. "Guys like him don't know squat about plumbing."

After breakfast, as she loaded the dishwasher, Carole tried to put to rest the niggling little worry that was growing in her mind. Frank would never, it was out of the question. But he did know people; everybody in Providence knew somebody who would, if you asked. But would Frank ask, or maybe just drop a hint? If he did say something in passing, about what a jerk Hosea was, for instance, somebody might take it the wrong way, depending on how much the guy owed Frank. Plenty of people owed Frank; he was a generous guy. If you were having a tough time and needed rent or a car payment, he was quick to pull out the fat roll of hundreds he kept in his pocket and peel off a few. "No problem," he'd say with a shrug. "Pay me back when you got it. No rush." And sometimes payback came in the form of favors: a free car repair, a dinner at one of the restaurants on Federal Hill, a pair of shoes or a new suit, a couple of cases of wine.

It wasn't that Frank was connected, no way. It was just the way things were in Providence. She figured the stuff he occasionally brought home was just the guy version of the favors she traded with her girlfriends, like babysitting, when the kids were little, or dropping off a tray of lasagna or manicotti when somebody died, or buying a case of cookies you didn't need and wouldn't eat from some cousin's little Girl Scout.

Sure, Providence had a bit of a reputation, but the days when Raymond Patriarca sat outside his Coin-O-Matic storefront and collected tribute from anyone who wanted to do business on Federal Hill were long gone. Things were different now, she reminded herself, and there was no sense in letting her mind run away with itself. Shame on her for even thinking for one moment that Frank could ever possibly be involved in a murder. She knew her husband inside and out, and while he might seem a little rough on the outside, she knew he was a big softy on the inside. She'd go crazy if she kept thinking like this, she told herself as she changed into her workout clothes. Better instead to work it off in the gym, on the elliptical, then finish up with some laps in the pool. And by the time she was back in the apartment, taking a shower, she was already thinking ahead to the rest of the day and trying to decide what to wear. Her Versace jeans, she thought, with a cashmere sweater and her new retro, faux-leopard-skin jacket. Cute. And, of course, her new Jimmy Choo stilettos.

She was greeted like a hero when she breezed into Macy's at Providence Place, but even so, she had to admit it was a poor substitute for her beloved Nordstrom, which was a victim of the financial crisis. Back then, in the good old days, she'd always stopped to give the piano player a hug and a ten, and he'd play her favorite song, "La Vie en Rose," for her. But times changed, right? And the girl at the Bobbi Brown counter was waving at her.

"Hi, Mrs. Capobianco," she chirped. "We have some fab new eyeliners."

"Not today," she called back, with a wave. "I'm in a hurry."

"Come in for a free makeover," the girl urged. "You'd look great in the new teal eyeshadow."

"I'll keep it in mind," promised Carole, hurrying on through the cosmetics department to the escalator. Up on the second floor, the girls in the designer collections waved to her. "Just arrived," one called to her. "Gorgeous, sexy spring outfits from Vince Camuto."

"Send me a text reminder," she called, waving her cell phone. "I don't have time today," she explained, making a beeline for the lingerie department, where she hoped to find a birthday present for Connie.

"She's a lawyer," she told the sales associate, Lily. She knew Lily from before, when she'd worked at Nordstrom.

"Wow, you must be really proud, Mrs. Capobianco."

"I am. But the problem is she has to wear such conservative clothes to work, and she works all the time. That's why I thought of lingerie. It can be lovely and lacy and sexy, and nobody sees it because it's under her clothes."

"Unless she wants them to," said Lily, with a naughty twinkle in her eye.

"Right," agreed Carole, with a smile. "And maybe I'll just look for a little something for myself. Something that Frank would like."

"Good idea," said Lily. "Black? Leopard print? Red?"

"Red," said Carole. "I heard somewhere that it's the color of sex."

She and Lily had a good laugh over that.

Twenty minutes later, she was back in her Porsche Cayenne, tapping her nails impatiently on the steering wheel as she waited in line at the exit. Parking for less than two hours was free, but you still had to insert the ticket in the machine. Really, why? she fumed, impatiently, as someone ahead was trying various credit cards.

Finally through the lift gate, she zoomed through a yellow light at the exit out onto Promenade Street, heading straight for the Hill and Scialo's bakery to order zeppole for the traditional Saint Joseph's Day celebration. Usually it was just family, but this year they wanted to show off the new apartment and were planning an open house.

"How many do you want, hon?" asked the counter girl, when it was her turn. There was almost always a line at Scialo's, and today was no exception.

"Two dozen?" Carole wasn't sure. The pastries were enormous and very sweet, loaded with whipped cream and lemon curd.

"You tell me, hon," said the girl, looking off into the distance.

"Two's probably not going to be enough. Give me four dozen."

"Okay."

Carole was adding up everybody she thought might come. "No, make it six."

"You got it, hon. They'll be ready for pickup in the morning on the nineteenth. Something for today?"

Carole looked around the bakery, studying the gleaming glass cases filled with cookies, pastries, cakes, and bread. "I'll take a loaf, and some cannoli. A half dozen. To take with me."

"No problem," said the girl, folding a box for the cannoli.

Leaving the bakery, Carole walked across the plaza to Venda Ravioli. Frankie Junior loved Pellegrino orange soda, and she thought she'd grab him some, plus some of their fabulous prepared takeout food, since she knew that he never bothered to cook for himself. There was no line at Venda and no numbers you pulled from a machine; you just had to catch the eye of the guy behind the counter. Carole never had any trouble with that.

"Hi, Mrs. Capobianco. What can I get for you today?"

"What's good, Gino?"

"The stuffed mushrooms, the lemon chicken breast, the veal, what can I tell you? It's all good."

"You're right. Just give me some of each, say a pound. And throw in some bean salad. The kid needs some vitamins."

"So this is for Frankie Junior?"

"Frank-O, that's what he wants us to call him," said Carole. "He thinks he's an artist."

"Well, here you go, for Frank-O. Hey, I'm a poet!" exclaimed Gino, handing over a stack of containers.

Carole chuckled. "You're a poet and don't know it," she said, taking the food.

She was back outside, stowing the groceries in the SUV and wondering if she had time to pop in on Mom and Big Frank, just to see how they were doing and maybe have a bite of lunch with them, when her cell phone rang. Probably the girls from Macy's, reminding her about those Vince Camuto dresses, she thought.

"Hi, Carole; thank God, I got you."

It was Paulie, Frank's brother, and he sounded upset.

"What's the matter, Paulie?" she demanded. "Tell me!"

"It's Frank . . ."

Carole's immediate thought was that big breakfast; he was a heart attack waiting to happen. "Is he okay?"

"Yeah, sure. Kind of. He's not sick or anything."

"Well, what is it?"

"It's the cops. They came this morning and arrested him. They said he killed some Hosie guy." "Hosea Browne?"

"That's it. How'd you know?"

"Just a guess," said Carole, ending the call. "Damn, damn, damn," she repeated, pounding her fist on the Cayenne's Carrara White Metallic roof.

Chapter Three

Climbing behind the steering wheel of the roomy SUV, Carole tried to think what to do. What were you supposed to do when your husband was arrested for murder? This was definitely new territory. She sat there for a minute, staring at her cell phone, scrolling down the list of contacts. Then she saw Connie's name. A no-brainer: Connie was a lawyer!

"Hi, Mom," she said, sounding harried. That's how she always sounded these days. They were working her like a dog at Dunne and Willoughby. "What do you want?"

"Sorry to bother you," began Carole, "but your father's been arrested for murder."

As intended, that got her attention. "What?"

"You heard me. The cops think he killed Hosea Browne."

"The venture capitalist?"

"Yeah."

"Wow."

"So what do I do?"

Connie sighed. "There's not much you can do except call his lawyer, but I bet Dad's already done that." She paused. "When was he arrested?"

"I'm not sure. Paulie just called me." Carole tapped her steering wheel with her nails. "You're a lawyer. Can't you get him out of wherever they've got him?"

"I can't get him out. Nobody can."

Carole was not used to taking no for an answer. "Why not?"

"Well, they're probably questioning him right now. And then he has to be arraigned—you know, formally charged with the crime. After that, a judge will set bail."

"Bail's no problem. How much do they want? I'll go to the bank and get it right away. Cash?"

Connie sighed again. "No, Ma. It doesn't work like that."

Carole was getting mad. What was with all this nonsense? "Why not?"

"Murder is a capital case. There has to be a hearing, and the judge will set bail."

"When will that be?"

"A day or two, probably. Daddy's lawyer will let you know."

"A day or two! That's crazy. Are they gonna keep him in jail?"

"Well, yeah, Ma. They think he killed somebody. They're not going to let him go free."

This was ridiculous, thought Carole. "Are you kidding me? The paper's full of people getting killed every day. The morning news is nothing but knife fights, drive-by shootings. Like that poor pregnant lady who got shot sitting on a bus and lost her precious unborn baby. Most of the time nobody even gets arrested. I don't know why they're picking on your father."

"Ma, this is different. That's street crime, mostly mentally ill people, gang fights, people on the bottom rung of the economic ladder. Dad is accused of killing Hosea Browne. He's a very important man. He's CEO of a venture capital company, a trustee at Brown University, and on the board of a couple of banks, too. He's got a finger in everything that happens in Providence."

"So you're telling me that Hosea Browne matters more than that lady on the bus? I thought this is America and everybody's equal."

"Come on, Ma," said Connie. "It's not fair, but that's the way it is. You know that as well as me." She paused. "They wouldn't make an arrest without some sort of evidence. Ma, you don't think it's possible Dad was involved somehow?"

Carole was outraged. "What are you saying? You think your father is a murderer!"

Connie was quick to defend herself. "I'm not saying that at all. I just want to know what you think is really going on here. The big picture."

"Well, I know your father is innocent! And no matter what they taught you at that goofy un-American law school, everybody in America is supposed to be innocent until they're proven guilty!"

And with that, Carole ended the call, wishing she could slam down the receiver, but you couldn't do that with a cell phone. Made you miss the good old days. She continued sitting in the car, staring at her phone, gradually becoming aware of a spicy, meaty scent. The food for Frank-O! Well, Connie was pretty much useless, which was not the return you expected for paying hundreds of thousands of dollars for law-school tuition, but that's what you got. She might as well take the food over to

Frankie Junior's place. He might even be home and have some ideas. She did her best thinking when she drove; maybe something would come to her.

Frankie Junior—she couldn't help it, she couldn't get used to this Frank-O business—lived in a tenement on the hill behind the Esplanade. In her opinion, it was an absolute horror, but she understood why he wanted to live independently. Not that she liked it, not when she and Frank would be more than happy to get him one of the cute studio apartments at the Esplanade. She was driving a bit too fast, coasting down the hill, and she had to brake hard in front of the ugly, brown-shingled building on Caverly Street that was built into the hill, with one side taller than the other.

Shaking her head over the building's somewhat dilapidated condition, she collected the bags of groceries and the bakery box and started the climb up to the porch. The door was unlocked, and she still had to climb another flight of stinky, rickety stairs to get to the apartment. That door was also unlocked, and she nudged it open with the pointed toe of her Jimmy Choo, grimacing at the sour smell that filled her nose. Frank-O definitely needed to do some laundry and change the sheets on his bed.

"Anybody home?" she called.

Nobody answered.

Sighing, she made her way through the clutter of dirty clothes, shoes, and books that littered the floor and went into the kitchen. Dirty dishes were stacked everywhere, the garbage was overflowing, a giant bluebottle fly buzzed at the window. She opened the refrigerator, which, thank goodness, was empty, and put the food containers inside, along with the soda and bread. She sure wasn't going to leave the bread out on the counter where whatever else lived in the place might get at it. There were some takeout menus stuck on the fridge door with magnets; she took one and, digging an eyebrow pencil out of her bag, wrote a note in giant letters over the notation for Family Dinner A: "Call me! Emergency! Love, Ma."

That ought to do it, she thought, hurrying out of there. She had more important things to do than worry about Frank-O's disgusting lifestyle. Back in the car, she had a sudden inspiration, remembering that kid Tom who lived next to Mom and Big Frank. Hadn't she heard somewhere he was a cop in the homicide division? It was worth a try. She had to call Mom and let her know what had happened anyway.

Mom's reaction was predictable. "My bambino!" she wailed. "My baby Frank! This can't be happening!"

"I know, it's all a big mistake. But in the meantime, I need some info. Remember that kid, Tom, used to live next to you? Isn't he a cop or something?"

"Little Tommy Paliotto. What a cutie. He's all grown up now. I thought he and Connie might've got together, both being interested in the law and all . . ."

"Right, Ma," said Carole, cutting her off. "Didn't I hear he works downtown in homicide? Something like that?"

"Yeah, he went to Northeastern up in Boston, got a degree in criminal justice."

"And he's a Providence cop now?"

"Yeah, a detective. I talked to his mother just the other day. He's married now and expecting a baby. Connie really missed her chance there."

"Yeah, too bad," agreed Carole. "Look, I gotta go. Give Big Frank my love, and don't worry; it's all a big mistake, and we'll get it straightened out."

Carole still had a couple of bars left on her cell phone, so she called 411 and got connected to the Providence Police Department's homicide division. "Detective Paliotto, please."

"Who shall I say is calling?"

Carole hesitated, wondering if she should give her maiden name. If she said Capobianco would she be labeled some sort of criminal, too? Then she reminded herself that even if Frank was accused, he wasn't convicted of anything. "Carole Capobianco," she said, in a firm voice.

The response was polite. "Sorry, Mrs. Capobianco. He's on another line. Can you hold?"

Carole checked her bars. She was down to one. "Okay," she said.

A minute or two later, little Tommy picked up, only now he sounded all grown up.

"Hi, Mrs. Capobianco. I bet you're calling about Frank."

"I sure am. What's going on?"

"Well, he's going to be charged with murdering Hosea Browne down at the Factory construction site."

"I know that. But why Frank?"

"Because the evidence all points to him," he said, matter-of-factly.

"What evidence?"

"He was at the scene..."

"Well, sure. He's got the plumbing contract. He's got to be there some of the time, right? Making sure the guys are doing a good job."

"Then there's the weapon, which the coroner thinks was a standard piece of copper tubing."

"So Frank is not the only plumber in the world, and there's lots of copper tubing around."

"Yeah, but Browne's secretary says he had an appointment with Frank, yesterday, at four o'clock, and nobody saw him after that until his body was discovered by the night watchman."

"Somebody could've killed him after the appointment, right?"

"Then there's the neighbors. We interviewed them first thing this morning, and they all remembered Frank saying he'd like to kill Hosea Browne."

"That was months ago, back in December," said Carole. "Frank was upset because we didn't get that apartment at Prospect Place."

"Exactly," said the detective. "In my business, we call that a motive."

Carole was about to say something she would have regretted, but that's when the phone gave a long beep and died. She sighed, tossed it in her purse, and started the car.

When she got back to the apartment, the landline was ringing, and she hurried to answer it, fending off Poopsies's frantic efforts to greet her.

"Hello," she said, putting the receiver to her ear and falling to her knees so Poopsie could lick her face. It was Vince Houlihan, Frank's lawyer.

"Mrs. Capobianco, I'm sorry to tell you . . ."

"I know all about it," said Carole, scratching Poopsie behind her ears. "They think Frank killed Hosea Browne."

"Right. Now I don't want you to worry. Frank did the right thing; he called me first thing. I've made it clear that he will not answer any questions unless I am present."

"That's good," said Carole. "How is he? Where is he? Can I see him?"

"He's being transported to the Intake Service Center at

the Rhode Island Department of Corrections. He'll have to be processed, but I think you can probably see him this afternoon. I'll try to set something up."

"Thanks," said Carole, in a small voice. All of a sudden, reality seemed to be crashing all around her. It was really true. Frank was accused of murder; he was in jail. He might spend the rest of his life in jail. Tears began rolling down her cheeks, and Poopsie gently licked them away.

"I'll be in touch," said Vince.

Carole got up and went into the bathroom, where she peed and smoothed some cooling Clinique Moisture Surge on her face. She put the cell phone on the charger, changed out of her heels and into her dog-walking boots, and put Poopsie on the leash for a quick walk. Back in the apartment, she made herself a salad, then found she couldn't eat it. Vince called and told her she could see Frank at four o'clock; he also told her the arraignment and bail hearing would take place tomorrow morning at ten.

"I'm confident he'll get bail," he said. "Bring your checkbook and Frank's passport. And, uh, dress conservatively, and it wouldn't hurt if you brought his parents along. They're pretty old, right?"

"Right," said Carole, getting the picture.

First things first, however. She had to decide what to wear to visit Frank this afternoon. She wandered into her gigantic closet, the one she'd had California Closets outfit for her, and studied her reflection in the three-way mirror. Funny, she thought, she looked just like she had earlier that day, before she'd learned that Frank was accused of murder. Her shoulder-length blond hair still needed a touch-up; the roots were showing, but that was kind of fashionable now. Her figure was still trim, but if she gave into her current craving for something chocolate, she'd start packing on the pounds. Note to self: eating wouldn't help. Neither would drinking, she told herself, resisting the urge to pour herself a stiff one. No, this was going to take self-discipline. She couldn't let herself go; she had to think of Frank.

She glanced around the closet, studying the lighted shelves holding designer bags and shoes, as if they were precious artifacts. Well, considering what they'd cost, they were. She studied the dresses, shirts, and pants, all hanging on one side, arranged by color. Lingerie and sweaters were folded in drawers on the other side. She perched on the stool in front of the vanity counter and thought: What was she going to wear? What would cheer Frank up?

Not the gray Armani suit she'd immediately thought of when Vince advised her to dress conservatively for court. That thing had bad memories, anyway, since she'd worn it at the ill-fated Prospect Place interview. No, she wanted something colorful, something cheery, something a bit risqué, for Frank.

She stripped off her cashmere sweater, noticing the lacy black bra she had on underneath. A glimpse of black lace, that was just the thing. On her feet, yanking open drawer after drawer, she finally found it: a fuzzy pink angora sweater with a revealing, deep V-neck. She slipped it over her head and studied her reflection. Perfect.

Not that Frank seemed to notice the trouble she'd gone to, when she was finally admitted to the visiting area. He was more interested in the squares of Caserta's pizza she'd smuggled in, in her Louis Vuitton bag. You weren't supposed to bring anything for the inmates, according to the big sign in the waiting room, but Carole had gone to school with one of the prison guards, Brian Dutra, and she slipped him a fifty, so he made an exception. He didn't even check the pizza to see if she'd hidden a file inside, not that she had.

"This is a hell of a mess," complained Frank, taking a big bite. He was sitting on the other side of a table, and they were alone, apart from a watchful prison guard, in a big room that looked like a school cafeteria and smelled strongly of disinfectant. Except for a brief hug, they weren't supposed to touch, which Carole found difficult since she was a hugger. "While I'm rotting in here, we're losing money, you know. That contract has late penalties, and now I don't know how we're going to make the deadlines."

"You'll get out, Frank. Vince said so."

"Paulie?"

"He called me to tell me you'd been arrested."

"I mean about the job. Can he handle it?"

"He didn't say anything about that," admitted Carole.

"It's a conspiracy, I tell you. A big WASP conspiracy to destroy Capobianco and Sons, that's what it is. We had the low bid, so we got the job, but it didn't sit well with Chase and Mooney," said Frank, starting on his second piece of pizza. "Those guys think they're so superior 'cause they've been in business since indoor plumbing was invented, they figure they're doing you a favor to even put in a bid, and then price everything too high like you gotta pay for the privilege of getting them to work for you."

"I don't think . . ."

"It is." Frank nodded, chewing away. "A big conspiracy. I'm not kidding. You get too successful, they start going after you. They want to bankrupt me and put me in my place, then Chase and Mooney will be the only big plumbing outfit in Providence."

"Don't talk like that, Frank," said Carole, alarmed. "That's what the cops think, that you had a motive because you were mad we didn't get into Prospect Place."

"Is that what they think?" Frank leaned back in his chair. "Not to worry, babe." He popped the last bit of pizza into his mouth. "Thanks, hon, that sure hit the spot," he said, giving her a smile. "You go on home now. I'll see you tomorrow."

Carole stood up and blew him a kiss, then turned and hurried out the door. She didn't want him to see her crying.

Next morning, the Superior Court was packed. Not only had Frank's parents come, but almost everybody from the Hill had crowded into the room to show support for one of their own. Connie couldn't make it; she'd called and said she had to work on a motion, whatever that was, that one of the partners wanted ASAP. But Frank-O was there, greeting his mother with a big hug. He'd dressed for the occasion in a dark suit a size or two too big; Carole guessed he'd either borrowed it or bought it in a thrift shop, and he'd slicked down his hair. It was still blue, of course. But the color wasn't so noticeable as when he wore it moussed and gelled into spikes.

"Thanks for coming," she whispered, squeezing his hand as they took their seats in the front row, right behind the table where Frank and Vince were sitting. Frank was wearing the same outfit he'd worn to the Prospect Place interview; Carole had delivered it to Vince's office yesterday, after visiting the jail.

"Thanks for the food," said Frank-O. "It was great."

She looked at him. "Did you eat it all?"

"Yeah, me and some guys. It was great."

"You're welcome," she said, as the bailiff called the room to order. "All rise for the Honorable Judge William Wilson."

Carole's heart sank as a wizened little man in a black robe took his seat behind the bench. Frank turned around and gave her a look, as if to say the judge was further proof of his WASP conspiracy theory.

Judge Wilson, however, was unimpressed with the evidence the prosecution presented and refused to comply with the DA's demand that bail be denied. "Five hundred thousand dollars," he said, "and Mr. Capobianco must surrender his passport." The business was quickly completed, Frank was released, and a joyful throng issued out onto South Main Street, where they encountered a barrage of questions from the assembled media.

Microphones were thrust in Frank's face, but he just waved and smiled, letting Vince do the talking. "My client welcomes this opportunity to demonstrate his complete and utter innocence," he declared. "And he also extends his deepest sympathy to the Browne family."

"Yeah, right," murmured Frank, leaning into her ear and giving her a hug as the cameras clicked around them.

Then they went on up the Hill for a celebratory family lunch with Mom and Big Frank and Frank-O at Costantino's that seemed to go on and on as the chef produced specialty after specialty and bottle after bottle was opened, different ones for each course. They were finally eating the tiramisu when Carole remembered Poopsie.

"We better get home," she said, rising and tapping Frank on the arm.

"What's the hurry?" he asked, pulling her back down into her chair. "I've been eating prison food."

"One, maybe two meals," she said.

"That so-called breakfast was enough to convince me I don't want to go back," declared Frank, and everybody laughed.

It was after three when they finally staggered home; one of the boys from the restaurant drove the Cayenne, and they gave him taxi money for the trip back, as well as something for his trouble. They'd hardly got through the door and Frank was groping Carole's butt when a familiar odor reached them.

"Well, I guess we didn't name her Poopsie for nothing," said Frank, handing Carole the roll of paper towels.

Carole was just putting the last of the dinner dishes in the dishwasher when there was a tap on the apartment door. She wasn't expecting anyone, so she peeked through the peephole, surprised to see Connie standing in the hall. "Come on in," she said, greeting her daughter with a hug. "What brings you here?"

"The case, Mom. I've been worried about Pop. I came right over after work."

"You just got done with work now?" asked Carole, noticing that Connie was still dressed in her business suit but had pulled her shirt out of the waistband and had swapped her heels for a pair of running shoes. "It's almost eight! That's ridiculous. How are you supposed to have a life?"

It was a shame what this job was doing to her, thought Carole, studying her daughter. Connie had always been a pretty girl, with a heart-shaped face, big hazel eyes, and a head of abundant brunette hair that she wore long. Only you couldn't tell how beautiful she was because that gorgeous, naturally wavy hair was pulled back into a bun, there were dark circles under her eyes, and she was developing a worry line from furrowing her lovely arched eyebrows. At least she'd managed to keep her figure, although that suit was looking as if it was a size too large.

"My life is just fine," said Connie, firmly. "It's Pop I'm worried about. How's he holding up?"

Poopsie, seeing her adored Connie, had jumped down from her favorite spot on the couch and greeted Connie by rolling on her back and baring her tummy. Connie bent down and politely gave her a couple of rubs, after which Poopsie rolled over and sat on her feet, taking possession.

"See for yourself," said Carole, tilting her head toward the big leather recliner, where Frank was dozing, snoring gently, after eating most of a pizza for dinner. Carole had begged off cooking, saying they'd had such a big lunch, and ordered delivery. She'd had one slice, and Frank ate the rest of the pie.

"I guess he's not too stressed, then," said Connie, scratching the dog behind her ear. "That's a relief. Right, Poopsie?"

Poopsie lifted her snout, inviting Connie to scratch her chin.

"Come on into the bedroom," invited Carole. "We can talk there, and I've got a new pair of shoes to show you."

Connie and Poopsie obediently followed Carole down the short hallway to the master bedroom, where Connie sat herself on the king-size bed. Poopsie leaped up and sat beside her, placing her chin on Connie's thigh. Carole disappeared into her enormous closet and returned with a pair of Ferragamo sneakers.

"They're real nice, Mom. Are you taking up jogging?"

"Me? What, are you crazy? They're for walking Poopsie."

"Your mommy will be the most stylish dog mommy at the dog park," crooned Connie, allowing the dog to give her a doggy kiss.

"I can't take her to the dog park; she fights with all the other dogs," admitted Carole, sitting alongside Connie on her free side, holding the shoe in her hand. "Tell me what you really think?"

"The shoes are really cute."

"I don't mean the shoes! Tell me the truth. Is your father in trouble?"

"Well, yeah, Mom. He's been indicted for murder."

"But he didn't do it. He's innocent."

"Vince Houlihan's a good lawyer; he'll put up a good defense."

"So Frank will get off?"

"I'd say probably; I'd put the odds at something like sixty-forty," said Connie.

Carole was right on it. "Sixty he'll get off, right?"

Connie laughed. "Yeah, Mom."

"Not great odds," said Carole, studying her daughter and noticing the dark circles under her eyes and the way she was holding the dog, almost as if Poopsie were a stuffed toy. Poopsie loved that sort of attention, but Carole wondered if Connie was making so much of the dog because she wasn't getting enough human affection. "Your birthday's coming," she said, thinking of a couple of eligible men she could invite. "Let's have a party."

"Mom, you know I hate parties, and besides. . . ."

Carole was quick to change course. "Just family."

"I was gonna say, I won't be here. I'll be in Buffalo then, for work."

"Like in Canada?"

"No, Mom." Connie was laughing and shaking her head. "It's in New York state, near Niagara Falls."

"Never been," admitted Carole, who had no plans of remedying the situation. "What are you going to do there?"

"It's for a case. The firm is representing the Oneida nation, who claim they were cheated out of their hunting grounds about two hundred years ago and want it back."

Carole shrugged. "Fat chance. I don't like the odds on that one."

"You're probably right," agreed Connie. "There's an entire subdivision built on it, but maybe we can get them some compensation. I'm going to be researching the old treaties and agreements, and I might have to go to Ottawa, too, which is in Canada. It's pretty exciting," she continued, growing animated. "It's my first company trip, and it's actually a pretty big case, if we win. A lot of money. Millions."

Poopsie had fallen asleep in Connie's lap and was twitching a bit, dreaming of chasing rabbits. "You know, Mom, I've been talking to this archivist; she's fabulous," said Connie, who was growing more animated. "You'd think something like government archives would be dusty and boring, but she makes it all sound so interesting. Like a trip into the past. I'm really looking forward to digging into this stuff."

"You better wear a mask," advised Carole. "Those old treaties are probably dusty, and you have allergies."

"Thanks for the advice, Mom, but I think you're missing the point. This is an exciting time for me. Like doors are opening, and my job is getting more fascinating every day, and I kind of feel like I'm getting more attention and opportunities than the other associates." She paused. "I don't want to get ahead of myself, but I'm beginning to think they're eyeing me for the partnership track. Like maybe this trip is a sort of test."

"You'll do fine," said Carole, automatically patting her daughter's hand. "But what are we going to do about your birthday?"

Chapter Four

At breakfast the next morning, Frank got right down to business.

"The way I see it," he said, stabbing a bright yellow egg yolk with his fork and smearing it over the white, "is that the only way I'm going to get out of this mess is if we figure out who killed that old bastard."

Carole stared at him. "Isn't that what the cops are supposed to do?"

"You said it, kiddo," replied Frank, waving his fork at her, "but they think they got their man, who just happens to be me. They're not gonna keep looking, are they? But we've got an advantage because we know they got the wrong guy. We know I didn't do it, right?"

"Right," agreed Carole, stirring her yogurt. "But how are we going to find the real killer? Maybe we should hire a detective? Somebody who knows what they're doing?"

"Nah," said Frank, shoving a toast triangle into his mouth, "nobody's gonna care like we care, right? And," he continued, taking a big slurp of coffee, "we can hit the ground running. We know the background."

Carole raised her expensively waxed and shaped eyebrows. "We do?"

"Sure." Frank was busy mopping up the last bit of egg with a piece of toast. "Don't you remember what he said at that meeting? About how he would tolerate no hanky-panky at the old manse there?"

"Yeah," she said slowly, "he did mention something along those lines."

"I been thinking about this. He did, and he's not, I mean he wasn't, the kind of guy who just throws words around. So that there is the motive. Somebody there at the condo has something they want to keep hidden, and the old bastard must've figured it out."

"Do you mean to say you think one of the other residents at Prospect Place killed Hosea Browne?" she asked, incredulously.

"Yeah."

Carole's eyebrows rose again. "And you think we can figure out this secret, a secret that this person is so desperate to hide that they killed Hosea? How exactly are we going to do that?"

"We're gonna investigate," he said, reaching for his phone. "We're gonna start with Connie over there at that fancy law firm. I'll do the questioning, you can take notes." He began dialing. "Go on, get something to write with."

Carole hopped up and grabbed the pad and pencil she kept handy for grocery lists. When she was back at the table, Frank switched to speaker phone, and Connie's voice suddenly reverberated through the apartment. Frank, being Frank, had the volume up to max. Poopsie, who had been snoozing on the couch, sat up and pricked up her ears.

"So, honey, I bet Hosea Browne had Dunne and Willoughby on retainer, right? I need some info about him and the rest of that bunch at Prospect Place..."

"Sorry, Dad, but there's this thing called client confidentiality. I'll get in big trouble..."

"This is your father making a simple request," said Frank, laying down the law. "Do you want to get in trouble with me?"

"Uh, no, Dad..."

"Now that's settled. What's the poop on this Hosea character?"

Hearing something like her name, Poopsie jumped down off the couch and crossed the living area, joining them at the dining table. She sat on the floor next to Frank, ears lifted and listening to every word.

"Well, he's a big shot. Comes from an old Yankee family; Brown University is named after one of them, but without the e. He's got, I mean he had, a finger in just about everything in Rhode Island: banking, real estate, politics, you name it."

Poopsie was hanging on every word. She adored Connie.

"What about his brother?" asked Frank. "I got the feeling old Hosea didn't think much of him, seemed to think he's irresponsible or something when it comes to money."

"Jonathan? I don't know about that. He's quite a bit younger than Hosea, maybe in his late fifties. He's an archaeologist, he was working at a dig in Peru, but he's coming home for the funeral and to take care of Hosea's affairs."

"Is he the heir?" asked Frank, as Poopsie began to scoot

around the apartment, tracking Carole, who'd disappeared into the bedroom.

"I can't say," said Connie, putting up a weak resistance.

"You know how I feel about that word," growled Frank. "There's no such word as can't."

"Yeah, he's the heir."

"And what about the others? That old bat, Millie something?"

"I don't know, Dad. Look, I gotta go. Somebody's coming."

"Okay. But do me a big favor. Keep your eyes and ears open. You hear anything interesting, let me know."

"Sure, Dad," said Connie, as Poopsie circled the table and lifted one forepaw, making a perfect point right at the phone.

"Look at that," said Carole, proudly. "She figured out that Connie's voice came from the phone."

"The dog's a genius," said Frank, sarcastically. "Maybe she can solve the murder."

Still pointing, Poopsie barked at the phone.

"I think she wants to hear Connie's voice again."

The phone rang, and Frank snatched it up. "Maybe she'll get her chance," he said, but it wasn't Connie. It was Paulie, and he sounded upset.

"Frank, I just want to let you know the cops are here, so mebbe you don't want to rush into the office this morning."

Poopsie was growling. She didn't think much of Paulie.

"Screw 'em. They can't touch me. I'm out on bail," said Frank.

"Just thought I'd let you know. They've got warrants. They want the contracts for the Factory job."

Poopsie was barking now. "So give 'em to 'em," said Frank, turning to Carole. "Can't you shut her up?"

Carole shrugged. "Ask him why they want the contracts."

"I guess they think there's something funny, I don't know. I think Chase and Mooney put 'em on to us, complaining we squeezed 'em out."

"Be quiet," Carole told the dog.

"That's crazy. We did Mitch Chase a favor, got 'em the HVAC."

"Yeah, well, I guess they don't see it that way," said Paulie.

"Shut the dog up," said Frank. "I'm getting a headache." Poopsie was running around in circles, barking her head off.

"Turn off the speaker," suggested Carole. "I bet that's what's bothering her."

"Gotta go," said Frank, slamming the phone down and making a grab for the dog. She eluded him and ran down the hall to the bedroom, where she scooted under the bed. Frank fell to his knees and tried to grab her, but she growled and snapped at his hand. "I'm gonna kill that dog," he threatened, as the phone rang again.

This time Carole got it. Good thing, she thought, because it was Frank-O, and Frank was in no mood to deal with his son.

"Hi, sweetie," she cooed, and Frank gave her a look.

"What do you mean?" Carole was asking. "Didn't we give you five thousand at the beginning of the term?"

Frank was listening, and he didn't like the sound of what he was hearing.

"That's all gone? And you haven't finished your project?"

"What's he making? The Leaning Tower of Pisa or something?" demanded Frank, angrily. Still beneath the bed, Poopsie was keeping up a low growl.

"He won't get any credit," Carole told him, "if he doesn't finish the project."

Frank was pissed. "What does he think I am, made of money?" he shouted.

Poopsie began barking.

"Enough, enough," said Carole. "I'll call you back," she told Frank-O, ending the call. "You," she said, pointing a finger tipped in Melon of Troy, "work off some steam at the gym. I'll take the dog out for a walk."

Frank took the elevator down to the gym, but Carole and Poopsie took the stairs. Carole was a bit nervous that Poopsie might not make it down four flights without an accident, but the frisky dog bounded down the steps, straining at the leash. Carole peeked cautiously through the glass window of the stairwell door into the lobby and, seeing the way was clear, made a dash for the door.

Once outside, Poopsie seemed to focus on the task at hand and began sniffing around the trees planted along Edith Street. Carole avoided the Esplanade's dog-walking area, where they might encounter another dog, and headed for her usual walk up Holden Street to Smith and around the statehouse. She charged up the steep incline, until she suddenly found herself short of breath and stopped. She inhaled a few times, leaning on a chain-link fence and taking deep yoga breaths, trying to relax. Honestly, she didn't know if she could take another morning as stressful as this one. Poopsie, however, obligingly squatted and produced a big poop, which Carole bagged. Proceeding more slowly, they headed for a trash can on Smith Street, crossing to the other side of the street when a black-and-white dog appeared. Poopsie, who was half his size, growled and barked and pulled at the leash, letting the black-and-white dog know she'd like to rip him to pieces.

"Sometimes," Carole found herself talking to the dog, "I'd like to let you go and see what happens."

The owner of the black-and-white dog gave Carole a wave and continued on his way; his dog did not seem impressed by Poopsie's theatrics and paused to raise his leg to mark a tree.

Lost in thought, worrying about Frank and Frank-O, Carole returned from the walk later than usual. It was almost ten when she got back to the Esplanade, and the concierge had left the *Journal* outside her door. She stooped and picked it up, removing the rubber band. When she unfolded it, she saw her own face staring back at her. The photographer had snapped the photo when they were leaving the courthouse, just as Frank whispered in her ear. They looked happy, as if they didn't have a care in the world. But that wasn't true, of course. Frank got bail, but he was still under indictment and was facing life in prison. Maybe he was right, she thought; maybe they did have to find the real killer.

Back in the apartment, Carole fed the dog and cleared up the breakfast dishes. She started the dishwasher and went into the bedroom to dress. She was pulling a sweater over her head when she heard Poopsie barking again. She went back to the kitchen to investigate and found the dog staring at the dishwasher, barking. Something was loose in there, rattling a bit.

"It's just the dishwasher, Poopsie," said Carole. "You hear it every day."

Poopsie clearly didn't like the dishwasher today.

"Quiet!" ordered Carole, in the authoritative voice the dog trainer had instructed her to use.

Poopsie ignored her and kept on barking.

"Please, Poopsie," pleaded Carole, "the neighbors are going to complain."

"*Woof, woof,*" replied Poopsie.

"I give up," said Carole, scooping up the dog and grabbing her purse and jacket. Ten minutes later, Carole found a parking spot right in front of her favorite manicure salon, Happy Nails. Poopsie, apparently soothed by the brief ride in the car, gave in to exhaustion and curled up in a ball on the back seat for a nap. "Good dog," said Carole, leaving the windows open a notch for air and locking the car. The temperature was only in the forties; the car wasn't going to heat up.

She was pulling the salon door open when she bumped into Susan Weaver, the real estate agent, who was just leaving. "Hi, Susan," she said. "I didn't know you got your nails done here."

"Always," said Susan, displaying her fresh French manicure for Carole to see. "I can't go with colors; doesn't look professional."

"So how's business?" asked Carole. "Did you sell that condo?"

"Not yet," said Susan. "And now that Hosea's gone, maybe I owe your husband a big thank you. . ." She stopped in mid-sentence, and her face went scarlet. "I didn't mean, I mean, well, it's crazy to think Frank would have killed Hosea to get an apartment, even if he did say what he said. I don't know what I was thinking. I didn't mean to imply that even for a minute I thought . . . absolutely not! Of course I'm absolutely positive that Frank is innocent."

"It's good to know people believe in him," said Carole, taking her hand and giving it a gentle squeeze.

"Of course I do," said Susan, making eye contact and assuming a sincere tone. "Everyone knows the cops have got the wrong guy."

"Thanks," said Carole, "that means a lot to me." She smiled and released Susan's hand. "What were you going to say, about Hosea being gone?"

"Just that he was the main impediment to the sale. Nobody was good enough. He turned down so many offers I wondered why he agreed with his brother to put the place on the market in the first place."

"Interesting," said Carole.

Susan pushed the door open and paused on the stoop to give her an encouraging smile. "Hang in there," she said, with a little wave.

Carole continued on into the salon, where she was greeted by Sonia, her favorite manicurist. "I thought you might be in today," said Sonia, taking her coat. "By the way, that was a nice photo in the paper."

"Do you really think so?" asked Carole, slipping into a chair. "I thought I looked old."

"Not a bit," said Sonia. "You looked happy."

"I was happy—well, relieved—but now I think we were celebrating a bit too early," said Carole, as Sonia got to work with the polish remover. "Frank's still got to go to trial."

"He'll get off," said Sonia.

"I don't know," admitted Carole, dipping her fingers into the soaking bowl. "I'm beginning to worry."

"You're not the only one with worries," said Sonia, assembling her tools. "You know that lady who just left..."

"Susan Weaver?"

"Yeah. She sells real estate, but she says things are not good. She's behind in her car payments, and this month, she says, if something doesn't happen soon, she won't be able to make her mortgage payment."

"Really?" said Carole, as Sonia began to work on her cuticles. "I never would have guessed."

"I know; she looks real rich, doesn't she?"

"She has to keep up appearances; it's part of the job," said Carole, reminding herself that even though she had her troubles, she didn't have to worry about having enough money, and she ought to be grateful.

"Well, it's all appearances, believe me. She could barely scrape up the money for the manicure, and she didn't even tip me; she said she'd get me next time."

"She's an excellent realtor," said Carole. "Things will turn up for her. I'm sure of it."

Sonia shook her head. "She seemed real depressed. Said she came so close..." Sonia held up her own perfectly manicured hand with her thumb and forefinger almost touching. "This close to selling a coupla-million-dollar condo, but some old man nixed the deal." Sonia raised her eyes and met Carole's. "Not just once, but every time she had a buyer, she said. He wants to get the right person."

This was interesting, thought Carole. Poor Susan; it would be awfully frustrating to come so close, to find buyer after buyer, and always be turned down.

"So what color are you thinking about?" asked Sonia. "Red? Pink? I have this new frost, Sunset Over Cairo . . ."

Carole didn't answer. She was thinking, wondering if Susan might have taken her frustration out on Hosea with a piece of pipe. She certainly had motive enough. If Hosea had accepted their offer of four million dollars, Susan would have netted around two or three percent, which would be eighty thousand. Even with taxes and expenses and whatever, it would have been a tidy haul. And even if the other offers had been less, say the asking price of two million, she would have cleared around forty thousand. Enough to make a lot of mortgage payments.

"You want to go with the frost?" asked Sonia.

"No," said Carole. "I'm thinking of something brighter. Something cheerful."

"How about Chapel of Love?" suggested Sonia, looking up as a woman in a fuzzy wool cape and clunky clogs opened the door. "Can I help you?" she asked. "I'll be free in a few minutes."

"Oh, no, I don't want a manicure," said the woman, who obviously went in for the natural look. "I just happened to notice a very unhappy dog outside, left in a parked car, and I wondered . . ."

Carole was quick to deny responsibility. "Sorry, I don't have a dog."

"It's barking its head off," said the woman. "People are so irresponsible. Imagine leaving a dog in a car like that."

"What can you do?" asked Carole, with a shrug. "At least it's not hot; the dog won't get heatstroke."

"Even so, it's very inconsiderate," said the woman. "Maybe I should call the animal control officer."

"Why don't you try the florist next door," suggested Carole, smiling and nodding until the woman left.

"Chapel of Love?" asked Sonia, holding up a bottle of pink polish.

"No," said Carole, scowling. "Something stronger. Like Vampire."

Chapter Five

That annoying woman who shunned hair dye and lipstick and wore ugly natural fibers was right; Poopsie was barking her head off when Carole got back to the SUV. Probably because the interfering woman had disturbed her when she approached the SUV and wrote a note about the danger of leaving a dog unattended in a car and stuck it under the windshield wiper. That was exactly the sort of thing that would drive Poopsie wild. Carole pulled off the note and tossed it in a nearby trash barrel, thinking it was a wonder that the woman who couldn't mind her own business hadn't bothered to inform her that an oversized car like the Porsche only got eighteen miles to the gallon on the highway and contributed to global warming. Climbing behind the wheel, she took a few yoga breaths and hoped that Poopsie would calm down when she started the car.

Poopsie didn't; she kept on barking and tried to jump into the front seat.

"No!" ordered Carole, using the authoritative voice the dog trainer had told her would guarantee instant obedience. "Sit! Quiet!"

Poopsie continue to bark and tried to slip through the gap between the two front seats. Carole grasped the steering wheel with both hands and rested her head on it; Poopsie immediately slipped by and seated herself in the front passenger seat, where she continued to bark. What was she supposed to do now? How was she going to get the dog to quiet down and go back to the rear seat, where she belonged? If only there was Xanax for dogs . . .

Carole lifted her head, inspired. That was it. They must have something like that, some sort of dog tranquilizer. She'd take Poopsie to the vet.

Shifting into drive, Carole zoomed out of her parking spot, cutting off a VW Beetle. Hey, she couldn't be responsible for everybody in the world, could she? She had problems of her own, namely this dog, who was driving her crazy. The vet, fortunately, had her office nearby, in Pawtucket. Carole was definitely rattled as she drove, but she began to feel calmer just spotting the vet's sign, and she almost felt normal when she parked. Poopsie, however, was still upset and barking frantically. There were a lot of other cars in the parking lot, so Carole figured it would be best to leave the dog confined to the car while she went in to ask for an emergency appointment.

"Sorry, hon, the doc's got an emergency; a Lab got hit by a car. We're all backed up," said the receptionist. She waved a hand at the waiting room, which Carole saw was packed with people and their assorted pets: cats, dogs, birds, even a rabbit.

"This is an emergency, too," said Carole. "My dog won't stop barking."

"That's Madame Pompadour, right?" asked the girl, pulling out a file and flipping it open. It apparently made absorbing reading. "She's a biter, I see," said the girl.

"That was an accident," said Carole, a bit defensive. "The veterinary assistant had her hand in the wrong place."

"Sure," said the receptionist, who had clearly been trained to agree with the clients. "Why don't you take a seat, and we'll see if the doctor can squeeze you in."

"I'm not kidding; the dog is out of her mind. I'm worried she's going to have a fit or something," explained Carole. "Maybe I could just buy some tranquilizers for her?"

The receptionist looked shocked. "The doctor will want to examine the dog before prescribing medication."

"Okay, I'll wait," said Carole, turning to go into the waiting room. She could hear Poopsie barking right through the walls and shut windows. Pausing in the doorway, she sighed and looked for a seat. Only one was empty, and she was surprised to discover it was next to Millicent Shaw, the old lady who lived at Prospect Place. She was dressed, as before, in a pleated skirt and twin-set combo, blue this time, and was holding a gray plastic cat carrier on her lap. Carole hesitated, afraid Millicent might not welcome her presence. Her husband, after all, was accused of killing her neighbor.

Millicent looked up, spotting Carole. Carole was ready to flee; there must be other vets in this town. But Millicent smiled at her.

"Don't be shy; take a seat," she said, patting the empty chair.

"Thanks," said Carole. "I was afraid I might make you uncomfortable."

"No, no." Millicent shook her head. "I'm sure the police have made a terrible mistake and your husband is innocent." She paused, reflecting. "I did so think you would have been a breath of fresh air in that musty old place. Hosea was wrong to vote the way he did. He won't allow anyone who's not a white Protestant and preferably a *Mayflower* descendant to buy that apartment, not that he would ever have admitted it. But I'm sure he didn't like your beautiful Italian name; he probably thought all Italians are in the Mafia or something." She snorted. "So ridiculous. The moment I heard dear Susan say Capobianco," she said, lingering over the syllables. "well, I thought of Florence." She turned to Carole, nodding. "It's my favorite city in the whole world."

"Mine, too," said Carole, who actually thought Florence was terribly overcrowded and often smelly. "I heard he turned down other offers," she added, recalling the gossip she'd heard at Happy Nails.

"Several. A lovely Black couple, an Asian professor, and oh, that wonderful rabbi and his wife," said Millicent, rolling her eyes. Her short, curly hair was snow-white, and she wasn't wearing a bit of makeup, Carole noticed, but she didn't look bad. Her skin was soft, and her cheeks were pink and firm, even though wrinkles sprouted around her eyes and mouth. Her eyes were bright, and she had a perky look about her, as if she found everything absolutely fascinating. "That was Hosea for you."

"He voted against them all?"

"It made me furious," admitted Millicent, patting her cat box. "Tiggles has an upset stomach."

Even through the wall, Carole could still hear Poopsie, who was still barking, but not quite as frantically as before. "My dog's having a panic attack," she said.

"Animals are so sensitive. I bet your dog is worried about your husband," said Millicent. She paused a moment, apparently lost in her own thoughts. "I abhor prejudice," she said, suddenly, startling Carole. "I absolutely detest it. I've seen it firsthand—you know, dreadful, hateful behavior—in the South. But it isn't just there, you know; it persists in many places today. And we in the North are certainly not blameless." She lowered her voice. "Hosea's ancestors, you know, made their money in the slave trade. Rhode Island was a major player."

"So they say," said Carole.

"It's only recently that we're beginning to come to terms with our history." Millicent peered into the carrier, checking on Tiggles. "The lynchings and the church burnings and the fear, it was a terrible thing. I was a Freedom Rider, you know. I went down to Mississippi in the sixties, with a group of Quakers and Unitarians to register Black voters."

Carole was impressed; she'd never have guessed that this little old lady with her pearls and her kitty-cat had done anything so daring. "You were part of history," she said.

"We made history, that's for sure, but things didn't change overnight. And when I got back North, I found parents in Boston were protesting when they began bussing to integrate the public schools. I was shocked!"

"There's a documentary about that. I saw the promo on PBS," said Carole. "I remember their faces, so full of hate."

"Exactly," said Millicent, just as her name was called. She popped right up, quite spry for someone her age, thought Carole. "It was nice talking to you," she said, before hurrying to follow the veterinary assistant.

Carole settled into her seat, trying to ignore Poopsie's barks and hoping she wouldn't have to wait much longer. The situation was getting on her nerves; she was worried about Frank, and that's probably what set Poopsie off. The little dog was terribly sensitive and tuned right in to her people's moods. Maybe she should have gone in for a yoga session, instead of getting a manicure, she thought. She knew her emotions were in turmoil, and it wasn't doing her or the dog any good. Or Frank, for that matter.

How could the cops be so wrong? she wondered. Why hadn't they dug a little deeper? If they had, they would have discovered that Hosea Browne wasn't a very nice guy and there were probably a lot of people who would have liked to kill him. Take Susan Weaver, for one; old Hosea had really screwed her, turning down those perfectly good offers. And what about the other applicants? Maybe they weren't about to take Hosea's rejection lying down.

Mentally, Carole tut-tutted. Wasn't discrimination in housing supposed to be illegal? How could Hosea get away with it? And if he was pulling stunts like that, how many other people had he offended? Maybe Frank was right, she thought; maybe the murder did have something to do with Prospect Place.

Of course, that was probably part of the cops' case against Frank: that he was so upset about being turned down that he offed the old Yankee. But Carole thought they'd have a hard time proving it. Truth was, a day or two after the Prospect Place interview, Frank had already forgotten about it. In fact, he'd never even mentioned Prospect Place again. He was like that; he didn't fret, he simply moved on. Nowadays, he seemed perfectly happy with the pool and gym and parking at the Esplanade; he especially loved the hot tub. There was no sign at all that he was sulking over the rejection.

But what about this new wrinkle that Paulie had mentioned, that Hosea's murder was linked to the Factory contract? That was troublesome, thought Carole, who knew enough about the building trades to know that there was inevitably some pushing and shoving and squeezing when a lucrative contract was in the offing. Hey, this was

Providence; that's the way things were. Competitors were warned off, palms got greased, everybody was happy. Nobody made a big deal about it. Look what happened to Buddy Cianci, for Pete's sake. He turned the city around when he was mayor, and everybody loved him for it, but the Feds got him on corruption charges and sent him to jail. Even so, most people thought he got a bum deal, and the conservative Providence Preservation Society even gave him an award, overlooking the inconvenient fact that he would be unable to attend the awards banquet due to incarceration. And when he got out of jail, he ran for mayor again and got elected to another term.

That all took place a long time ago, and a lot had happened in the meantime, like the recession and the Covid pandemic, but it was like that French saying, she thought, "The more things change, the more they stay the same." And Frank was a pretty smart cookie. Hadn't he invented the Bye-Bye Toilet? He was no dummy, and she was confident he always knew which side his bread was buttered on. And when it came to the Factory, Hosea was the butter; he was the guy with the financing. He held the purse strings, and there was no way Frank was going to kill the goose that laid the golden eggs, she decided, mixing metaphors. Having cleared that up in her mind, she reached for her cell and dialed Tom Paliotto, over at the homicide division.

"You know, Tom," she began, "I've been thinking about Frank's problem."

"How's he doing?" asked Tom.

"Okay, everything considered. He knows he's innocent, of course, and he figures the trial will show that."

"We've got the best justice system in the world," said Tom, diplomatically.

"Right," agreed Carole. "But trials are expensive and

take a long time, and while they're building a case against Frank, the real murderer is still at large." Carole was so involved in her conversation that she didn't notice the glances she was getting from the other people in the waiting room. "And it's really obvious to anyone who knows Frank that he would never do something like that."

"Kill somebody?" asked Tom, in a doubtful tone.

"I suppose everybody's got their limit and could get mad enough to kill somebody," admitted Carole. "But, for Frank, it would probably be someone in the family, like Frank-O," she added, chuckling.

"Frank-O?"

"Frankie Junior. He's an artist now. Wants to be called Frank-O. Like that guy who wrapped up islands in cloth and did a big deal in Central Park. Christo."

"Okay," said Tom, who didn't have a clue what she was talking about.

"Anyway, like I was saying, Frank would not kill Hosea Browne because Hosea Browne was controlling the cash for the Factory. He was the goose, you see, and Frank is way too smart to kill a goose."

Everyone in the waiting room was fascinated; they were hanging on every word Carole said. A couple of people were even chuckling, and Carole looked up. Eyes were quickly averted; smiles were covered.

"Well, hey, I'm at the vet's. I can't talk anymore. But keep what I said in mind, okay? And give my love to your mom." Carole sat, staring at the phone in her hand. What the heck, she thought, scrolling through her contacts to Susan Weaver's name. She still had her number from the time when they were trying to buy the apartment at Prospect Place. It wouldn't hurt, she thought, to get together with her and have a little chat, see if she had some information about the other residents, that blond couple and the professors. And the other applicants, too. If she was really as hard up as Sonia thought, she'd probably appreciate a free meal. But Susan didn't answer, and she got the recorded voice telling her to leave a message. She did, proposing they meet for lunch, soon.

She pocketed the phone and reached for a magazine, unwilling to meet the eyes of the other people in the waiting room. She flipped through the pages; it was some wordy news magazine, and she really couldn't get interested; her mind was going a mile a minute. What the heck were they doing in there, anyway? How long was this going to be? How much veterinary care did a parakeet really require, or a cat? And how could she get information about the Prospect Place residents if Susan Weaver didn't accept her lunch invitation? After all, she might be leery of getting involved with the wife of an accused murderer. No, thought Carole, she'd probably sell a condo to Satan himself if it was a cash offer. She smiled grimly to herself. How, she wondered, was she going to investigate, like Frank wanted? How do you get to know people you don't know? Hang around and accidentally bump into them? They had a name for that: stalking. No good. She didn't want to get into trouble, especially trouble that would make things worse for Frank. But there had to be a way . . .

"Mrs. Capobianco?" She looked up. It was the veterinary assistant, and not the one that Poopsie bit on her last visit. Small mercies, thought Carole.

"I'll just run out and get the dog," she said. "I'll be right back."

The girl smiled at her as Carole dashed for the door, her heels clattering on the vinyl floor. Out in the parking lot, Carole yanked the car door open and found the seat empty. What happened to Poopsie? Come to think of it, she hadn't been barking for a while. Had somebody dognapped her? It seemed unlikely, considering her personality, but she was a pedigreed pooch. Somebody might just be crazy enough, she thought, frantically yanking open the other doors, until she reached the driver's door. That's where she found the little dog, curled up in a tight ball, sound asleep in the driver's seat.

Chapter Six

Carole cooed to the dog as she gently lifted her up. Poopsie had that glassy-eyed stare she knew was trouble, and Carole handled her gingerly, fearing she might snap at her. Poopsie just closed her eyes, however, and resumed her nap, resting her chin on Carole's shoulder. The dog wasn't very big, small for a Brittany at about twenty-five pounds, but what with those killer heels and all, Carole was out of breath when she finally got into the examining room and set Poopsie on the stainless-steel table. She continued to coo softly and stroked her head, hoping to prolong her nap as long as possible, but Poopsie was definitely waking up.

"Give her a minute," Carole warned the vet, a plain young woman in a white coat and thick eyeglasses with round black frames. "She's just waking up, and it takes her a minute or two..."

"I thought you said she was barking hysterically," said the vet, reaching for Poopsie's neck.

Predictably, Poopsie snarled and snapped at her, but thanks to divine intervention or maybe just grogginess, she didn't connect. Carole exhaled a grateful sigh and looked upward, at the ceiling.

"Whoa," exclaimed the vet, jumping back. "She is skittish, isn't she."

"The trainer says it's fear aggression," said Carole, who was now struggling to keep a wriggling and protesting Poopsie on the table now that her fight-or-flight reflexes had kicked in.

"Yeah, well, I think you can let her down," said the vet, checking the chart. "My colleague examined her recently..."

"Only a month or so ago."

"Right. And she seems quite healthy. I have no problem prescribing something to relax her," continued the vet, scribbling away while keeping a nervous eye on the dog.

Poopsie was at the door, scratching furiously. "Why don't you take her out to the car? She'll be more comfortable there," suggested the vet. "I'll meet you at the front desk."

"Righto," said Carole, relieved, picking up the leash, which was trailing on the floor. She opened the door, Poopsie charged out, pulling her across the waiting room to the exit, where she again began her frantic pawing and scratching at the door. The same scene was repeated in the parking lot as the small dog dragged the grown woman to the car and waited, shivering, with her tail tucked between her legs, until Carole opened the door and she jumped inside. Carole marched back inside to face the music.

"I have to tell you," said the vet, peering through those glasses, "that unless you undertake an intensive program to train that dog, you are looking at trouble down the line."

Carole nodded obediently while groping in her bag for her checkbook. Been there, done that, she was thinking, but she didn't say it. Instead, she dutifully took the name of the trainer the vet suggested, wrote the check, and left holding tight to the vial of magic pills. Back at the car, she climbed into the back seat next to Poopsie and gently embraced her with one arm while tickling her chin with the other hand. Slipping a finger between her jaws, she gently pried her mouth open and poked one of the tablets down her throat. Quickly wrapping her hand around the dog's muzzle, she stroked her throat until she felt Poopsie swallow. "Better living through chemistry," she muttered, climbing behind the wheel.

She carefully maneuvered the big SUV out of the tight parking lot and headed back toward Providence, mentally checking her collected to-do lists. She needed salad for supper. She had to drop off the check for Frank-O. And she really ought to see how Mom and Big Frank were doing now that yesterday's jubilant celebration was over and the grim reality of Frank's situation was setting in, kind of like cold, bleak January coming right after Christmas.

Traffic was light on Route 95, and she was making good time, so she decided to zip along Valley Street and on to Federal Hill to Venda for a prepared salad and some more stuff for Frank-O, since he was a bottomless pit and always needed more nourishment, taking advantage of the fact that Poopsie was now sleeping like a dream in the back seat.

She was heading back home with a couple of bags of groceries in the rear when a rag-tag procession of people carrying signs caught her eye, walking along the sidewalk in a straggly line. She'd seen other processions like this before, usually organized by a parish priest agitating for the homeless or the hungry or the unborn, but this group was a lot more flamboyant than those faithful souls. These folks were dressed in colorful clothes; they were banging drums and tooting horns; they even had a huge puppet that several of the marchers were carrying on poles. She smiled, watching the show pass by, until she spotted a familiar head of spiky blue hair. Frank-O!

"Hey, Frank-O!" she called, steering the car alongside and lowering the window. "Way to go!"

Frank-O didn't notice her at first, but one of his companions did and pointed her out to him. Smiling, he left the group and ambled toward her parked car, still carrying his sign. "Gentrification kills art!" it read, above a sketch of a smocked artist complete with beret and paint palette facing a wrecking ball.

"What's with the demonstration?" she asked.

Frank-O bent down and stuck his head through the open window, and she had a déjà vu moment, remembering him doing the same thing as a scrawny Little Leaguer. Now he was so big that his broad shoulders filled the whole window opening, and it was hard to believe she had actually given birth to him as a tiny, seven-pound baby.

"It's about the Factory, the way it's displacing all these artists and small tradesmen," he explained. "Where are they going to go?"

"They can stay right where they are," exclaimed Carole. "They're not tearing those old buildings down; they're just rehabbing them. It will be better, all nicely landscaped and cleaned up."

"Oh, yeah, it'll be nice all right, but they won't be able to afford the new rents."

Carole rolled her eyes. "Sure they will. They'll make more money because people won't be afraid to come down to Valley Street and will stop avoiding the area." She waved her arm. "Nobody picks up litter, it's a maze of chain-link fences and weeds and hand-lettered signs. Where exactly are these businesses? I tried to find that table and chair place a couple of months ago, and I got kind of lost, so I parked to figure out where I was, and some weird-looking guy was staring at me. I got out of there fast."

"That weird-looking guy was probably a great artist, on the verge of being discovered," said Frank-O.

"I think he was a wino," said Carole. "But anyway, I've got some groceries for you."

"Great," said Frank-O, watching as the tail end of the procession wound its way past the parking lot. "Can you drop them at the apartment? I'm kinda busy right now."

"Okay if I leave them on the porch? I don't want to climb the stairs."

"Sure, Ma." He withdrew his head from the car. "And remember how I told you I need some money for art supplies?"

"Oh, right," said Carole, reaching for her bag, but stopping when a niggling little thought popped up. She turned and raised a freshly manicured finger. "Hold on here," she said. "Are you aware that this money you want me and your father to give you comes from this very project that you're demonstrating against? How do you think your father makes his money?"

"From those toilets, Ma."

"Yeah. And where do they put those toilets? In projects just like this one, all over the country. And where is your father works hard to keep his brother and mother and father living in the style to which they've become accustomed? And to which you seem to be taking for granted?" she finished, ungrammatically.

"Look, I don't have to agree with everything my father does..."

"But you'll take his money?"

"Well, Ma, I don't want to, but I've got to, don't I, if I'm going to finish my sculpture project? Art supplies are expensive, and this is a big project; it needs a lot of stuff." He shook his head mournfully. "I wish it was different, but it isn't."

"Okay, okay," said Carole, digging into her oversized purse. "I've got it right here." She was holding the folded check in her hand, and he started to take it, but she didn't let go. "But listen to me, Frank-O. I don't want your father knowing that you're demonstrating against his project, okay? Not a word to Frank, right?"

"I promise, Ma."

She let go of the check and smiled fondly as he ran off to catch up with the demonstrators, just like he used to run off to join his friends when he was a kid on the Hill. Nostalgia, it'll get you every time, she thought, blinking back a tear. What happened to that cute little kid? Where'd he go?

Carole was still thinking fond thoughts about her not-so-little boy when she dropped off the groceries for him. Then, remembering she wanted to touch base with Frank's parents, she circled back to Federal Hill, where Mom greeted her by engulfing her in a big, welcoming hug. Mom wasn't exactly fat, but she did carry an extra fifteen pounds or so, and hugging her felt a bit like hugging a marshmallow. She wore her gray hair short, didn't bother with makeup, and favored elastic-waist pants and arch-support Skechers sneakers.

"How're you doing, sweetie?" she asked, concern clouding her big brown eyes. "Is Frank holding up okay?"

"You know Frank. Nothing short of a nuclear bomb bothers him."

"That's my boy," crowed Big Frank, who was cooking up his gravy. The whole house smelled like tomatoes and herbs and garlic; the scent wrapped around you, like a favorite old sweater.

"Y'eat?" asked Big Frank, turning to her.

Now retired, Frank favored comfortable track suits and used more than a little dab of the Brylcreem that left comb tracks in his plentiful, steel-gray hair. He was remarkably light on his feet for such a big man; he'd boxed a bit in his youth and had kept himself in shape. The boxing explained his crooked nose—broken in a fight, along with quite a few teeth—but dentures gave him a perfect smile. She planted a kiss on his freshly shaven cheek. "Not yet"

"Sit," he ordered, waving his ladle at the kitchen table. "How 'bout a bowl of minestrone? I know you like to watch your weight."

"That would be great," she agreed, although Big Frank's minestrone, which was loaded with pasta and beans and topped with a big handful of cheese, was hardly low-calorie. She'd skip the bread, she promised herself, and besides, it had been a tough, calorie-burning kind of day, what with wrestling the dog and shopping for Frank-O.

Mom set the table for Carole, setting down a big basket of bread and offering to pour her a glass of wine. Carole asked for Pellegrino, instead, and was surprised when Mom poured a big glass of Chianti for herself and joined her at the table.

"I'm worried about Frank," she said, by way of explanation. "The stress is killing me."

"I'm telling you, stop worrying," said Big Frank, whacking a garlic clove into small pieces with a chef's knife. "He's innocent; he'll get off."

"I don't know," sighed Mom, watching as Carole spooned up the delicious soup. "Look what they did to Buddy."

"That was a long time ago; Buddy's gone, rest his soul. Things have changed. And besides," he added, waving the knife, "Buddy wasn't exactly innocent, like Frank."

"Even so." Mom was shaking her head. "I don't like it. And what's going to happen if Frank goes to jail? Paulie can't run the business by himself. We'll all be ruined."

"We've just got to have faith, Mom," said Carole, who was slathering butter on a piece of bread, a sure sign of her distress. "I saw Frank-O," she said, changing the subject. "He was part of a demonstration; they were marching on Pleasant Vallely Parkway."

"Such a good boy, trying to save the unborn babies. Or was it the homeless?" asked Mom.

"The artists," said Carole, as Big Frank added another ladleful of soup to her bowl.

"Bless them," said Mom. After a moment she added, "Frank-O sure reminds me of his father, when he was younger."

Carole couldn't really see the similarity, but before she could follow up on that thought, Big Frank was asking, "So what's the plan? Has Houlihan come up with a line of defense?"

"Not that I've heard," admitted Carole, raising a spoon full of beans and tomatoes to her lips. "But Frank has some ideas of his own. He thinks it was somebody at Prospect Place who killed the old guy, probably because they have some deep, dark secret. That Browne was a stickler; he insisted he wouldn't tolerate any impropriety in his family home." She dipped her spoon into the bowl and swirled it around thoughtfully. "Frank thinks we can investigate ourselves, but I don't see how. We tried to get some info about Hosea from Connie; he was a Dunne and Willoughby client, but she couldn't tell us much because of attorney-client privilege."

"That girl works too hard," said Ma, lifting her glass. "She's so conscientious."

"I know, Mom." Carole took a sip of water. "I wish she'd find a nice fellow and start a family."

"From your lips to God's ears," said Mom, crossing herself. "I think Frank might be on to something. If anybody wanted to kill that old meanie, it was probably his neighbors. After all, they were the ones who had to live with him."

"The real estate lady, Susan Weaver, had a motive. He nixed every offer she brought him, costing her a hefty commission, which Sonia at Happy Nails says she needs real bad." Carole polished off the last of her soup and shook her head when Big Frank raised his ladle, offering more. "I've invited her to lunch, so I can question her. But how do I get to talk to the others? I can't just knock on their doors and invite myself in; they'll tell me to get lost."

"Especially if they're guilty," said Big Frank, pounding away at some veal cutlets with a mallet.

"Hold on," said Mom, checking her phone. "I got an idea. I saw something when I was looking for casting calls."

Behind his wife, Big Frank made circles around his ear with his forefinger, indicating his wife was crazy. Carole smiled at him, while Mom scrolled down the screen. She knew Mom was an enthusiastic amateur actress who always had a lead role in the parish musical every year. She'd also snagged a few minor parts at Trinity Rep and frequently got hired as an extra when movie crews filmed in Providence. Her last appearance was as a mourner in a mob funeral scene for a TV pilot that never got picked up.

"Here it is!" she exclaimed. "Help Wanted. Cleaning person for Prospect Place condo. Call Angelique at 401-565-2368."

"I'm not a cleaning lady; I have a cleaning lady," said Carole, holding out her hands. "And besides, I just got a manicure."

"Well, if you think a manicure is more important than your husband's freedom," said Big Frank.

"I can lend you my rubber gloves," added Mom.

"Look at me," said Carole, framing her face with her hands. "Do I look like a cleaning lady? My dye job alone costs more than I pay my own cleaning lady."

"You can go in disguise," said Mom.

"Yeah, but I'm no actress, like you. I couldn't convince anybody that I know how to clean. It's been years since I ran a vacuum."

"I'll go, too. We'll be a team. I'll do the talking; we'll pretend you don't speak English." Mom was warming to her theme. "That will be even better because they'll talk freely in front of you, thinking you don't understand."

"I think that kind of thing only happens in movies and mystery books," said Carole.

"It's worth a try, isn't it? Do you have a better idea?"

demanded Mom. "Honestly, sometimes I think you wouldn't mind if Frank went to jail."

"Well, I wouldn't mind for a couple of days," admitted Carole, with a sly smile. "But eventually I'm sure I'd miss him."

Behind Mom, still at the stove, Frank was heaving with laughter. Mom, however, wasn't amused. "Oh, you can joke; you didn't go through labor for forty-eight hours to deliver a ten-pound baby Frank, did you?"

"No, Mom," admitted Carole, "but I have had to put up with him for longer than you did. He was twenty-one when he got married, and that was twenty-seven years ago this October."

Mom wasn't listening; she was already on the phone calling Angelique Poole. In a matter of minutes, they had set up an interview. "Tomorrow, ten o'clock. My partner and I will be there," she was saying, giving Carole a look as she hung up the receiver. "So be here at nine-thirty and look like your cleaning lady."

"I can't, Mom. She's Black."

"You know what I mean," said Mom.

"Okay, it's worth a try," said Carole, rising from her chair. She never ate this much and felt stuffed, but in a good way. Big Frank was busy filling a big plastic cooler with packages of frozen food for her.

"I got some manicot'," he told her, piling on the containers. "Some gravy, some chicken parm, some cacciatore."

"Great. Frank's got to keep up his strength, right?"

"Right, baby," he said, giving her a hug. "Want me to carry it out to the car for you?"

"Sure, thanks," said Carole, figuring he wanted to get her alone, out of Mom's hearing.

He was already out the door as Carole gave Mom a parting hug. "I'll see you tomorrow," she promised. "I'll wear polyester."

"Good girl," said Mom, patting her on the back. "No heels."

"Right, Mom."

She followed Frank outside, finding him standing by her car. "What'sa matter with the dog?" he asked. "She's out like a light, didn't even wake up when I opened the door."

"She's on tranquilizers," said Carole. "Wouldn't stop barking this morning."

"She's probably worried about Frank," said Big Frank, nodding wisely. "I just want you to know, you gotta take this serious. I know Mom thinks he's gonna get off 'cause he's innocent, but there's other stuff going on here. There's plenty of people wouldn't mind seeing Frank go down, you know?"

"Yeah," agreed Carole, giving him a parting hug. "The price of success, I guess."

Then she was back at the wheel, starting the car and studying her freshly done nails. How was she ever going to convince anybody she was a cleaning lady with nails like these? She'd have to cut them, that was that. She sighed and was starting to back out when her phone rang. She braked and, seeing Susan Weaver's name, swiped it.

"Hi, Susan," she said, cheerily. "I was hoping we could get together for lunch."

"Thanks, that would be nice. I checked my schedule; how about noon tomorrow?"

Carole calculated. She had the interview at ten; it would be tight, but she figured she could be dressed and ready by noon. "Okay," she agreed. "What's convenient for you? Red Stripe?"

Susan said Red Stripe, a French-themed bistro, would be perfect. "See you then," said Carole, ending the call. She checked the backup camera screen and began rolling out of the driveway, deciding this investigating wasn't so hard, after all. In fact, she thought to herself with a little giggle, it was actually kind of fun.

Chapter Seven

Poopsie was still out like a light when Carole parked the Cayenne in her favorite spot in the garage, on the second level near the pedestrian bridge. She knew she couldn't manage to carry the big cooler up to the apartment, so she left the sleeping dog in the car and went on down to the lobby to check the mail and borrow one of the wheeled carts the concierge kept for the tenants' use.

Barry was on duty today, sitting behind the slab of angled steel that had been salvaged in the rehab and recast as a modernistic, industrial-chic desk. Carole loved the desk, but she wasn't that keen on Barry, who was a stickler for detail. That meant she'd have to sign the cart out and, worse, return it. Big pain.

"Hi, Barry," she said, giving him a big smile. "I need to use the cart."

"Sign here," he said passing a clipboard across the desk to her. He pursed his lips and leaned toward her, whispering, "There's a note from the management in your box."

"I probably got an award for being the best tenant," she joked. That was one of the things, maybe the only thing, she didn't like about renting: the way the management bossed the tenants around. Considering how much they were paying every month, you'd think they would be treated like valued customers, customers who were always right, right? Wrong. The management held all the cards; they wrote the rules, and the tenants were supposed to knuckle under and follow those rules, or else. Opening her mailbox and pulling out the assorted bills and letters, Carole knew exactly what the complaint was this time.

> Dear Mr. and Mrs. Capobianco:
> As property manager, it is my responsibility to inform you that I have received numerous complaints from tenants concerning your dog, which barks excessively and persistently, according to reports. These reports, I might add, have been confirmed by building staff.
> Pets are allowed in the building at the discretion of the management, as long as they do not interfere with the comfort and enjoyment of the other tenants. For further details, see Section VI, paragraph 3 of the Rental Agreement.
> Unfortunately, this is not the first time there have been complaints concerning your dog, and if the situation does not improve, there is a strong possibility that we will no longer be able to accommodate your pet here at the Esplanade.
> Sincerely yours,
> Doriss Chomsky,
> Property Manager

Carole read the letter as the crossed the lobby, pushing the rumbling cart ahead of her. Who was this Doriss woman? Whoever she was, Carole was positive she'd never actually met her. She must spend her days hiding in some back office. And so much for the two-thousand-dollar pet deposit they'd paid; it didn't seem to have bought them much. Not to mention the two hundred dollars she'd tipped Barry at Christmas. Good luck next year, she thought, stuffing the paper in her purse and pushing the button for the elevator. When it arrived, Joao, the Brazilian kid who collected the garbage and vacuumed the halls, was inside.

"Hi, Mrs. Capobianco," he said, noticing the cart. "You need help with something?"

Carole cheered up; some people evidently appreciated their Christmas tips. "I do," she said. "Thanks."

Joao took charge of the cart as they rode up to the second floor.

"So how's the family?" she asked, as they made their way to the garage.

"My mom's doing better; she doesn't miss Brazil so much," he said. "But the weather! She hates the cold!"

"Me, too," sympathized Carole. "But spring is almost here. The days are already getting longer; warm weather is on its way."

At the car, Carole unlocked the door, and Joao lifted out the cooler, while Carole roused Poopsie. The dog was groggy, but she followed Carole on the leash, weaving unsteadily from side to side.

"Is your dog sick?" asked Joao, his soft brown eyes full of concern.

Carole loved this kid. "She was barking this morning, so I gave her some tranquilizers. They made her sleepy."

Joao nodded as he held the garage door for her. "Dogs don't like apartments; they like the country. And if you gotta live in the city, you gotta make sure they get a lot of exercise."

"I think you're right," agreed Carole.

"I'm talking from experience, y'know. I got a dog."

"Yeah? What breed?"

"Pit bull."

"Oh," replied Carole, a bit surprised. Joao was more interesting than she'd thought.

Returning to the building, they encountered Tilly, another staff member, wrestling with a massive, industrial carpet-cleaning machine. Seeing her, Carole had an idea.

"Listen," she said, waving a hand at the cooler, "I got all this food here. Frank's father made it and we can't eat it all. Do you want some?"

"Sure," said Tilly, promptly switching the noisy machine off.

"You're very generous," said Joao, as Carole popped the lid on the cooler.

"What do you want? Lasagna? Manicotti? I've got it all," said Carole, passing out half a dozen packages. Down at the far end of the hall, she spotted Pinky, the super, and his assistant, Wilson, and waved at them.

"What's this?" asked Pinky, looking at the cooler.

"Frank's dad loves to cook, but I don't have room in my freezer," said Carole. She actually had plenty of room; in fact, she relied on Big Frank's cooking to feed Frank, since she didn't really like to cook much herself. She was willing to make the sacrifice, however, if she could win them over with the food. "Can I convince you to try some of his cacciatore? It's sooo good . . ."

"I don't need no convincing," said Wilson, stretching out his hands, dark chocolate brown on the backs and pink on the palms. "Say, what's the matter with your dog?"

Poopsie was standing unsteadily with her legs splayed out, looking woozy.

"She was barking this morning, and I don't want her to disturb the other tenants, so I got some tranquilizers for her. I don't think it will be a problem anymore." She made eye contact with them, one at a time, her arms full of frozen food. "Will it be a problem?"

"Dogs bark; it's natural," said Pinky, accepting a couple of containers of cacciatore, a container of gravy, and a chicken parm.

"Boss is right," agreed Wilson, topping his load with a foil-wrapped baton of garlic bread. "Thanks, Mrs. Capobianco."

"I got a couple more," coaxed Carole, studying something lumpy wrapped in white freezer paper. "Looks like osso buco to me. You ought to try this. It's delish."

"You sure, Mrs. C?" asked Joao. "There's nothing left for you and Mr. C."

"No problem; we got plenty upstairs," fibbed Carole, handing them over. "But, hon, do me a favor? Return the cart for me?"

"Sure thing," said Joao. "Want me to put the cooler back in your car?"

"You're a peach," said Carole, handing over the keys and scooping up Poopsie, who was about to topple over. Next time, she thought, stepping into the elevator, she'd try giving the dog half a tablet and see how that went.

When Frank got home, she suggested going out for dinner, explaining she'd given all of Big Frank's food to the building staff so they wouldn't turn Poopsie in if she started barking again.

"A little insurance?" asked Frank, cocking an eyebrow.

Sounded like a good idea to Carole. "Can you get dog insurance? In case she bites someone?"

"We got a hefty umbrella policy," said Frank, landing

heavily in his La-Z-Boy and clicking on the TV to the sports network. Poopsie, who was starting to come around, made it up to his lap on the third try and settled down, just like she always did, so he could scratch behind her ears. "You know," he continued, "I could go for one of 'em big, thick burgers they got at Trinity Brewhouse."

About a gazillion calories, thought Carole, not to mention the mountain of fries they came with. And, of course, the beer. Liquid bread, they called it because it was loaded with carbs. But, hey, anything to keep Frank happy. And they had salads. "Fine with me," she said.

Neither one of them thought to remember that the pub was right down the street from *The Providence Journal* building, making it a favorite hangout for reporters. The bar was overflowing when they arrived and were seated at a booth.

"IPA for me," Frank told the waitress. "Chardonnay for you?" he asked Carole.

"Sure," agreed Carole, who said she had heard Frank's name mentioned by some guy at the bar.

"What's going on?" demanded Frank, as Carole opened her menu. "They talkin' about me?" He was ready to go over and punch somebody.

"Hold your horses," advised Carole, reaching for his arm. "They're reporters, and you've been in the news lately."

"I don' care who they are," growled Frank. "I don't like bein' talked about."

"You're news, Frank," said Carole. "You better get used to it."

"Well, I'm not," he said, starting to rise. "Let's go someplace else."

Looking across the room, Carole recognized Adrienne Viola, the *Journal*'s chief investigative reporter, heading for the stairs to the basement restrooms. "I gotta use the ladies' first," said Carole.

Frank scowled. "Already? Shoulda gone before you left the house."

"I did," snapped Carole. "It's a woman thing. I had two kids, and I don't have to account to you for my bladder or my . . ."

"Nah, nah." Frank was holding up his hands as if to ward off some witchy spell and backing off. He hated what he called "woman problems," joking that feminine "plumbing" was a mystery to him and he wanted to keep it that way.

Downstairs, Carole was standing at the sink and patting her expensively highlighted hair when Adrienne came out of a stall.

"Don't mind me," said Carole, stepping aside so Adrienne could use the sink. "I'm just freshening up." She started groping in her bag for her makeup case.

As Carole expected, Adrienne, a petite brunette with a pixie cut, wasn't about to let an opportunity like this pass. She was a reporter, alone in the ladies' room with the wife of an accused murderer, a plumbing contractor who was rumored to be connected, but if he wasn't, which most people thought was unlikely, he certainly knew people who were. There could be a story here. "So how's Frank holding up?" she asked, turning on the tap.

"He's fine," said Carole, sounding like a well-prepped wife. "He knows he's innocent, and he welcomes the opportunity to prove it."

Adrienne soaped her hands.

"He's got nerves of steel," said Carole, hoping she could get some information out of Adrienne without actually giving her any.

"It's not just the murder," continued Adrienne, lathering up. "There's all that talk about the Factory contracts."

"You can't believe everything you hear," said Carole, unzipping the pouch and pulling out a lipstick. "What exactly are people saying?"

"The usual," replied Adrienne, rinsing her hands. "Threats, payoffs, that sort of thing."

Carole sighed. "That's just because Frank's Italian..."

"I know." Adrienne was drying her hands with a paper towel. "That's what I told my editor, but he went ahead anyway and assigned an investigative team to the project. He's even hiring a forensic accountant, and those guys don't come cheap."

Leaning into the mirror, applying her Chanel Rouge Absolu, Carole recognized the *I'm really your friend* tactic. She decided to play along. "What's a forensic accountant?"

"Fancy bookkeeper, knows how to spot fraud."

Carole didn't like the sound of this, but didn't want to seem concerned. "Are you on the team?" she asked.

"No. I'm covering the city council meeting tonight. Some of the folks from Valley Street who are being displaced by the Factory are scheduled to speak." She studied her reflection in the mirror and ran her fingers through her hair, fluffing it up. "Ought to be interesting. Those artists are a lively bunch."

"Artists!" snorted Carole. "Far as I know, it's mostly chop shops and T-shirt printers down there."

"Them, too," admitted Adrienne, laughing as if Carole had made a joke.

Carole smiled, too. It never hurt to have a reporter on your side.

When Carole got back to the table, she found Frank had

gone, leaving a couple of crisp twenties under his empty glass. Her untouched wineglass sat on one of those cardboard coasters, so she took a big swallow and went outside, shrugging into her fur-trimmed jacket.

"What now?" she asked, slipping into the car beside him. He had the engine running.

"Let's get a pie at Caserta's," he said. "I couldn't take it in there; they were all giving me looks, you know," he explained, with a shrug. "Bunch of a-holes, pardon my French."

Caserta's wasn't too busy on a weekday night, and they got a table in the rear, after ordering a nine-square pie and a salad for Carole. Unlike just about every other pizza in the world, including those in Providence, Caserta's pizzas were square. "We can take the extra home," said Frank, as they seated themselves and waited for their number to come up.

"What did you get out of Viola?" he asked.

Carole raised one delicately arched brow, remembering the sheer agony of getting it waxed into shape. "I didn't think you noticed," she said.

"I see more than you think," replied Frank, with a grin and a wink.

Carole felt warm all over—you had to love the guy. He was annoying, for sure, but so damn cute. "The *Journal*'s assigned a team to investigate the Factory, including a forensic accountant."

Frank nodded. "Viola's on the team?"

"No, she's covering the Factory neighbors' protest at the City Council meeting tonight." As soon as the words were out, Carole knew she'd made a mistake. What if Frank wanted to go, to defend the project? And what if Frank-O was there, too? She could already see the headlines.

"Somebody's always got a beef," muttered Frank, as their number was called and he got to his feet. Returning with the pie, he announced his decision. "I guess we might as well go. We might pick up some information for our investigation, right?"

"I don't think so, Frank," protested Carole. "After all, you yourself said Browne was probably killed by somebody from Prospect Place."

"Yeah," said Frank, getting most of a piece of pizza in one bite. "But the first rule of investigation . . ."

"There are rules?"

Frank gave her a look. "Yes, there are rules, and rule number one is to keep an open mind, and rule number two is to gather as much information as you can. We're going to the meeting."

"Okay, Frank," said Carole, nibbling at her slice. "Where's my salad?"

The City Council's chamber was packed when they arrived, and the crowd of artists and tradespeople was spilling out into the hall. This was not a problem for Frank, who ploughed his way through, with Carole following in his wake, like Moses leading the Israelites through the Red Sea. Once inside, he made his way down to the front row, where he tapped on somebody's shoulder. The guy, startled, jumped up when he recognized Frank, first nudging the guy next to him, who also got up. Now Frank and Carole had front row seats.

When stuff like this happened, and it happened quite a bit, Carole was always amazed—and worried. "Who are those men?" she asked.

"Guys I know," said Frank, shrugging and slapping his hands, palm down, on his knees, which were spread wide apart. Frank wasn't really that big a man, but he took up a lot of space.

Carole looked around while they waited for the council members to appear. Being in the first row, she couldn't easily see the back of the room to find out if Frank-O was in the crowd, but she sincerely hoped he wasn't, and if he was, that he would keep quiet. The view of the front of the room wasn't very inspiring. The place could use a coat of paint, and she didn't much like the color, whatever it was supposed to be. The fluorescent lighting was out of date and very unflattering; the place could use a redo. And so, she thought, could the council members, who she judged a scruffy lot as they filed in and took their seats. All except for the president, a young guy oozing ambition with moussed hair, an overlong red tie, and a blue Brioni suit, copying you-know-who. And there was a distinguished-looking old guy with white hair and a bow tie—the East Side's representative, she was willing to bet on it.

"I'm calling the meeting to order," said the president, banging his gavel. "We'll begin with the usual public comment period."

A forest of hands shot up, and Carole crossed her fingers. No blue hairdo, please, she prayed, every time a new speaker was recognized. They all said pretty much the same thing: they enjoyed low rents in their studios and workshops and would be driven out of business by the Factory. Providence would lose valuable diversity; artists would be forced to relocate to Pawtucket, depriving the city of vision and creativity, not to mention the probable loss of a number of first-class auto body shops.

Finally, Frank was allowed to speak.

"This is a load of crap," he began. "Let's cut through the bullshit here, pardon my French."

A few people laughed, but Frank was undeterred. "This place you're all so crazy about is one big dump. You people ought to be ashamed of yourselves. Why do you want to live and work in these crappy conditions? Low rent is good for you, I get that, but considering the money you save, how come you don't buy a gallon of paint? It's cheap enough. Or pick up the trash; that don't cost nothing. The place is a health hazard. I see rats down there, garbage everywhere. So, the way I see it, take your filth and crap and your precious creativity to Pawtucket. I won't miss it. We're gonna make this a place people can be proud of; that's all I have to say."

While Frank was talking, Carole managed to angle herself so she could see more of the room. She looked for Frank-O but didn't see him. She spotted Adrienne and a couple of other reporters and photographers; the cameras were pointed in Frank's direction. And she spotted somebody familiar. Stu something. Stu from sixth grade; he hadn't changed a bit. Sempione. That's it. Stu Sempione. She'd know him anywhere. He was a big tattletale who'd gotten her and her friends in trouble plenty of times. "Sister, I saw Carole stick her chewing gum under the desk," he'd say. Or, "Sister, I saw Carole roll up her skirt when she left school yesterday to make it shorter."

What had become of Stu, she wondered. Hadn't she heard something, something that she'd thought was terribly fitting, and thus funny? Like he'd become a cop. An undercover cop, that was it. And was that Frank-O standing next to him?

On the way home, she asked Frank if he'd seen Stu Sempione.

"The narc?"

"Is that what he is? A narc?"

"Yeah," said Frank.

"So why was he at the meeting?" asked Carole. "I thought the cops were interested in fraud."

"'Cause of the artists," said Frank, taking a corner a mite too fast, so that Carole had to hang on to the grab bar over the door. "Those creative types like to experiment with hallucinogens, mushrooms, crap like that. Expand their minds."

"Oh," said Carole, as a broad avenue for future worry opened before her. "You don't think Frank-O uses, do you?"

"Better not," said Frank, flooring the gas to make a yellow light. "I'll kill him if he does."

Chapter Eight

Next morning, Poopsie woke Carole as usual, nudging her with a cold nose and demanding her walk. And, as usual, Carole splashed some cold water on her face, ran a comb through her hair, and pulled on her track suit, boots, and jacket. Poopsie wore her pink rhinestone collar.

Carole felt a sense of relief as Poopsie dragged her down the four flights of stairs; she'd felt uneasy about the effect the tranquilizers could have had on the little dog. She'd wanted to calm her down, not knock her out. Truth be told, Carole didn't much like drugs at all. If she had a headache, she'd lie down on the couch for half an hour and see if it went away rather than take anything, even an aspirin. If she had an upset stomach, it was clear fluids for a day or two rather than Pepto-Bismol.

It was a puzzle, though, she thought, checking the lobby to see if it was empty before making the dash for the door. Why wouldn't Poopsie stop barking yesterday? Today she seemed fine, sniffing her way up Edith Street, pausing to squat at the last tree.

While she waited for the dog to finish, Carole assessed the weather. It was a damp, drizzly morning, too cool for comfort. She shivered as they started the climb up the hill toward Smith Street and decided to take a shorter route, turning down West Park, where there were houses on only one side of the street. The other side ran along the back of the Esplanade property, behind the garage, and was largely unkempt and perfect for dog-walking purposes. Nobody expected you to scoop the poop here, although Carole did.

She was debating with herself whether to give Poopsie another dog pill or not. She sure didn't want another barking episode, but she also didn't want to dope the dog unnecessarily. Poor little thing, thought Carole, studying the dog. Her senses were so finely tuned that she was easily upset. Brittanys were bred to find birds in the brush and could hear tiny noises that humans couldn't. That was it, Carole decided. Poopsie had probably heard something yesterday that set her off, something that she couldn't hear. And today, whatever that was, it was apparently silent.

Poopsie suddenly scooted off, and Carole followed with a lurch. They were at the corner of Caverly Street, and she could see Frank-O's building. There were lights on in his apartment, so she decided to pay a quick, surprise visit, just to see if he was all right. It wasn't that she thought he was doping himself with heroin or LSD or cocaine or ecstasy, nothing like that. She just wanted to know if he'd found the groceries she'd left for him yesterday and if he'd remembered to put the food in the fridge.

"C'mon," she coaxed the dog, who hesitated at the door. "We're going to visit Frank-O."

Hearing the name, Poopsie lifted her ears. She loved Frank-O and obediently followed Carole inside and up the creaky, uneven stairs. Poopsie gave each step a thorough examination with her nose, and Carole figured there must be quite an assortment of aromas: Chinese food here, pizza there, even a hint of New York System hot dogs. Those last, she thought, were a Providence recipe that would certainly surprise a New Yorker. Poopsie was prancing eagerly when they reached Frank-O's door and wagging her tail. Carole knew she was anticipating at least a pizza bone from Frank-O.

When there was no answer to her repeated knocks, Carole tried the knob, and the door opened. Calling Frank-O's name, she stepped inside. Poopsie went in, too, and immediately began checking out the pizza boxes that littered the floor.

Carole stepped gingerly over the mess: food containers, clothes, shoes, books. A couple of canvases were propped against a wall; a wooden crate held jars and tubes of paint. A coffee can sitting on a windowsill bristled with paint brushes. In the kitchen, the sink was overflowing with dirty dishes, and the bags of groceries had been set on the cluttered table; the plastic packages of food were still inside the bags. Sighing, she dumped most of it in the trash, salvaging only a couple of packages of cheese that she put in the fridge among the containers of half-eaten food. What a way to live!

Dismayed, she checked Frank-O's bedroom, but his unmade bed was empty. Either he had turned into an early riser, thought Carole, or he was shacking up with some girl. Or maybe he couldn't stand his own mess. As in the rest of the apartment, every surface was covered with clothes and books and shoes. The fug was unpleasant, so she cracked the window an inch to let in some fresh air and withdrew, ignoring the adjacent bathroom. She was not going to look in there, no way. Poopsie, however, found it fascinating, so Carole tried not to look as she grabbed the leash and pulled her away from the overflowing wastebasket, which had a used condom dangling over the side. Yuck.

On the bright side, she told herself, as she returned to the Esplanade, Frank-O was practicing safe sex, and she hadn't found any sign of drugs. No zip bags of pot, no vials of crack, no packets of white powder. Still, she couldn't help worrying. Where was Frank-O? As usual, Frank had an answer. "Probably got lucky with some artsy-fartsy broad," he said, with a shrug. "That kind have loose morals."

Recalling that dangling condom, Carole was inclined to agree. She tidied up the breakfast dishes, gave Frank a goodbye kiss, and went into the bedroom to get dressed. How exactly did a cleaning lady dress? Her own cleaning lady, Thomasina, went in for white shoes and hospital scrubs, but she was a top-of-the-line professional, referred by a top-notch service, and spoke in a clipped, British accent. That wasn't quite the look she and Mom were going for, thought Carole, flipping through the rack in her closet.

Well, she finally decided, the track suit she was wearing was probably the best she could do, and the dog-walking boots were appropriately worn. She pulled out one of Frank's sport shirts; it was a boldly patterned Tommy Bahama, but it was pretty old. It looked awful when she put it on over the track suit, so she kept it on and went over to her vanity table and sat down, staring at her face in the make-up mirror. Thomasina wore bright red lipstick, carefully applied, and gigantic gold hoop earrings. Again, not the downtrodden look she was going for. She dabbed on a bit of moisturizer and some lip gloss and figured that was all she could get away with. As for her hair, she left it uncombed and topped it with an old PawSox baseball cap. Honestly, she decided, taking one last look in the hall mirror as she left the apartment, she looked more like a clown than a cleaning lady.

"Not bad," said Mom, greeting her at the door, dressed in the costume she wore as Golde in last year's Parish Players' production of *Fiddler on the Roof*, "but we gotta do something about your hair. Those highlights probably cost ten dollars a foil..."

"More like twenty, Mom."

Mom raised her eyebrows.

"Seb is an artist," explained Carole.

"Seb?"

"Short for Sebastian."

"Oh." Mom was bent over, rummaging in a cardboard carton full of costumes she used for auditions. When she pulled out a polyester housedress, Carole recoiled in horror.

"I can't wear that," she protested. "It's orange."

"It's perfect," declared Mom. "We'll add a wig to cover your hair and maybe a little kerchief, give you an Eastern European look."

In for a penny, in for a pound, thought Carole. "Okay."

"Aieee!" shrieked Mom, reprising her performance as Golde. "Your nails!"

"I know." Carole splayed out her hands, displaying her gorgeous one-inch Vampire red nails. "I just couldn't cut them."

"All right," said Mom, diving under the kitchen sink. "Rubber gloves. If she asks, we'll say you have very sensitive skin."

"Okay," agreed Carole, taking the bright pink latex gloves. "Anything to save my manicure."

It was amazing, the way clothes changed your outlook,

thought Carole. She was trudging along Prospect Street with Mom, her pink-rubber-gloved hands shoved deep in the pockets of an old work jacket that belonged to Big Frank. Her head itched under the wig, which was tied on tight by the babushka scarf, and everything was slightly out of focus due to the reading glasses Mom had stuck on her nose. It was only a disguise, but it made Carole want to run and hide herself.

Oddly enough, even though Carole was acutely self-conscious, the people they passed didn't seem to see them at all. This was weird, thought Carole, who always got noticed and often got smiles from other people. It was as if the ugly clothes and dull brown wig had made her invisible. By the time they reached Prospect Place and she'd followed Mom up those ugly gray stone steps to ring the bell, she felt unworthy even to enter the imposing mansion. What was she doing here?

When the door opened and she saw Angelique, perfectly coiffed and dressed in a chic little black dress with a flower-printed scarf at the neck, she wished the earth would open and swallow her up. "You must be Mrs. Nowak and Mrs. Pijar," she said, stepping back so they could enter the hall. "Come right in."

"Goot morgning," said Mom, assuming what she thought was an Eastern European accent.

"My apartment is one flight up," said Angelique. "Follow me," she continued, climbing up one or two stairs and then pausing. "While we're here, you can look around you; this is the area you will be responsible for. The hall, the stairs, windows, and there is also a basement area."

"Ver' goot," said Mom, nodding. Carole nodded, too, for effect.

Angelique paused outside the door to her apartment, indicating the hall, which was spacious and contained several large pieces of furniture: a table, a pair of wooden armchairs, and several large paintings. Heavy drapes hung at the two enormous windows, which were deeply set and had cushioned window seats. "As you see, this is more than the usual condo cleaning job. You need to know how to care for antique furniture, paintings, and rugs, as well as the silk curtains."

"Beeshwax," declared Mom. "Besht for wood."

"Exactly," said Angelique, opening the door and ushering them inside her apartment.

Behind her, Mom met Carole's eyes and gave her a thumbs-up. In response, Carole stuck up one of her pink latex thumbs. Surreal, real surreal, she thought, keeping her eyes down and scuttling along behind Mom.

"You, I take it, are Mrs. Nowak?" Angelique was addressing Mom, who nodded. "And you are . . ." she began, looking Carole over from head to toe.

"Mrs. Pijar," supplied Mom. "Her English not yet goot. Sheesh from Dubrovnik. Jusht come lasht mo'."

Carole picked up her head at the word *Dubrovnik*, hopefully indicating it was a familiar word she recognized, then returned her gaze to the floor. Dusty, very dusty, she saw, and covered with a turquoise rug with pink flowers. And French women were supposed to be so chic. Glancing around, she noticed the walls were lined with bookcases containing strange objects, like broken bits of statuary and crockery, as well as books. Lots of books. Well, she thought to herself, both Angelique and her husband were professors, so they probably would have books.

"I think we'll go in the kitchen," suggested Angelique. "Follow me."

Once again, they made a little procession through a

smaller room, which was obviously a study, and down a dark hallway. Angelique pushed open the swinging door, and they were suddenly zapped by a flood of bright light that poured from countless ceiling fixtures and bounced off polished stainless-steel appliances and caromed off snowy white marble counters and glossy white subway tile walls, ricocheting from one surface to another until finally crashing into their dazzled eyes.

"Wow!" exclaimed Carole, blinking furiously and slipping out of character.

"Exaktly," chimed in Mom, giving her a warning look.

"This is where I am most at home," explained Angelique, in her light French accent. "I've cooked all my life. I teach confectionary at Johnson and Wales." She waved a hand toward a table set by the window. "Sit down, please, and I'll give you some tea, and we can talk."

After she had filled their cups with lightly scented chamomile tea and set a plate of golden madeleines on the table, Angelique began explaining the job. "It's just one morning a week, and only the public—no, that's not the right word," she said, pausing thoughtfully, "the *shared* spaces in the building. The foyer, the stairs, the halls. But, as I indicated, these areas contain valuable carpets and furniture that require special care."

"In Dubrovnik, my friend Mishus Pijar worked in big hishtorical palash," affirmed Mom.

"Yesh," agreed Carole. "Palash."

"She kleen golt gilt, shilk, cryshtal, all verry, verry olt and delikat."

Carole nodded furiously, avoiding eye contact. Angelique was giving her odd little looks; she was no dummy, that was for sure, and Carole was afraid she was getting suspicious.

"You teech canty?" asked Mom, going on the offensive.

Angelique laughed, setting her fragile cup on its saucer. "I do. I teach in the culinary department at Johnson and Wales. My specialty is pastry, candy, anything with sugar and butter." She slid the plate of madeleines toward them. "Try these, I made them myself."

Mom took a bite. "Mmm," she said. "Ver goot. I ne'r het befoor."

"They're a French delicacy. I'm from France, you see."

"Yoo English ver' goot," declared Mom. "Yoo here lonk?"

"A couple of years," said Angelique. "I met my husband on vacation in the French West Indies, on Saint Martin. It's very popular with French people. We met, we fell in love, and I ended up here. *C'est l'amour, n'est-ce pas?*"

"Ah, l'amoor," said Mom, nodding wisely. "And how you say? Privak work, for utter tenansh? Ish poshible?"

"Perhaps," said Angelique, with a shrug. "You'd have to arrange with each one separately."

"Yoo?" asked Mom. "I notish mush dusht."

Carole figured Mom had blown it, but Angelique just laughed, a tinkly little charming French laugh. "That's my husband; he gets upset if anything is moved. My kitchen, you see, is very clean."

"Yesh, verry," agreed Mom, nodding away.

"Well," said Angelique, rising and indicating the interview was over. She ushered them back through the apartment, speaking as she went. "I have some other people to interview, but I'll let you know in a day or two. And, oh, the pay is fifteen dollars an hour, is that acceptable?"

"For two?" demanded Mom, snapping to attention at the top of the stairs.

"No, no, fifteen hours each, for four hours a week,"

said Angelique, proceeding down the stairs. "That's sixty dollars each. Okay?"

"Sheventy-five," said Mom, unable to resist bargaining. They were at the door, so it was a last-ditch attempt.

"I will take that under advisement," said Angelique, closing the massive front door behind them.

Once outside, on the stoop, Carole began laughing so hard she had to hold her stomach. "I thought I'd die in there," she declared. "Dushty? What sort of accent is that?"

Mom raised herself to her full five feet one inch. "I'll have you know I got an A in that dialect class I took at Providence College." Mom was always taking acting courses. "And anyway, I think she fell for it."

"I think she did, thanks to you," admitted Carole, as they headed back along Prospect Street to the car. "Do you think we'll get the job?"

"I wouldn't be surprised," said Mom. "Madame Angelique can be as snooty as she wants, but we're probably the only ones who'll take the job for such crummy pay."

It was already almost twelve when Carole dropped Mom off at home; she didn't have time to change or she'd be late for lunch with Susan Weaver. She couldn't go the way she was, though, so she yanked the scarf and wig off as she drove back across town to the East Side, where Red Stripe was located, near Wayland Square. She plunked her makeup bag in her lap and brushed on some bronzer as she drove. Stopping at a traffic light, she dabbed on some mascara and lipstick, and she brushed her hair as she crept along on Waterman Street. Finally reaching the parking lot off Wayland Street, she wiggled out of the jacket and housedress; the navy blue velour track suit wasn't what she would normally wear to lunch, but lots of women did. As for the grubby boots, hopefully Susan wouldn't notice.

Reaching down to the floor, where she'd hidden her Prada bag, she grabbed it and hopped out of the car. She hurried down Angell Street, already fifteen minutes late.

Susan was seated in a booth and was checking her watch when Carole arrived, giving her a big wave as she sailed across the bistro's dining room and plunked herself down at the table. She was opening her purse, which she'd set down on the banquette, and discovered the five fingers of a rubber glove sticking out of the black bag, looking like five little pink balloons.

"Thanks for waiting," cooed Carole, as she tried to unobtrusively stuff the uncooperative pink latex—it looked for all the world like a bright pink cow's udder—back inside her bag. "I think I'll have a drink. How about you? Some chardonnay?"

Chapter Nine

When Susan hesitated, Carole decided to make it clear that lunch was her treat.

"Let's say it's my way of making up for the Prospect Place sale," she said, signaling the waiter. "Please have whatever you want."

"You don't need to do this," said Susan. "It wasn't your fault; you were certainly well-qualified buyers."

"I know, but I want to," insisted Carole, as the waiter approached, and she ordered the two glasses of wine. "I don't suppose," she continued to Susan, "now that Hosea is gone, that maybe there's a chance for us to get that place?"

"I don't know," admitted Susan, shrugging. "It all depends on the brother, Jon. From what I gather, he's some sort of Indiana Jones type, digging away at an archaeological site in Peru. Probably some remote location in the mountains or something. It may be some time before he can get back to Providence. I think that's why they haven't announced a funeral yet. I think they're waiting for him."

"I was wondering about that," said Carole, as the wine

arrived. She hoisted her glass in a toast, clinking with Susan's. "Salute!"

They both took a sip of wine and then bent their heads over the menu. Carole ordered a salad, with the dressing on the side, and Susan went for steak frites, which Carole thought indicated either a very high metabolism or the need to fill her stomach on somebody else's tab. "Do you want to switch to red?" asked Carole, indicating the wine.

"No, no, this is plenty for me. I have to get back to work."

"I don't usually drink with lunch," said Carole. "I've had kind of a stressful day."

"That's understandable," sympathized Susan. "Of course, I'm sure Frank is innocent, but even so, it must be a very difficult time for you."

"You have no idea," said Carole, twirling the stem of her wineglass between her fingers. "Or maybe you do. It must have been very disappointing for you when Hosea Browne nixed the sale."

"Not just you guys, but a couple of others, too," exclaimed Susan. She leaned forward and lowered her voice. "I had high hopes for one couple, lovely professionals, but Hosea voted no. I'm sure it was because they were Black. He said it was for their own good; they'd be happier someplace else, with their own kind!"

"That's what he said about us," said Carole, "but he was right. I am happy at the Esplanade. I love our gorgeous new apartment."

"But you're still in the market?" asked Susan, anxiously.

"Sure, if the right place comes along." Carole took a sip

of wine. "Frank hates paying rent. He doesn't believe in it. And there are so many rules. You know, I can't even hang a wreath on my apartment door at Christmas!"

"It's always better to own. I'll keep you in mind," promised Susan, as their food arrived. "But you're still interested in Prospect Place?"

That ship had sailed as far as Carole was concerned, but she didn't want Susan to know that. "Frank loved it," she said, with an encouraging smile.

"It's a fantastic property. Unique, with all that history," said Susan, with a sigh. "But Hosea's death has put everything on hold. It's a great address, and people are lining up to buy in, but I can't even show the condo until Jon Browne arrives from Peru, whenever that is. And even then, we'll have to wait for the funeral," she continued, "and then nobody knows what will happen because it's part of Hosea's estate. There'll be lawyers, bankers, claims, and counter-claims; it could be months before it's back on the market."

Susan looked so mournful that Carole reluctantly crossed her off the list of suspects. It seemed clear that she was one of the very few people who would actually prefer that Hosea Browne were still alive and therefore wouldn't have murdered him. But what about the other Prospect Place residents?

"You know," she began, spearing a piece of lettuce, "Frank has a theory that somebody at Prospect Place killed Hosea Browne."

"Really?" Susan's eyebrows shot up quizzically, and Carole noticed she needed a waxing. "Whyever would one of them do that?"

"Remember how he said that he wouldn't tolerate any

impropriety in his family home? Frank thinks somebody up there has a dirty secret they want to hide."

"Everybody's got secrets," agreed Susan, slicing into her steak. "Believe me, in this business you see a lot! But the Prospect Place bunch all seem pretty respectable to me."

"What about Millicent Shaw?" asked Carole. "Doesn't she seem too good to be true?"

Susan shook her head. "She's a real lady, with those lovely, old-fashioned manners. She's been nothing but sweet to me; she even sent me a handwritten note of encouragement after Hosea turned you down."

"What do you know about her?" persisted Carole.

Susan chewed thoughtfully. "She seems to be one of those rare people who always looks for the good in others. One time, I complained to her that we'd never find a buyer who would satisfy Hosea, and she just laughed, said he was a relic from an earlier time. But then she went on and said that wasn't always such a bad thing, that some of those old-fashioned virtues, like honesty and fair dealing, were in short supply these days, something like that."

"I'd call it turning a blind eye to bigotry, but then I'm not a Pollyanna like Millicent," said Carole, softening her declaration with a smile. "What about the Pooles? They seem a bit of an odd couple. She's quite a bit younger..."

"He's a fusty old thing, isn't he? I suspect he's pretty upset about losing Hosea. They were birds of a feather."

"Somehow I can't see Hosea approving of Angelique, though. She's so French."

"Are you kidding?" protested Susan. "They say the way

to a man's heart is through his stomach, and Hosea was no different. All she had to do was cook him a tarte tatin or something and he'd be a goner, head over heels with her."

"He looked pretty skinny to me," observed Carole. "Like he didn't really care about food."

"Trust me. He might have lived on a steady diet of English muffins and tea, but that doesn't mean he didn't appreciate free food when it was given to him. I brought some doughnut holes from Dunkin' to my first meeting with the Prospect Place owners, and he ate almost all of them."

Carole pushed a piece of frisée around her plate. "What about the professor?" she asked. "How was he like Hosea?"

Susan was making steady progress on her meal, chowing down on the steak and frites. "I think Angelique was his one moment of madness," she said. "His head is in the clouds; at least it was whenever I had any dealings with him. He just sort of nodded along, and I knew he wasn't really hearing a word I said." She laughed. "Like Hosea, he lives in an alternate reality. I once saw him on Benefit Street, walking along, reading. Reading a book, while he walked. Can you imagine?"

"Not on Benefit Street," said Carole. "The paving is so uneven it's practically impossible to walk there in heels."

"You said it," agreed Susan, finally putting down her fork and coming up for air. "This is so good, and it's so nice to just sit and chat with you like this. I've been so"—she paused, searching for the right word—"busy lately."

"Me, too," said Carole. "Would you like some coffee or tea? Some dessert?"

When Susan admitted that she wouldn't mind, Carole

asked the waiter for the dessert menu. "Go for the profiteroles," she urged, when he brought them. "They're delicious."

"Want to share?" asked Susan.

"Sure, I'll have a bite," she said. "And two coffees," she told the waiter. "*S'il vous plait.*"

"You speak French?" asked Susan.

"Tourist French. My mother lives in Paris, so I've picked up a little bit."

"Lucky you," enthused Susan. "It must be great having family in Paris."

"Sometimes," said Carole, noncommittally. "What about those Lonsdales? Frank calls them 'the skim-milk couple.'"

Susan laughed, nodding. "Mark and Celerie? I don't imagine Hosea had any trouble approving them," she said. "I don't know much about them. He's a banker; she's got an interior-design business. Somehow I think there might be some trust fund money in their background, but I'm just speculating."

"What makes you think that?"

"Well, those units start at well over a million, and even though they've got the smallest one, up on the top floor, it seems like a lot of money for a young couple to come up with."

Carole was inclined to agree. "Some people have it all, don't they? Rich parents, naturally blond hair, perfect teeth." Carole sighed. "Of course, she is named after a vegetable."

"You're not so badly off yourself," said Susan, smiling as the dessert and coffee arrived.

"It wasn't always like this," said Carole, grinning mischievously. "You know that old commercial? Frank made his money the old-fashioned way—he earned it."

When Carole left the restaurant, she had to admit to herself that, although she'd enjoyed the meal and Susan's company, she hadn't really gotten any incriminating information out of her. And now she was almost three hours late for Poopsie's eleven o'clock walk. The poor dog hadn't been out since early morning, about eight hours ago, and that was a long time to expect her to wait. The poor thing was probably frantic.

Carole paid the parking fee and zoomed out onto Angell Street, tapping her foot impatiently at the red light. Damn, damn, damn, she thought. The Wheeler School would be letting out soon and the street would be packed with school buses and kids. And then there was Thayer Street to get through, with the absent-minded professors and the entitled Brown kids wandering this way and that, heedless of traffic. The local streets were a nightmare, but at least she didn't need to take the highway, which was way worse, nothing more than a nerve-wracking high-stakes game of bumper cars.

Oh, well, she told herself as she crept slowly along in the narrow streets, there was nothing she could do. She couldn't be where she wasn't, and she was trying to get home as quickly as she could. Frank had told her to gather as much information as possible, because you never knew exactly which little bit was going to be the final piece of the puzzle. When she looked at it that way, her lunch with Susan hadn't been a waste. She'd definitely picked up some interesting and possibly valuable background information.

Finally making it through the stop sign by the Hillel Club, Carole broke free of the congestion and accelerated up the hill and through the light at Prospect Street, which was, amazingly, green. She was on the way down the hill, toward the oldest Baptist Church in America, and picking up speed when the light on Benefit Street turned yellow, a clear invitation to speed up. She pressed her foot down on the gas; she could make it, she knew she could, because she'd done it a million times, when suddenly—what the hell?—a ridiculously tiny little mini car pulled out of a parking spot and stopped right in front of her, even though the light was still golden amber.

"Gold means go," screamed Carole, slamming on the brakes and hanging on to the steering wheel for dear life. It wasn't like she could avoid a crash; the street was lined with official RISD vehicles on both sides, and the Smart car was directly in her path.

The noise of the impact was horrible—first, the big, loud, hollow bang, followed by the grating crunch of metal tearing, glass smashing, horns honking, tires popping, and radiators hissing.

Carole quickly climbed onto the street, where she saw that, except for some minor scratches, the Cayenne didn't appear to be seriously damaged. She gasped in horror, however, when she saw the damage to the Smart car. It was completely demolished, and she was horrified to see that the driver, a man, was unconscious, face down over the steering wheel. Not dead, please God, she prayed, standing helplessly in the street. Should she try to get him out? What if the little car burst into flame? She started toward the Smart car, but was stopped in her tracks by a RISD security guard, one of several who came running to the accident. They quickly took charge, insisting on leaving the injured man in place until the EMTs arrived. Soon there were police cars and an ambulance and fire trucks, all with lights flashing. The jaws of life were employed to pry the little car open, and the driver was finally extracted. Carole couldn't watch but turned away, a sick knot in her stomach, as he was rolled away on a stretcher.

"So what happened, Mrs. Capobianco?" demanded one of the cops, after examining her license and registration. "The guy stopped for a yellow light or something?"

"It was worse than that," said Carole. "The road was clear, but all of a sudden he pulled out of a parking spot right in front of me and stopped. There was nothing I could do. I braked hard, but it was too late."

"Must be from out of town," suggested the cop, shaking his head and clucking his tongue. "What was he thinking?"

They both watched as the stretcher was slid into the ambulance, the doors slammed, and it took off with siren screaming and lights flashing.

"Was he hurt real bad?" asked Carole.

The cop shrugged. "Them little cars is nothing more than sardine cans," he said.

"I feel terrible," said Carole.

"Nothin' you could've done," said the cop, consoling her. "'Course, I'm gonna have to charge you with something since you did rear-end him."

Carole braced herself. What would it be? Vehicular homicide? Manslaughter? Speeding or, at the very least, failure to use caution. Would she have to go to court?

"Illegal parking," said the cop, handing her the summons and the accident report. "Fifty-dollar fine."

"Illegal parking?" she asked incredulously, as the Smart car was cranked up onto a wrecking truck and driven off.

"Lady, you're parked in the middle of the road. You can't do that."

"Right," said Carole, taking the papers. "I'll move my car right away."

"You do that," said the cop, with a dismissive nod.

Still shaken by the accident, Carole drove home slowly and carefully, to a steady chorus of outraged honks. The other drivers didn't seem to appreciate her cautious approach as she switched on her signal indicator and braked to make a slow turn onto Holden Street and repeated the process at Edith Street. "Get a rocking chair, Granny," yelled one guy, zooming past her in a Range Rover.

"Get one yourself," she yelled back, using the brake the whole way down the hill and turning into the garage. There she flipped on her headlights, just to be on the safe side, and circled slowly up the ramp until she got to her favorite spot and found it vacant.

Grateful for small mercies, she carefully checked that everything was off before turning off the engine, which gave a hiccup before falling silent. That had never happened before, and she wondered if the collision had broken something in the engine. She decided she'd better have the car inspected before she drove it again and made a call to Johnny D's Auto Care. She spoke to Aaron, her favorite mechanic, and after sympathizing with her about the accident and making sure she was okay, he promised to pick the car up right up away. Then, suddenly remembering Poopsie's predicament, she hopped out, hurried across the bridge, and pounded the elevator button. It seemed to take forever, but it finally did arrive, and she got up to the fifth floor, where she hurried down the long hallway to her apartment at the end; she was fumbling with the key, and she could hear Poopsie whining and jumping, scratching at the other side of the door. Finally, it opened, and she scooped up Poopsie, grabbed the leash, hooked it on the dog's rhinestone collar, and set her down in the hallway for the dash to the stairs.

Chapter Ten

Whew! What a day, Carole thought, as Poopsie dragged her down the four long flights. When the ceilings are eighteen feet high, the stairs are twice as long. Then, after taking her paranoid peek through the glass window in the lobby door, she ran across the polished concrete floor, Poopsie making silly little swimming motions as she struggled to get her footing on the slick surface, and they made it outside.

Carole let out a long, relieved sigh, and Poopsie squatted just outside the door. Not the best spot, since they were right in the path of a rather distinguished-looking, sixtyish gentleman in a topcoat carrying a briefcase. Carole gave him an apologetic grin; he gave her a disapproving glance and made a slight detour downhill from Poopsie. A tactical mistake, since the yellow stream headed straight for his lovely, polished brogues. Carole gave the leash a yank, but Poopsie was not about to cooperate. She didn't like this man; she could apparently sense his disapproval and was determined to let him know it by nipping at his ankles as he danced past.

The gentleman was spryer than he looked; he not only

avoided the nip but gave Poopsie a sharp little kick as Carole dragged her up the street, legs stiffly splayed out in resistance. It wasn't until they reached Holden Street that the dog gave in and trotted along, stopping now and then to sniff something that caught her interest.

As she reached the corner of West Park, Carole suddenly realized she didn't need to walk the dog any farther in this darkening drizzle; she had already done all her business. She could go home and recuperate from the day's stresses with a nice cup of tea and a TV soap, maybe catch the last few minutes of Jennifer Hudson. She needed some downtime, a chance to process the crash and to sort through the information she'd gathered from Angelique and Susan. But when she got back to the apartment, she discovered Frank had come home early and had found the accident report she had dropped on the console table by the door.

"What the hell is this?" he demanded, waving the paper in her face.

"No big deal," said Carole, soothingly. "I rear-ended this little car that popped out in front of me on a hill, when I was trying to make the light."

"I've told you, time and time again, you drive like a maniac."

"I do not. Even the cop thought it was tough luck. He gave me a parking ticket."

Frank wasn't buying it. "You smash into somebody's car and you get a parking ticket?"

"'Cause I was blocking the road. He told me to get out of there, and I did." She was hanging up her jacket. "The car's fine, hardly a scratch; the airbags didn't even deploy. And I'm okay, too," she added, turning to face him. "Not that you bothered to ask!"

If Carole had hoped that Frank was going to suddenly realize the error of his ways and engulf her in a loving and forgiving hug, offering apologies for being such a callous brute when she was actually an accident victim deserving tea and sympathy, she was about to be disappointed.

"And the other guy?" he demanded, waving the report in her face.

"Uh, well," confessed Carole, "it was a very little car, and they had to take him to the hospital."

"Minor injuries?"

"He was unconscious, and they had to use the jaws of life . . ."

"Ohmigod!" exclaimed Frank, pacing back and forth, clutching the accident report in his fist and pumping it up and down. "What have you done?"

"It wasn't my fault," insisted Carole. "Really. The guy must be an idiot. Who pulls out without looking, hunh?"

"Maybe somebody who just got off a plane from Peru and isn't used to city traffic," said Frank. "Do ya think?"

An awful suspicion was growing in Carole's mind. "This guy's from Peru?"

"Yeah. And you know what his name is?"

"I haven't actually read the report because of the dog," said Carole, noticing for the first time that Poopsie had jumped up on their twenty-thousand-dollar, custom-made sectional and was tossing the Fortuny silk pillows around in an effort to find a biscuit she had hidden there. "Stop that!" she ordered the dog, who paused to give her a challenging stare before resuming the task at hand. "I was late getting back to walk the dog because I spent the most of the day investigating, like you wanted."

"Investigating is fine," growled Frank. "Sending Jonathan Browne to the hospital is another."

"The Jonathan Browne? Hosea's brother?"

"Yeah," said Frank, reaching for the scotch.

While Frank made himself a drink, Carole started calling hospitals. She finally discovered that Jon Browne has been admitted to Rhode Island Hospital and was in stable condition following surgery. She took down his room number and got right on the horn to Frey Florists over on Radcliffe Avenue; they had gorgeous arrangements, and she ordered a huge bouquet to be sent to him in the hospital. She struggled a bit over the wording of the note; she didn't want to admit culpability—that was the first rule of accidents—so she settled for a simple "Wishing you a speedy recovery."

That done, she went back to the living room, where Frank was in his usual spot in the leather recliner with Poopsie on his lap, watching the sports network. Carole replaced the cushions on the sectional and sat down.

"That Jonathan Browne got here from Peru awfully fast," said Carole. "I had lunch with Susan Weaver today—you know, the real estate lady—and she said he was sort of an Indiana Jones, off digging up bones in the Andes."

"Yeah, well, when there's a lot of money lying around, people tend to be in a big hurry to hear what the will says," observed Frank.

"He's probably already rich," speculated Carole.

"You're never rich enough," said Frank, scratching Poopsie behind her ears. She closed her eyes and extended her neck, letting Frank know he was the best ear-scratcher in the world and pointedly ignoring Carole.

"Do you think there'll be a funeral? Should we go?" asked Carole.

"Probably one of those memorial services," suggested Frank. "Not worth the trouble, really. Won't be any tears with all those stiff-upper-lip types. Besides," he added, "we probably wouldn't be welcome. I wouldn't be surprised if they think we've got some sort of vendetta going and will pull out knives from our socks."

"Vendetta? Socks?"

"Yeah, like we're out to destroy the family."

"I know what vendetta means," said Carole. "But that's crazy. Why would we do that?

"We wouldn't. But you gotta admit, Carole, it don't look good. They think I killed Hosea, and here you go, smashing into his brother and sending him to the hospital."

"But I didn't know who he was," said Carole.

"Try telling that to the judge."

Carole stared at him. "I haven't been charged with anything."

"Not yet," said Frank.

Carole leaned back against the cushions. Was he right? Were the cops going to put two and two together and come up with five? Was she going to get slapped with driving to endanger or maybe attempted vehicular homicide? It was too awful to think about; she needed a drink.

In the kitchen, she poured herself a big glass of chardonnay with shaking hands, then carried it into the bedroom, away from the noise of the TV. There she stood at the window, hoping to calm herself by looking at the view she loved so much. There was the Coca-Cola sign, a flamboyant swirl of red neon in the evening darkness. The streetlights marked out Promenade Street, running along the Woonasquatucket River, which gleamed like a ribbon of black satin. Farther along, in the distance, she could see the streaming white and red lights of the cars on Route 95; the evening rush hour was in full swing. Beyond, she saw the bridge over the highway that led up to the Hill, where the lights from the houses and restaurants gave the misty air a soft, golden glow.

She took a swallow of wine, holding it in her mouth and savoring the fruity, buttery taste. Then she swallowed, tasting the lingering touch of bitterness, and took a deep yoga breath, concentrating on letting the tension out. Only after three breaths, in and out, did she allow herself another sip of wine.

She was feeling better already. She loved it here, high up, looking out at the city and thinking of all the people hurrying home to their families, all the people gathering together with their loved ones around their dinner tables, all the moms cooking meat loaf and pot roast and pork chops, and all the kids doing homework or playing video games until they were called to supper.

Then, suddenly, her peaceful reverie was shattered by the scream of sirens, lots of sirens. At first, she didn't see anything; she couldn't tell where the fire trucks were headed, but then one and then two and then more all went roaring past on Promenade Street. She followed their progress, watching as they began to gather just past the bridge to the hill, where Valley Street began, at the Factory.

"Frank!" she screamed. "There's a fire at the Factory!"

"Whuh?" Frank had been dozing; he struggled to upright the chair and untangle himself from the dog. He took a quick look out the window and headed straight for the closet to get his coat.

"You're going over there?" Carole didn't think it was a good idea.

"Sure, I'm goin' over there. Some of the guys might still be there, working late."

She looked at the clock; it wasn't six yet. The clouds and rain had made it seem later than it was. "I'll go with you," she said. It had long been understood between them that if one of their employees had been injured, she would be the one to break the news to his family.

What a day, she thought, zipping up her parka. She hadn't changed out of her velour track suit and was still wearing her dog-walking boots. She hadn't even had a chance to do her hair or put on her rings. She grabbed her bag, slung it over her shoulder, and hurried over to the garage with Frank.

"Where's your car parked?" he asked, as they jogged along.

"We gotta take your truck," she said. "The Cayenne's at Johnny D's."

He stopped and stared at her with narrowed eyes. "I thought you said the Porsche was okay..."

"I'm just having Aaron look it over to make sure."

He let out a big sigh and led the way to the truck. Exiting the garage a bit too fast, he avoided Promenade Street, which was crowded with fire trucks and police cars, and wound his way through the side streets, past the rows of three-story tenements with their steeply pitched roofs and porches stacked one above the other. Spotting a police barrier on Valley Street, he turned abruptly and parked in the lot behind the Coca-Cola bottling plant, and they hurried across the street, holding hands, to join the crowd of onlookers.

"Where's the fire?" demanded Frank. You could smell the smoke, but there were no flames shooting out of the windows of any of the buildings, at least not that they could see. Nevertheless, the fire department was responding as if it were a major fire, with lots of engines. Their lights were flashing, illuminating the entire area in an eerie, pulsating, red light.

Hoses were snaked through the area, firemen were running this way and that, cops were setting up yellow sawhorses to keep everyone back. Frank wanted to get in there; he wanted to know firsthand what was going on, but the cops wouldn't let him. "Too dangerous," one was saying, when suddenly there was an enormous boom and a giant fireball exploded out of one of the hollow, black buildings.

"What the hell!" exclaimed somebody.

"Propane," said Frank. "Musta been a tank in there. Probably other explosives, too."

"Move back, move back," ordered the cops, lifting the sawhorses and forcing everyone to the far side of the street.

"I thought all the buildings were empty," said Carole.

"The artists, they squat; soon as you kick 'em out of one place, they pop up somewhere else," said Frank. "And that art stuff is flammable: paints, tanks for welding—you name it, they got it in there."

"You know, Frank-O hasn't been spending much time in his apartment. You don't think he's down here, do you?"

"Doesn't he work over at the school? Don't they have studios there? We pay 'em enough."

"Of course. You're right. That must be it," she said, as an ambulance began making its slow way down the street and onto the fenced building site.

"They musta found somebody," said a man in the crowd.

And indeed, two helmeted firemen were running to meet the ambulance, carrying an unconscious victim between them in a classic firemen's hold.

"I didn't know they really did that," said Carole, straining to get a glimpse of the victim. But all she could see was a glimpse of purple hair. Probably an artist, she thought, like Frank-O, with his blue hair.

She sent up a little prayer for the kid, gazing at the red

light that was bathing the scene, giving it a surreal glow. Everything was red, she was thinking, and what did you get when you mixed red with blue? Purple, you got purple.

"Frank-O," she screamed, shoving her way through the crowd and breaking free from the cop who tried to stop her. The ambulance drivers were beginning to close the doors, but paused when they heard her shrieking. "That's my son!" she was yelling frantically, crazy with terror, running as fast as she could to the ambulance. "That's my baby!"

Chapter Eleven

The ambulance ride was horrible. Carole perched on a little jump seat thing as they bounced over the potholed streets, rushing Frank-O to the hospital. She couldn't even hold his hand because the EMT was between them, bent over Frank-O, whose face was covered with an oxygen mask. Since she couldn't reach his hand, she grabbed his ankle, holding on for dear life as if by hanging on to him she could keep him from slipping away.

Through the windows in the rear doors, she could see the headlights of Frank's GMC truck; he was following close, slip-streaming behind the ambulance. She couldn't see his face, but she knew how he looked: his jaw set, his eyes straight ahead, fixed on the ambulance containing his wife and son. Nothing was going to come between him and that ambulance. Nothing.

It seemed to take an eternity before they swooped down the ramp beneath the hospital and braked outside the emergency room. The EMTs must have alerted the ER that they were coming; people in scrubs were waiting for them, and as soon as the stretcher was unloaded, they rushed it inside. Carole ran after them, only to be blocked by a large woman with frizzy gray hair.

"I'll need some information," she said, taking Carole's arm and attempting to steer her toward a desk.

"That's my son!" protested Carole. "I have to be with him."

"Against policy," insisted the woman, as Frank suddenly loomed behind Carole.

"Let go of my wife," he said.

The woman looked up and, seeing Frank's expression, let go. Frank was in motion, and the woman stepped aside, letting them continue through the swinging doors to the curtained bay where Frank-O was being treated. Frank pulled the green curtain aside and demanded, "How's he doing?"

A number of doctors and nurses were bent over Frank-O; one seemed to be in charge and was talking steadily to the others, who responded with curt answers. It was enough to drive you crazy, thought Carole, who wanted to scoop up her baby in a big hug and make everything all right.

After getting a nod from the guy in charge, one of the team members broke from the group and approached Frank and Carole. He tried the arm tactic on Frank, but it didn't work; if Frank didn't want to move, he didn't move. "How's my boy?" he asked.

"Let's go outside," said the doctor, Dr. Huang, according to the name embroidered on his white coat.

Carole felt desperate; she was hanging on to Frank's hand. All she could think of was that awful nightclub fire years ago when a rock band's pyrotechnic display sparked a quick-moving fire. A hundred people were trapped inside and died in the flames; others made slow and agonizing recoveries, but were scarred for life, both physically and emotionally.

Frank glared at the doctor. "I got a simple question for you," he said. "Is he gonna make it?"

The doctor looked at Frank as if he were seeing him for the first time, then nodded and pulled down his mask. Carole thought he looked about sixteen years old.

"Is he burned or what?" demanded Frank.

"As far as we can tell from the initial exam," said the doctor, holding up a cautionary hand, "he does not appear to have any burns, but . . ."

Frank let out a big sigh of relief. Carole waited to hear the rest.

". . . smoke inhalation is our major concern right now," continued the doctor.

"But you're giving him oxygen, right?" asked Frank.

"Smoke inhalation is tricky," warned the doctor. "The symptoms tend to get worse before they get better."

"Meaning?" asked Carole.

"He will have to be watched very carefully, especially for swelling; we have to make sure his airways remain open and that his brain hasn't been oxygen starved. We'll sedate him tonight, to keep him comfortable and allow his body to begin healing. He'll be in the ICU, where he can be monitored."

"But he's in no immediate danger?" asked Frank.

"Can we stay with him?" asked Carole.

"Once he's settled in the ICU," said the doctor. "But I have to warn you, if his condition changes, you may have to leave." He was looking past them, at the woman with frizzy gray hair who was hovering behind them. "But now I think you have to provide some information to admissions."

Frank gave him a look, but the doctor wasn't fazed. "Like

I said, your son is in no immediate danger, and we'll let you know as soon as you can see him."

"Okay," said Carole, taking Frank's arm. "Let's get this over with."

One thing about Frank, he didn't skimp when it came to health insurance for his workers or his family. Even the admissions clerk was impressed when he handed over his card and her computer produced the platinum plan. Frank-O was on the move by the time they finished, and they followed the little procession to the elevator that took them up to the ICU. There, the beds were arranged in a circle of curtained bays surrounding a central nursing command post. Everything was high-tech; Frank-O's bed was surrounded by an array of beeping and flashing monitors. Frank-O himself was quiet, a peaceful little island surrounded by all the machinery.

There was one recliner by the bed, and the nurse brought a small armchair for Carole; they sat and watched and waited. Eventually, Frank dozed off, but Carole remained awake, watching every rise and fall of her son's chest. Her thoughts wandered back to the night he was born and how she'd held him to her breast, concentrating on every swallow of milk that he took as if she could will him to feed and grow and thrive. She eventually began to relax when she became convinced that he was a normal, healthy baby, but whenever he got sick, even with a little cold, the old anxiety would reassert itself. Then she would hover over him, willing him to get well with every fiber of her body. And it was physical as much as mental; she was rooted in place and couldn't pull herself away until she knew he was going to be okay.

Carole was unaware of the hours passing, but the sky was pink with dawn when a nurse urged them to go home.

"He's really doing fine," she reported, after checking his vitals. "Why don't you go home and get some rest, eat something..."

Carole suddenly remembered that they hadn't had any supper the night before. And poor Poopsie! She must have been upset, alone in the apartment all night. And by now she would be more than ready for a walk. But still, Carole was reluctant to leave.

"He'll be here when you get back," the nurse told her, brushing Frank-O's hair off his brow. "Honest. And we have your cell phone number if there are any changes."

"Okay," said Carole, rising stiffly from her chair and bending over Frank, gently waking his shoulder until he woke up.

"Whuh... what's the matter?" he demanded, snapping to attention.

"Nothing. The nurse says he's doing fine and we can go home, get a shower and something to eat."

Frank looked at the bed where Frank-O was still sleeping. "I'd feel better if he was awake," said Frank.

"He's sedated," said the nurse. "They won't be waking him up until this afternoon, at the earliest."

Frank yawned and stretched, then stood up. "Okay," he said, holding up a finger, "but the least little change, you give us a call, right?"

"Right," agreed the nurse.

The way home took them past Connie's condo, and Carole suggested they stop in and tell her about her brother. "I want to do it in person, Frank," she told him. "They've always been real close, and I know she's going to be upset."

"Okay," agreed Frank, whose stomach was rumbling. "Not too long, though."

"Sure," said Carole, thinking she would stay as long as she was needed.

Frank parked in the visitor spot in front of Connie's town house, and together they walked up the little path and stood on the stoop. Carole rang the bell, and they waited for what seemed a long time before a puzzled Connie opened the door. She was dressed for work in a gray pantsuit and holding her purse and a tote bag, ready to leave. "Mom! Dad! What are you doing here?"

"Uh, we got somethin' important to tell you," said Frank.

"I was just leaving," said Connie.

"We're comin' in," said Frank, starting through the doorway and forcing Connie to step aside. Carole followed him.

"So what's so important that it's going to make me late for work," snapped Connie, impatient to leave.

"It's your brother . . ." began Carole.

Connie's eyes widened. "Ohmigod, is he okay?"

"He's in the ICU; they're keeping an eye on him."

Connie sat down on her sofa; she went in big for the retro-fifties look, and it was lean and minimalist, behind a kidney-shaped coffee table. She picked up the one throw pillow; it was a bull's-eye pattern, and she held it in her lap, hugging it. "The ICU. What happened?"

"There was a fire down at the Factory, and they pulled him out, unconscious," said Frank.

"Was he, um, burned?" Connie could barely make herself say the word.

"They say not, but he's got smoke inhalation," said Carole, seating herself beside Connie and giving her a hug.

"That's awful. Can I go see him?"

"Maybe this afternoon," said Frank, who had plopped himself down, mansplaying his legs, on an uncomfortable upholstered chair with bare wood arms. "They say they're going to try to wake him then."

Connie had gone white as a sheet. "What?"

"They've got him sedated, for now," offered Carole, taking her hand and squeezing it.

"Uh, so what's the plan?" demanded Frank, standing up. "We gotta get some breakfast; we were at the hospital all night."

"I'd offer you something," began Connie, looking blank, "but I don't think I've got anything."

"That's okay, honey," said Carole, still holding her hand. "You go on to work; keep yourself busy, that's the best thing. I'll let you know if anything changes. Your dad and I are gonna eat something and shower and head back to the hospital."

Frank was ready to go. "So, uh, let's get a move on."

"Right." Carole and Connie stood up. Carole wrapped her arms around her daughter in a big hug, gave her a kiss on the cheek, and released her. "You'll be okay?"

Connie nodded. "Sure, Mom. It was just the shock."

"Not the best way to start your day," said Carole, giving her another squeeze.

Frank had opened the door and was standing in the doorway, jingling the car keys. "I'm coming," said Carole, in a warning tone. She turned to Connie and made eye contact. "You drive carefully now, extra carefully."

Connie offered a little smile. "I will, Mom." She gave her mother a quick hug. "Go on, Dad's hungry."

"He's always hungry," muttered Carole, following her husband out the door.

They were just finishing breakfast—for once Carole skipped the yogurt and ate scrambled eggs right along with Frank, though she gave her bacon to the dog—when the phone rang. It was Mom, announcing that Angelique Poole had called and offered them the cleaning job at Prospect

Place. "She wouldn't go for seventy-five, though, said sixty-five was the best they could do. She wants us to start today."

"I can't today," wailed Carole. "Frank-O's in the hospital."

Mom was on it in a flash. "What happened?" she demanded. "Is he going to be okay?"

"He's in the ICU," said Carole.

"Aiee!" exclaimed Mom.

"He was in that fire at the Factory last night . . ."

"It was all over the news this morning. They said they'd recovered a victim, but Mother of God, I had no idea it was Frank-O."

"He wasn't burned, but he got smoke inhalation."

"Ohhh! Mamma mia!"

"They've got him sedated, and they're monitoring his condition."

"That poor baby! I'm on my way; I'll be there in half an hour."

"We're going back, too. We'll see you there," said Carole.

But Frank, who'd been listening in, had other ideas. "Look," he said, leveling his gaze at her over his coffee mug, "you might not get another chance to get into Prospect Place," he said. "I think you and Mom should go."

Carole was horrified. "But what about Frank-O?"

"Far as I could tell, he didn't know we were there. And those nurses are top-notch; they know what they're doing. And that nurse promised to call if there's any change, and since her name plate said Julia Rosetti, I know she'll keep her word 'cause I know her father and her grandfather."

"But he's my baby!" protested Carole.

"Yeah, well, what about me?" demanded Frank. "If you

remember, I'm under indictment for murder and could go away for life if that DA has his way."

Carole bit her lip, torn between her husband and her son.

"He's doin' okay," Frank reminded her. "I'll go and stay with him, and I'll call you if anything happens."

Carole considered. "Okay," she finally said, "but you call your mother. I don't want her thinking that I don't love my son."

Frank narrowed his eyes. "With you, it's always the zinger, isn't it? Like I don't love him?"

Carole was tempted to remind him of the long list of issues he had with his son, beginning with his blue hair dye, but decided against it. There was no point starting something she couldn't finish. "I've got to get dressed for my cleaning job," she said, leaving him at the table with the dirty dishes. "Oh, and tell her she's got to drive. My car's still at Johnny D's. I figured I might as well get it detailed while he's got it." She paused. "It was starting to smell kind of doggy."

Frank was in the shower, and the dirty dishes were still there when she emerged from the bedroom in her mousy-brown wig, polyester housedress, and sweatpants. She started clearing the table and was loading the dishwasher when Frank appeared in crisp, clean clothes and freshly shaven. "What the hell?" he exclaimed.

Carole straightened up so he could get the whole effect. "It's my cleaning lady outfit. I don't want anybody over there to recognize me."

"Your own mother wouldn't recognize you," said Frank, laughing.

"How you can laugh at a time like this..." protested Carole, until she caught a glimpse of herself in the hall mirror and began to laugh, too. "You're right, my mother would die if she saw me like this," she admitted, thinking it was a good thing her mother lived far away, in Paris. She reached for Poopsie's leash and handed it to Frank. "I'm late," she said, grabbing the reusable grocery bag she'd hidden her Prada bag in and reached for the doorknob. "You'll have to walk the dog."

Mom was just pulling up in a beat-up old Corolla when Carole stepped outside. Frank was across the street, studying the sky and refusing to acknowledge what the dog was doing beside him.

"Where'd you get the car?" she asked, struggling to open the stiff, creaky door.

"I borrowed it from Christina Fornisanti 'cause Big Frank needed the truck," said Mom, beginning a slow chug up the hill while Carole battled with the seat belt. "Are you sure we're doing the right thing? I don't like this, leaving Frank-O all alone at the hospital."

"Frank's going," said Carole, finally snapping the belt.

"So's Big Frank," admitted Mom, "but still . . ."

"It might be our only chance to investigate at Prospect Place," said Carole. "At least, that's what Frank says." She paused, thinking, as they slowly rolled past the statehouse. "It's easy to forget, now that he's out on bail, but this thing hasn't gone away. Frank's still under indictment, and the DA is busy building a case against him. We can't relax; we've got to find the real murderer, or Frank could go to jail for life."

"It's like some wicked *strega* put a hex on us," said Mom, braking hard as the Corolla began rolling down the hill, picking up speed. "First Frank and now poor Frank-O. What next?" she asked, as the car shuddered to a stop at the light.

"You can't think like that, Mom," protested Carole. "We've got to stay positive."

"I hope I've got a green light on the hill," said Mom, making the turn onto College Street and beginning the steep climb. "I don't think the brakes will hold if we don't."

But it wasn't stopping that was a problem on the hill; it was getting up it. The aged Corolla inched along; somebody behind them honked, and Carole was wondering if she should get out and walk to lighten the load on the car. Mom wondered about an alternate route, but finally, through sheer persistence and the power of positive thinking, they made it to Benefit Street, the halfway point. The hill was even steeper on the other side of Benefit, so Mom made an executive decision and turned right, creeping past the RISD Faculty Club and art museum to George Street, where the hill leveled out. That meant circling around the Brown campus, and they were running late when they finally got back to Prospect Street.

"What are we going to do?" asked Mom. The street was packed solid with parked cars in every legal space.

Carole looked at her Cartier Tank watch and saw it was already ten past eight. Angelique had specifically warned them not to be late.

"Park in front of the old armory," said Carole.

"It's posted."

"We don't have any choice. We could drive around for hours and not find anything legal."

"What if it gets towed? Christina needs the car this afternoon..."

"Look, we'll get started on the job, and as soon as Angelique leaves, you can come out and move the car, right? Take the space."

"Okay," agreed Mom, sliding into the illegal spot and braking. She looked upward, apparently having a word with the man upstairs, or perhaps calling on her guardian angel, then wrestled the door open and began hauling cleaning supplies out of the trunk. They hurried down the street, making a fine picture in their thrift-shop outfits and bristling with mops and brooms, finally hauling themselves up those forbidding gray stone steps to the front door.

Angelique was waiting for them in the hall. "Finally!" she fumed, tapping her foot, shod in a running shoe. "It's about time you got here. I have commitments, you know. My students expect class to begin at exactly nine."

"We're very sorry," said Mom, momentarily forgetting her accent.

"Pukking," hissed Carole, breaking her vow of silence. "Pukking."

"Ahhh," exclaimed Mom, getting the message. "No pukking shpot for car," she said, adopting her accent. "Verrrr shorry."

"I know it's difficult," acknowledged Angelique, "but in future you'll have to allow extra time." She paused. "Now, about the payment..."

Mom couldn't help it; she had to haggle. "One hundert dollah fifdy, sheventy-five for herrr, sheventy-five forrr moi."

Angelique took a deep breath. "We agreed in our phone conversation that the payment would be sixty-five each, one hundred thirty total."

Mom gave a shrug.

"I left a check for you on the hall table."

"Shek no goot," declared Mom. "Kash."

Angelique tapped her foot. "I'm afraid I don't have that much cash on hand, so take the check this week, and I'll have cash for you next week."

"No!" Mom shook her head stubbornly. "No bank, shek no goot."

Angelique glanced at her watch, clearly at a loss what to do.

Mom made a big show of relenting. "Iss okay," she purred. "Yoo pay kash nex week. Tree hundert total, yess?"

Angelique surrendered. "Yes," she moaned, grabbing the coat and briefcase she had ready on a hall chair. "Cash next week," she promised, hurrying out the door.

"Watch where she goes," hissed Mom. "We'll grab her parking spot."

Carole obliged, first peering out the sidelight beside the door and then, as Angelique proceeded out of view, opening the door and watching from the stoop. But Angelique didn't get in a car; she began jogging, then running down the street as Carole watched, amazed. The woman was going to run all the way across town to Johnson and Wales!

Chapter Twelve

"So?" said Mom, when she stepped back inside. "You want the keys?"

"She didn't take a car," said Carole.

Mom's eyebrows shot up. "What?"

Carole shrugged. "She runs to work." After a moment, she added, "I guess that's how she stays so thin."

"That's un-American!" exclaimed Mom.

"Well, she is French," said Carole, picking up the duster.

It wasn't even eight-thirty yet, and she figured the professionals who lived in Prospect Place didn't keep plumber's hours and were probably still home, finishing up their breakfasts. With that in mind, she and Mom began dusting and vacuuming the front hall and stairs. Good thing, too, because first Mark Lonsdale came down the stairs, carrying a briefcase, only to be followed a few minutes later by his wife, Celerie, who was toting a couple of big wallpaper sample books. Neither one took any notice of Carole and Mom beyond a little nod and a "good morning."

Professor Poole appeared soon after, carrying an old-fashioned, accordion-style briefcase that was full to bursting with books and papers that threatened to spill out. He made it halfway down the stairs, saw them, and immediately turned around and went back up. Reappearing, he smiled apologetically and tapped his forehead to indicate that he had forgotten something, before making his wordless exit. That left the building empty except for Millicent Shaw, who had the garden-level apartment, actually the basement. Carole knew she didn't work and was afraid she might pop up with an offer of tea and cookies, but she left the house shortly after the professor, carrying an armful of Whole Foods grocery bags.

"We've got at least an hour," said Mom. "Where should we start?"

"Hosea Browne's apartment," said Carole, reaching for the knob and finding the door locked. "Darn," she said, checking out the mechanism. "It's one of those old ones with the bar that slides across. A credit card won't work."

"I thought of that," said Mom, producing a thin knitting needle and poking it through the large keyhole. A jiggle here, a jiggle there, a firm push, and the door creaked open.

"Spooky." Carole giggled nervously, following Mom into the dimly lit apartment.

"Yeah," agreed Mom, busily switching on lights. "This place is like a mausoleum. And how come, if he was so rich, everything looks like it's falling apart?" She pointed to the threadbare Oriental rug. "I mean, even the Salvation Army wouldn't take that."

Carole was looking around, studying the dusty old drapes, the gilt bull's-eye mirror topped with a ferocious eagle, the enormous highboy atop spindly legs, and wondering where to begin. "Be careful," she warned Mom. "I bet a lot of this stuff is very valuable."

"You kidding?"

"No, Mom. You wouldn't believe the stuff that decorator friend of Connie's wanted me to buy. Antiques, she said, but it all looked old and dingy to me. She said it was the responsible thing to do, you know, good for the planet."

"I don't mind antiques," said Mom, "as long as they look new."

"Me, too," said Carole, pausing to study a dark oil painting of a sailing ship that hung on the wall between the two tall windows. "The *Orion*," she said, reading the blackened brass plate on the frame. "It looks like it's going down in a storm."

Mom pointed to some dark figures in the water. "Looks like a bunch of folks are drowning," she said, shuddering. "Why would you have a gloomy picture like that when you could have a nice Thomas Kinkade with that pretty glowing light?"

"Dunno, Mom," said Carole, standing in the middle of the room with her hands at her side. "What are we supposed to look for?"

"Evidence," said Mom, heading for the kitchen. "Like maybe a blackmail letter, something like that."

"I don't think he'd hang something like that on the fridge with a souvenir magnet," said Carole, going in the opposite direction and looking for a study, or at least a desk. She found it in the next room, a musty-smelling gentleman's retreat with leather chairs, floor-to-ceiling bookcases, and a huge mahogany desk.

"Wow," said Mom, following her. "I wish we'd had this stuff for Professor Higgins's study when the Parish Players put on *My Fair Lady*."

Carole was bent over the desk, flipping through folders containing brokerage statements, bank statements, stock prospectuses, annual statements, departmental budgets, budget proposals, and minutes of meetings. Turning on Hosea's computer, she found his email contained more of the same. "It was all about money with him," she said with a sigh.

"Money is a big motive," said Mom, nodding sagely.

"Yeah, but you'd need an accountant to make sense of all this. I sure don't know what any of it means," said Carole. "Except that he seems to have a lot of the green stuff."

She was feeling depressed and anxious, convinced that the morning had been a waste, and wishing she hadn't given in to Frank but had gone to the hospital instead. When her cell phone rang, she snatched it frantically, terrified that Frank-O had taken a turn for the worse.

"*Bonjour, cherie,*" chirped a voice. Her mother's voice.

"Wow," said Carole, "they've really improved long distance. You sound like you're . . ."

"At the airport!"

"DeGaulle?" asked Carole.

"*Non, cherie*, T. F. Green!"

"You're here in Providence?"

"*Mais, oui!*"

"*Quelle horrible surprise,*" sighed Carole.

Paula Filardi Prendergast was not amused. "What do you mean? Aren't you happy to see your mother?"

"Sure I am, Mom . . ."

"Call me Polly."

"Right. I forgot. Sorry. It's just that this is such a bad time."

"It seems to me that there's never a good time with you," complained Polly.

"That's not true. It's just that Frank-O is in the hospital . . ."

"*Mon Dieu*! What's wrong?"

"He was in a fire."

"A fire! Is he okay?"

"They've got him sedated. They say he's doing fine, but I don't think we'll really know until he wakes up." Carole sighed. "And then there's Frank; he's under indictment for murder."

"I knew they'd catch up with him sooner or later," said Polly.

"How can you say that?" demanded Carole. "He's innocent."

"Of course he is," said Polly, stifling a giggle. "Now, *cherie*, you can't leave me here at the airport. How soon can you come get me?"

Carole looked at Mom. "I'm kind of tied up until noon," she said.

"Noon!" exclaimed Polly, so loudly that Mom could hear her across the room. "I can't wait that long. What kind of daughter are you, anyway, who would leave her mother friendless and alone in a foreign country . . ."

"Mom, this is not a foreign country. You're American, remember?" Paula Filardi had been a typical Federal Hill housewife when Carole was growing up, but when her second husband, Carole's stepfather, died shortly after Carole's marriage to Frank, she took a job as a social secretary for a wealthy Newport socialite. She quickly adopted a new name, Polly, and a new husband, Jock Prendergast, owner of two Kentucky Derby winners. The marriage didn't last, but the nickname did. As soon as the divorce was finalized, Polly packed up her bags and her generous settlement and moved to Paris, where she'd lived in expat comfort ever since.

"I know I'm an American, but try telling that to those customs agents. This cute little dog ratted me out. In my defense, I didn't know you can't bring in unpasteurized cheese. I had that bleu d'Auvergne that Frank likes, but they took it! And then they searched all my bags. I had to watch as they pawed through my lovely Chantal Thomass lingerie. It was so embarrassing." She let out an exasperated breath. "You're never too old for pretty lingerie, never! But the way they looked at me, you'd think they'd never seen a black lace thong or a bustier."

That was the last thing Carole wanted to think about. "Mom, why don't you call an Uber?" she asked, lighting on a solution to the problem.

"An Uber! Who do you think I am? Some college kid, coming home for the weekend?"

Carole took a look around the apartment and decided she was wasting her time. She could spend the rest of the morning searching, but she wasn't going to find anything, and there was no point in keeping her mother waiting at the airport. The sooner she got her settled, the better. "I'm on my way," she said.

"What about the cleaning?" asked Mom, as Carole headed for the door.

"Do you really think they'll notice?" asked Carole, waving her hand at the hallway. "And we did most of it, anyway."

"Okay," said Mom, picking up her bucket of cleaning supplies. "Let's go."

But when they got to the Corolla, they discovered they weren't going anywhere. An ugly yellow boot had been fastened to the rear wheel.

"What am I going to do?" wailed Mom. "Christina Fornisanti has to babysit her grandkids this afternoon over in Warwick."

Carole was tapping her foot, but it didn't have the

same effect in her flat, dog-walking boots as it did in her Louboutins. "Okay, Mom, this is what we're going to do. You call Ginny Ferrara—she knows somebody in the parking division, or maybe she knows somebody who knows somebody. I know there's some sort of connection. Here, take this," she added, stuffing a bunch of fifties in Mom's hand. "For expenses. Meanwhile, I'm calling an Uber."

They both got busy on their phones, Mom working through her network of contacts and Carole heading for the corner, where she waited for a silver Mercedes SUV. Her mother wouldn't settle for less, she knew.

When the car pulled up, she hopped inside and sailed off, giving Mom a parting wave.

Carole realized she was still in her cleaning lady disguise and probably looked as if she didn't have two cents to her name. "This isn't how I usually look . . ." she began.

"Whatever," said the driver, with a shrug. "Your card went through; that's all that matters to me. So is this some sort of prank? Like that old TV show? You know, the one where they pull tricks on people?"

"No. This is actually my life," said Carole, with a sigh. Things were certainly not going her way; she had a lot on her plate, for sure, but she wasn't about to bare her soul to an Uber driver. "Can you kind of hurry up?" she asked. "My mom's waiting at the airport."

"Once we're through town, things should open up," he said, referring to the stop-and-go traffic. He was right; they made good time, but Polly had been waiting close to an hour by the time Carole arrived. She was standing outside the terminal, impatiently drumming her fingers on her crossed arms, alongside a small mountain of Louis Vuitton luggage. She despised the current trend for wearing a comfy track suit for travel and was wearing instead a classic black-and-white tweed Chanel suit, complete with patent-leather Chanel pumps and the trademark quilted bag. She even smelled like Chanel, having doused herself liberally with Coco.

"Carole?" Polly pulled back when Carole jumped out of the car and attempted to embrace her.

"Yeah, it's me, Mom. I mean, Polly."

"What did you do to your hair?"

"It's a wig," said Carole, pulling it off.

"And why are you dressed like this? Has the IRS finally caught up with Frank?"

"I'll explain later," said Carole. "Hop in the car."

Polly slid gracefully into the back seat, looking like Catherine Deneuve. "I have quite a bit of luggage," she told the driver, expecting him to load it.

"I'll pop the hatch," he said.

"Well, really," declared Carole, who had joined her mother in the back seat. She was pretty sure that he wouldn't have dared to treat her like this if she weren't dressed like a cleaning woman, and she wasn't going to put up with it.

"Bad back," he said, with a grimace, leaving Carole no option but to climb back out and load the suitcases into the car. When the cargo area was full, she put the rest in front, next to the driver, who was looking increasingly miserable. No doubt he was thinking he'd priced the trip too low.

"Look, this is for you," said Carole, slipping him a fifty.

"Okay, where to now?"

"The Esplanade," said Carole.

Fortunately for her, Will, the nice concierge, was on duty when they pulled up at the entrance, and he hurried out to help her unload the bags onto the luggage cart.

"Nice place," said Polly, leading a little procession across the lobby to the elevator. "How long have you been here?"

"A couple of months," said Carole, pushing the elevator button. She was suddenly exhausted and leaned against the wall. "Thanks for helping us," she told Will, with a wan smile.

"No problem, Mrs. Capobianco." He waited until they'd gotten in the elevator and then pushed the cart in after them. "There have been some complaints about your dog this morning."

"My son's in the hospital," said Carole.

"I didn't realize," he apologized. "You know I'd be happy to walk her for you."

If only, thought Carole, thinking of the one time she'd attempted to hire a dog walker. The poor kid had quit, giving up dog walking to take a job as an exotic dancer at the Foxy Lady. "Not a good idea," she said. "Poopsie doesn't like changes in her routine."

And Poopsie didn't like the cart coming into the apartment, or Will, either, but as soon as she caught sight of Polly, she went into a gleeful frenzy of jumping and barking and rolling on her back, until she finally subsided at Polly's feet and gazed up at her in blatant doggy adoration. Polly returned the favor, dropping gracefully to her knees and scratching beneath the little dog's rhinestone collar, sending her into ecstatic wiggles. "*Tu es gentille, n'est-ce pas?*" crooned Polly. "*Quel bel chiot!*"

Poopsie couldn't agree more about being a sweet dog and a pretty puppy and followed close on Polly's heels as Carole showed her around the apartment.

"Who was your decorator?" she asked, staring at Frank's enormous La-Z-Boy with a horrified expression.

"A friend of Connie's from school came over, but I didn't really like her ideas," confessed Carole. "We kind of compromised on the sofa and the dining set, but she wanted to cover the windows with elaborate swagged and fringed curtains, so we parted ways."

Polly studied the huge windows, which were at least twelve feet high. "They're *fantastique*," she declared. "So much light, and the view! *Formidable*!"

"The windows are the same in every room," said Carole. "Come see the guest room—your room," she quickly corrected herself.

Carole was especially proud of the guest room, which she'd done in pale blue raw silk with Matouk linens and a pale beige mink throw, genuine fur—not faux—across the foot of the bed. The windows there overlooked the river and the trees that grew along its banks.

"This is nice," admitted Polly. "Very luxurious, but I really think you should do something with the windows."

Carole studied the narrow silver blinds that came with the apartment; they were serviceable and attractive, in a basic way, but she agreed.

"Do you know another designer?" asked Polly.

Wheels began to turn. "I do," said Carole, thinking of Celerie Lonsdale. She liked the idea so much that she gave her mother a big hug and a smacking kiss on the cheek. "You are *fantastique*," she declared, thinking that hiring Celerie would be a lot better approach to gathering information for the investigation than pretending to be a cleaning lady. And she wouldn't have to wear this horrible housecoat.

"I'm going to change and go over to the hospital," she told Polly. "You can get settled here or come with me, whichever you want."

"But of course I will come with you," declared Polly. "But first I want some fresh air. *Allons-y, Madame Pompadour*," she called, and Poopsie obediently sat at her feet while she fastened the leash and calmly trotted out the door at her heel.

An hour later, Carole looked like herself again. Her blond hair with buttery highlights flowed down to her shoulders, her face was freshly made up, and she was wearing a coral cashmere wrap sweater, skinny jeans, and ankle boots with stiletto heels. She tossed on a short fur jacket, and they left the apartment.

The morning paper was lying on the floor, just outside the door, most likely thanks to Will, who must have brought it up. Carole stooped and snatched it up, wondering if there was anything about the fire.

There was, she discovered, as she unfolded the paper. A huge picture of the flames erupting from the building and the firemen carrying Frank-O took up most of the top half of the front page.

"*Sacre bleu!*" declared Polly, reading over Carole's shoulder. "He's lucky to be alive."

"I know," said Carole, wondering for the first time if perhaps the fire wasn't an accident but had been deliberately set. She wasn't alone. According to the paper, the state fire marshal had declared the fire suspicious and was conducting an investigation.

Chapter Thirteen

Frank-O was awake when they got to the hospital, but he didn't look at all good. He wasn't sitting up but was lying with his head slightly elevated, and he could only muster a whispered "Hi" for his mother and grandmother. His color wasn't good, he had blue circles under his eyes, and his breathing was ragged despite the oxygen tube taped to his nose.

He also wasn't alone. A guy in a blue fireman's jacket with brass buttons and a cap was sitting by the bed, a laptop computer open in his lap. Another guy, in jeans and a sweater, was holding a cell phone, recording.

"What's going on?" demanded Carole, ready to defend her baby from all intruders. "Who are you, and what are you doing here?"

"I'm Assistant Deputy Fire Marshal Brian Salvati," said the guy in uniform, belatedly removing his cap. "I'm just asking a few questions about the fire."

"And videotaping the answers?" Carole was furious. "Has my son been informed of his rights? How come there's no lawyer here?"

"He was informed of his rights and waived them," said Salvati.

Carole turned to Frank-O. "Is that true?" she demanded.

"Yeah, Ma," he whispered.

Polly busied herself by refilling the water glass that stood on his bedside stand and held it so he could drink from the straw. "Thanks, Nana," he whispered, before taking a sip.

"Look at him!" said Carole, waving her hand. "He's in no condition to be questioned, and he's just a kid. You come in here looking all important and official in your uniform, what's he gonna say?"

"It's okay, Ma," whispered Frank-O. "Honest. I don't know anything," he added, before he was overtaken by a series of chesty coughs.

"We understand from your son that there were a number of artists squatting in the building," said Salvati. "Do you know anything about that?"

"I know nothing about it," declared Carole. "I don't know anything at all. And I think it's time for you to get out of here."

"Fine, that's fine," said Salvati, holding up his hands in a gesture of surrender. "But it might be better for your son if he cooperated with the department. Maybe you want to think about that."

"What do you mean?" demanded Carole.

"Well, one theory is that the fire started when somebody was cooking up some meth..."

Carole was furious. "Are you implying that my son is operating a meth lab?"

"All I'm saying is that, if he cooperates, we can cut a deal..."

"Get out of here!" shrieked Carole, as Frank strolled into the room.

"What's goin' on here?" he demanded. "Is this a party or something?"

"How about a nice hello for your mother-in-law who just got here from Paris?" said Polly, giving Frank a flirtatious smile.

Frank stared at her. "What are you doing here?"

"What? Like I can't visit my daughter? My grandson?"

His gaze shifted to the two investigators. "And who are these guys?" demanded Frank. As soon as he learned they were there to question Frank-O about the fire, he pulled out his cell and called Vince Houlihan. He explained the situation to Vince, listening intently to his replies. While he was involved in the conversation, Carole made her way to the head of the bed, where she smoothed Frank-O's hair and adjusted his covers. Polly, meanwhile, wasted no time joining Salvati and the videographer, who were holding their ground at the foot of the bed.

"So tell me," she began, in classic Polly fashion, batting her eyelashes, "it must be very exciting to investigate fires. And dangerous, too."

"Oh, I don't know about that," said Salvati, obviously flattered by her attention.

"But you have to deal with such dangerous people," cooed Polly. "Arsonists!"

Carole couldn't believe it. It wasn't bad enough that her mother was flirting shamelessly with these fire-cops—at her age, no less; she was pushing sixty-five—but she was practically incriminating poor Frank-O when he was lying in bed and too weak to defend himself. "Mother!" she warned.

"Do you have one of those fire dogs?" asked Polly.

"Sure do," admitted Salvati.

"What's its name? Is it a Dalmatian? With spots?" continued Polly, cocking her head.

"Cinders. She's a black Lab."

"Ooh, I love Labs."

"Me, too," chimed in the guy with the cell phone. "I got a mix, named Snickers."

"Aren't you lucky," purred Polly. "I'd love to have a dog, but, you know, I have such an unsettled lifestyle. I'm back and forth between here and Paris, and, well, it wouldn't be fair to the poor creature, what with these ridiculous immigration rules. Quarantines and things." She smiled. "Do you know you can't bring unpasteurized cheese into the US? You'd think a big country like this could handle a little bitty piece of cheese!"

The two investigators were shaking their heads, agreeing with her, when Frank hit the red button on his cell. "Okay!" he announced, in a voice that made it clear there would be no further discussion. "These guys are getting out of here, now." He jerked a thumb toward the door. "You wanna talk to my son, you call my lawyer, Vince Houlihan, first. Got it?"

The videographer was already on his way to the door, followed by Salvati. "Sure," he said, pausing in the doorway. "It was very nice to meet you, ma'am," he said, twirling his hat in his hand and smiling at Polly.

"A pleasure, I'm sure," said Polly, giving him a big smile. "*A bientot*, as we say in France. That means, until next time."

"*A bientot*," he replied, with a nod toward Frank.

"Did I say get outta here, or what?" growled Frank, and Salvati quickly replaced his cap on his head and beat a hasty retreat, his shoes squeaking on the vinyl tile floor.

"What are you trying to do?" demanded Frank, turning on Polly. "Whose side are you on here?"

"I was just trying to help," said Polly.

"Well, from now on, don't. Just mind your own business, okay?"

"*Bien sur*," said Polly. "I guess I'll go down to the cafeteria for a *café*. Anybody want something?"

Frank and Carole shook their heads, but Frank-O had a request. "Ice cream?" he asked.

"I'll see what I can do," promised Polly, clicking out of the room in her neat Chanel pumps.

"What is going on?" demanded Frank, closing the door behind her. "When did she get here? Why is she here?"

"She called this morning, from the airport, when I was over at Prospect Place with Mom. I don't know why she's here, but she is, so I'd like you to treat her like an honored guest, since she happens to be my mother. Okay?"

Frank's eyes widened in horror. "She's staying with us?"

"Of course she's staying with us," said Carole.

"My life is over," said Frank. "They might as well put me in jail."

"Get a grip," ordered Carole. "We've got more important stuff to worry about right now." She turned to Frank-O. "So how are you feeling, baby?"

"Rotten," he replied, in a hoarse voice. "I got a sore throat, and it feels like I got an elephant on my chest."

"What did the doctor say?"

"Haven't seen one."

"Figures," snorted Frank. "So what were you doing down there at the Factory, anyway?"

"Nothing."

"What do you mean 'nothing'? You musta been doing something."

"No, nothing. I was meeting a friend . . ."
"Who?"
"You don't know him." Frank-O maintained eye contact with his father as he continued. "An artist. Said he'd help me with my project. Feedback, you know? So he said come on by; he's been squatting there."

"Is that where the fire started? In his squat?"

"I don't know. I was waiting around for him; I had a coffee, so I drank some of it, and I was wandering around, looking for his studio. Then I kinda got lost; I was in this corridor, and it was getting smoky, and I turned to leave, and the smoke was getting thick, and I was trying to get back to the door, so I could get out, and that's all I remember."

Carole was horrified by her son's close call; she wanted to scoop him up in her arms and hug him, but since she couldn't do that, she just grabbed his hand and pressed it to her lips. "You were lucky the firemen found you in time. Think of what could've happened."

"Yeah," grumbled Frank, as Polly returned, carrying a Popsicle.

"I hope orange is okay; it's all they had," she said, peeling off the paper wrapper and handing it over to Frank-O. "And the *café*, just awful. I couldn't drink it."

"Orange is great," he said, struggling to sit up.

Carole handed him the switch that operated the bed, and he gradually rose to a sitting position, licking on the Popsicle. He still looked awful, she thought; his skin actually seemed gray, but at least he was beginning to look and act like himself. When he reached for the remote and switched on the TV, she decided he really didn't need company.

"I guess we better let you rest," she said.

"Yeah, I got business," said Frank.

"Thanks for coming," he said, his eyes on the TV as he flipped through the channels. "See you later."

Frank, Carole, and Polly began the long walk through the hospital corridors that took them to the parking garage. As they were passing the emergency room, Frank spotted an acquaintance, Mitch Chase, also leaving, with one hand wrapped in a thick, white bandage.

"Hey, Mitch! What happened to you?"

Mitch, a tall man with receding hair, dressed in a Carhart barn jacket and jeans, greeted them warmly. "Frank! Carole! And this is your mom, right? I guess you're all here to see Frank-O. So how's the kid doing?"

"It's a miracle he wasn't killed," said Polly.

"I think he'll be fine," said Carole. "Thanks for asking."

"So what happened to you?" asked Polly, her eyes full of concern.

"I burned myself, it's nothing. How's your kid? I heard he was in the fire. That was sure some blaze."

"He's gonna be okay. Were you at the Factory, too?" asked Frank, keeping his tone casual. "Is that how you got burned?"

"Nah. I was cooking bacon." He shrugged. "It's not too bad, second degree, but I thought I better play it safe, get it looked at."

"Very wise," said Polly, making her eyes big. Carole couldn't believe it; the woman simply couldn't resist flirting with anything in pants. Mitch was at least twenty years younger than she was.

"So what happened? How'd the bacon get out of control?" asked Frank; at the same time, Polly wanted to know what the doctor told him.

Tony ignored Frank and answered Polly. "You know, keep it clean; come back if there's any sign of infection . . ." He sighed, a big sigh, as if he were carrying the weight of the world on his shoulders. "Like I need this right now, right? I got that HVAC contract down at the Factory; you know, it's a big job, I got a lot invested in materials. I hired a couple of guys, Guatemalans, terrific workers and cheap, too, but now I don't know where things stand. You too, right, Frank? We might be taking a big hit, if they decide to demolish the place."

Polly's eyes were round. "Would they?" she asked, dramatically.

"They're not gonna do that," said Frank.

"How can you be so sure. Interest rates are killing the real estate market; the developers might decide to put off the project, wait for the economy to improve. It's like a big spiral, one thing happens, then another, and pretty soon it's a full-blown recession with plenty of misery to go around, what with the old guy getting killed and now the fire and Frank-O, and you know there's gonna be an investigation . . ."

"Yeah, well," said Frank, shaking Mitch's good hand and slapping him on the back. "It'll work out; things usually do."

"It was so nice to see you," said Polly, giving him a little wave as Carole pulled her along.

Frank was thoughtful as they continued their walk to the garage. When they passed through the fire door into the gritty parking area that smelled like exhaust, he finally spoke. "I wonder if the fire marshal questioned Mitch," he said.

"Why would they? He burned himself cooking bacon. That's got nothing to do with the fire at the Factory," said Carole. "See you later."

"Yeah, right," said Frank, heading for his car.

Carole watched him go; she loved that wide, rocking, bulldog gait of his. He was headed up the ramp when she noticed a car door open and quickly shut, only to reopen when Frank was past. Carole recognized the man who got out; it was Stu Sempione, the narc.

"What are we doing here in the parking?" asked Polly, giving her a concerned look. "We came in an Uber."

"Oh, I forgot. My car's in the shop; we've got to get another Uber," said Carole. "And I'm so hungry? Do you want to grab something in the cafeteria since we're here?"

"*Non! Tres, tres horrible,*" she said, shuddering. "I just bought the Popsicle."

"So you want to get a bite somewhere? Or should we just go home and have a salad?"

"Oh, Carole," began Polly, somewhat embarrassed. "You know what I would really love? One of those New York System franks and a big coffee milk."

Carole raised an eyebrow as she reached for her phone. "Really? That's what you want?"

"*Vraiment.* They don't have anything like them in Paris."

"I bet they don't," said Carole, as they strolled toward the parking garage exit. As far as she knew, they didn't have New York System franks anywhere beyond Rhode Island, and as far as she was concerned, that was a good thing. The world wasn't ready for the oniony local delicacy.

An hour or so later, Carole was still tasting the sauce

from the New York System hot dog, even though she'd gone through most of a roll of Tums. She and Polly were walking Poopsie on the statehouse lawn. Carole would have preferred to go by herself, but Polly insisted she needed some fresh air to clear her lungs after the airplane flight and the hospital visit. "I just can't handle that artificial air," she complained.

Carole had to admit, it was a nice, sunny day, a fact she hadn't really noticed until now. Maybe what Polly was saying was right; maybe Americans didn't know how to enjoy life the way the French did. And it was pleasant here, on the huge lawn, as long as you ignored the cars that swooped by on the nearby street.

"And the Italians, too," continued Polly, oblivious to the roar of traffic. "They take time to eat with their families; they think nothing of taking an hour or two for lunch, and always with wine, followed by a little siesta."

"How come they don't get fat?" asked Carole, who rarely ate more than a salad for lunch, with nothing stronger than a glass of Pellegrino.

"I've given a lot of thought to this," admitted Polly. "It's the lifestyle. They eat small portions, they eat lots of fresh fruits and vegetables, and they're active; they don't drive around in giant SUVs and get lunch from fast-food drive-thrus."

"I dunno," sighed Carole. "I'm always walking the dog, I never eat fast food, but it's still a struggle."

"Perhaps it's your metabolism," replied Polly, with a shrug. "Madame Pompadour here manages to look very trim indeed, but then, she is French."

Poopsie was walking along beside Polly, actually heeling, for the first time Carole could remember. She wasn't pulling at the leash; she wasn't growling and attempting to attack other dogs, and she wasn't even nipping the heels of passersby. She was simply walking along like the dogs in obedience-training videos. It was completely unnerving, and further proof to Carole, as if she needed it, that she wasn't half the woman her mother was.

"So is Frank really in big trouble?" asked Polly. "Will he go to jail?"

"He didn't kill Hosea Browne, but I don't know if a jury will believe it."

"I saw CNN on the plane, and they said that guy in South Carolina who killed his wife and kid is getting a retrial or something."

"Somehow that doesn't make me feel better," said Carole.

"I know," declared Polly, "you need cheering up. We should go shopping. Aren't there some cute little stores around here?"

"Yeah, Mom. We're right by Providence Place. It's a mall."

"Good. I will buy you a gift, a hostess gift, a thank-you."

"Now that you mention it, Ma—I mean Polly—how long do you think you'll be staying with us?"

"Six weeks, I think. I want a chance to really visit with my daughter and her wonderful children. How is Constancia, by the way?"

Carole swallowed hard. Six weeks! Wait until she told Frank.

Polly headed straight for the mall, while Carole headed home with Poopsie because dogs weren't allowed in Providence Place. She was worrying about how she was going to break the news to Frank about her mother's plans when she turned the corner onto Edith Street and noticed the Cayenne was parked in front of the door and Frank's brother, Paulie, was getting out.

"Thanks, Paulie," she said, noticing he looked as if he hadn't slept last night, with deep circles under his eyes. Of course, Paulie always looked like he was carrying the weight of the world on his shoulders.

"No problem," he said, keeping his distance from Poopsie as he handed her the keys. "How's Frank-O?"

"He's got a ways to go, but he's on the road to recovery," said Carole, keeping a firm hold on the dog. For some reason known only to Poopsie, she'd never really taken to Paulie.

"Doesn't rain but it pours, huh? Those fire marshals were at the office first thing this morning, asking lots of questions."

"So? None of us had anything to do with the fire, right?"

Paulie nodded, jerking his head up and down. "Nothing at all," he said, a bit too quickly, like a kid caught near the cookie jar with crumbs on his shirt. But that was crazy, thought Carole. Why would Paulie set a fire at a project that was making the Capobiancos a ton of money?

"Do you want a ride back?" she asked.

"Nah. One of the guys followed me." He jerked his head toward a little Civic behind the Cayenne.

Carole smiled. "You think of everything. Thanks, again."

"Yeah," he said, giving her a little salute and hopping into the Civic.

Funny, she thought, how much better she felt having her car back. Wheels equaled freedom and independence, which she needed right now. She decided to delay telling Frank about Polly's plan until she found the right moment.

First things first, and she had to move the car into the garage. "C'mon, Poopsie," she said, opening the car door. "We're going for a ride." Poopsie hesitated, sniffing the new car smell. "It always smells like new after the detailing," she explained. Poopsie didn't seem convinced and gave her head a good shake before deciding to leap in. "Sorry, but it's a very short ride," she added, as she started the engine and turned into the garage entrance.

Later that night, Carole finally broke the news about Polly to Frank, and he took it better than she expected, maybe because after her bath she'd slipped into the new peignoir set her mother had bought for her at Macy's. It was cream-colored chiffon, trimmed with lace, and didn't leave much to the imagination as she twirled about to give him a better view.

He was sitting in bed, reading *Sports Illustrated*. "Va-va-voom," he said, tossing it aside. "Where'd you get that?"

"My mother gave it to me. A hostess gift." Carole sat on the side of the bed and tickled Frank's chin. "She's going to be with us for a while. Maybe even six weeks."

"Well, she can stay with us as long as she likes," declared Frank, "as long as she keeps giving you stuff like this."

"Have I got your word on that?" asked Carole, slipping out of the peignoir and letting it flutter to the floor. The gown beneath was nothing but a wisp of silk.

"Ooh, baby, I'll give you whatever you want," said Frank, flipping back the duvet. "Now see what Papa's got for you!"

Chapter Fourteen

Next morning, Carole was surprised to find Polly sitting at the dining table when she and Poopsie got back from their walk. "Must be jet lag. I didn't sleep a wink last night," explained Polly, who had made coffee and was sipping a cup, poring over a magazine. Carole had picked up the morning paper on her way home and gave it to her, then went about her usual morning routine of feeding the dog and cooking eggs for Frank.

"I can't believe he eats that every morning," said Polly, as the bacon started sizzling. She was nibbling on an English muffin, which she put down with a sigh. "I don't suppose you can get decent croissants around here?"

"Croissants aren't exactly health food," said Carole, breaking a couple of eggs into the pan. "Frank!" she called. "Eggs are on!"

He appeared a minute or two later, unshaven and with mussed hair, in his rumpled pajamas and robe. Polly gave him a disapproving look but, wisely, didn't comment on his appearance. She herself was a picture of perfection: her hair was freshly styled, her face washed and moisturized, and she was dressed in an oversized white shirt and black leggings, with ballet flats on her feet. Frank ignored her and sat down heavily in his usual chair. Carole brought him a big mug of coffee, and he reached for the paper, which was unopened, lying beside Polly's plate.

"Ya don' mind, right?" he growled as he flipped it open and glanced at the headline: DA CONFIDENT OF CONVICTION IN BROWNE CASE, grunted, and tossed it aside in favor of the sports section. He was engrossed in a story about a promising rookie player when Carole brought him his plate, and he continued reading while he ate.

Carole, however, read every word of the headline story about the DA while she ate her whole-wheat English muffin and eighty calories worth of peach yogurt. "The DA says he wants to go to trial as soon as possible," Carole advised Frank.

"Good luck with that," replied Frank. "Vince has got other plans."

"Like what?" asked Carole.

"Delay, delay, delay, that's the name of the game—at least that's what he told me. The more motions you file, the longer you put it off, the case loses steam. Stuff gets lost, people's memories aren't so good. I think he's filing a motion for change of venue, says that'll use up a good six months. Then he's got a bunch of other stuff, says he can put off the trial for at least three years."

"That wouldn't work in France," said Polly.

"I'm not sure it's going to work here," said Carole. "I hope he's got a better defense strategy than that."

Frank was mopping up the last of the egg yolk with a piece of toast. "You and Mom find out anything yesterday over at Prospect Place?" he asked.

"Not much," admitted Carole, "But we're going back next week. And I've got an interview with Celerie Lonsdale this afternoon. I asked her for some help with window treatments."

"Window treatments! I'm looking at a couple of million in legal fees and you're talking window treatments?"

"Calm down," said Carole, placidly stirring her yogurt. "The windows are just an excuse. I'm going to pump her for information about Prospect Place, just like you want."

"Oh," said Frank, getting a sharp look from Polly. "That's a good idea."

"Yeah, I guess so," said Carole, licking her spoon. "I feel like I'm poking around in the dark. I don't know what to ask her."

"What've you got so far?" asked Frank.

"Not much," admitted Carole. "The real estate lady, Susan Weaver, seemed to have a big motive for getting rid of Hosea Browne because she's definitely got money problems. But when you think about it, she was better off when he was alive. He was difficult, but she could probably find some nice WASPy buyer for him sooner or later. Now that he's dead, there's all sorts of legal complications that could hold up the sale for years."

"She could've lost her temper and whacked him on the head," said Frank.

"I don't think so. A real estate agent has to be pretty good at controlling her temper, don't you think? And she's supposed to be quite successful."

"I thought you said she was having financial problems," said Frank. "People do weird things when they're under stress."

"It sounded like a cash-flow issue to me, and you know

how that goes. One month you're rich, the next you're hitting the food pantry."

"You wouldn't know where the food pantry is," countered Frank.

Polly giggled. "That'll be the day. Carole showing up in her Louboutins and Vuitton purse." She picked up an English muffin crumb with her finger and put it in her mouth. "But it is true, about stress. It can really mess with your mind."

"Okay, so we keep Susan Weaver on the list of suspects, but I'm pretty sure we can cross off Millicent Shaw. She's too nice to kill anybody."

"Those are the ones you have to watch out for," said Polly, darkly.

"If you met her, I think you'd agree with me," replied Carole. "She's just the sweetest old thing. And that's another point: she's really old. Too old to bop somebody on the head hard enough to kill them."

"Not so," said Polly, poring over the Living section. "It says here that seniors are joining gyms in droves, especially older women. They're working out with weights."

"That's just what we need," muttered Frank, pushing his chair back from the table and heading for the bathroom, bringing along the sports section. "Old ladies with dumbbells. What next?"

"I don't know," said Carole, propping her cheek on her hand. "I wish Mom and I had found out more over there at Prospect Place, especially about the Pooles. They seem like an odd couple to me. Angelique doesn't seem like the sort of woman you'd expect a fusty old bachelor like the professor to marry."

"Angelique Poole? Is that her name?" asked Polly.

"Yeah. Do you know her?"

"No, but I see here that she's offering a class in French pastry this weekend. Fifty dollars a person, and you get to eat everything you make. Shall we go? Maybe I can strike up an acquaintance with her and pump her for information." She paused. "I'm sure she'll know where to get good croissants."

"I'll try anything that will keep me out of that wig and rubber gloves," said Carole, beginning to clear the table.

An hour later, dressed in her usual skinny jeans and heels, she was back at the hospital visiting Frank-O. Polly came, too, and Mom was already there with a jumbo beaker of Big Frank's homemade eggnog, declaring that it would be soothing on his throat and was packed with nutrition. "You'll never get better on the poor excuse for food the hospital gives you."

"It's not so bad," said Frank-O. "I like those mashed potato mountains with the little crater on top for gravy." He was looking better, thought Carole, and even had a little pink in his cheeks. Speaking was also a lot easier for him, although he still sounded quite hoarse, and he wasn't coughing as much.

"Those potatoes taste like wallpaper paste!" protested Mom.

"Yeah, I know," admitted Frank-O with a smile. "But I still like them."

He had made substantial headway on the eggnog, however, when a nurse appeared and began taking his blood pressure. "Looks like you're going home tomorrow," she said, unwrapping the cuff with a ripping sound.

"What!" exclaimed Carole. "Tomorrow! He's sick. Too sick to go home!"

The nurse looked at her. "Sorry, you'll have to take it up with your health insurance. They say he's ready to go."

"The insurance! Since when do they decide?"

"Honey, it's a new world," advised the nurse. "They call the shots."

"Not in France," said Polly, smugly. "They have free health care."

Carole figured Frank would work it out with the insurance company, but in the meantime they could certainly cover the hospital cost. "If money is the problem..."

"Listen, Mom," interrupted Frank-O. "I don't want to stay. I'm okay, really, and I want to go home."

Carole looked at him, speechless. The kid couldn't take care of himself under the best of circumstances. How was he going to manage in his weakened condition? He could hardly breathe, so how was he going to get up the stairs? And what about meals? Who was going to cook for him? Was he just going to lie around in squalor, waiting for one of his buddies to bring in a pizza or some Chinese? If only he could stay with her, but her mother was in the guest room. He could bunk on the couch, but that wouldn't be too good, not with the way he and Frank didn't get along so well. It would be hell, but if that's what she had to do, that's what she'd do.

"Okay," she said. "You'll come home with me."

"Where's he gonna stay at your house?" asked Mom. "You got your mother, don't you? And you know how Frank likes his routine; he wants to watch what he wants to watch on TV when he wants to watch it. And don't get in between him and his bathroom! How are you going to take care of Frank and Frank-O at the same time?"

"I'll manage," said Carole, noticing that Polly was definitely looking nervous.

"I could go to a hotel," she said, without enthusiasm.

"I got a better idea," said Mom. "Frank-O should come and stay with me and Big Frank. We got plenty of room, and Big Frank'll feed him up good."

It was an offer from heaven. The woman was a gray-haired angel in a roomy turquoise polyester sweatshirt with matching elastic-waist pants and arch-support Skechers. "That okay with you?" she asked Frank-O.

"Sure, sounds great," he replied, reaching for the TV remote. The small movement started up a bout of coughing, and Mom hurried to give him a drink of water.

"You behave yourself; don't give your grandparents any trouble," warned Carole. "If your dad hears . . ."

"He won't be any trouble," said Mom, beaming at her grandson. "We're happy to have him."

"This is such a relief, I can't tell you," said Carole, checking her Cartier watch. "Oh, God, I've got to get back. I've got that meeting with Celerie Lonsdale." On her way to the door, she paused, remembering Polly. "Do you want to come?"

"I think I'll stay here, catch up with Giovanna," said Polly.

Polly almost asked who the hell was Giovanna, when she remembered that was Mom's name.

"That'll be nice," said Mom, shooing Carole out the door. "Go on."

Carole left in a flurry of hugs and kisses, getting back to the Esplanade just as Celerie Lonsdale was arriving in her little white van. With her shoulder-length blond hair, Hermès scarf, cashmere jacket, and tweed pants, she might have stepped from the pages of *Town and Country* magazine. She was very excited, she told Carole, as they went up to the apartment, to be working in the building, which she found quite impressive. "The space!" she declared, waving her arm at the enormous lobby. "That's what's so great about these old factories—they have so much room. And these tall ceilings!"

When they got to the apartment, Poopsie took an immediate dislike to Celerie, and Carole shut her in the master bath. Once the dog was safely confined, she gave Celerie a tour of the apartment, steeling herself for a critical review.

But Celerie seemed to approve or was too smart to disapprove until she was sure she had the job, at which time she could offer some tactful suggestions. So Carole was surprised when Celerie exclaimed, apparently genuinely impressed, "This is charming! Who designed it?"

"I did, with a little help from my daughter's friend who's studying design at RISD," admitted Carole. "It was fun."

"You did a great job," declared Celerie. "Big spaces like this can be tricky. But you picked furniture that fits the space, and the colors are wonderful. You really have an eye."

"Well, thanks," said Carole, warming to the woman despite herself. Flattery was powerful stuff and hard to resist. "My big problem is the windows."

"They're sure big." Celerie waved an arm at the huge expanse of glass that filled most of the exterior walls of the apartment. "The silver blinds are a good start."

"They came with the place," said Carole. "I don't want to get rid of them; I just want to soften the look. Make it less industrial and more boho."

Celerie was resting her chin in her hand, studying the situation. "What I wouldn't give for windows like these," she said. "Our apartment is so tiny, and the ceilings are quite low because we're up in the attic."

Carole saw an opportunity to steer the conversation in the direction she wanted to go, and she seized it. "But Prospect Place is wonderful, with all that amazing carved woodwork. We would have loved to live there." She paused. "Maybe we'll try again."

"And leave this?" exclaimed Celerie, determined to get, and keep, the decorating job. "Frankly, I think this is much nicer. You'd be crazy to give it up."

"I don't know," grumbled Carole. "Some of the people here aren't quite as nice as you people over at Prospect Place. There's a lot of kids, and they can be really noisy."

"Well, that's definitely not a problem at Prospect Place; it's quiet as a tomb," admitted Celerie. "Mark and I are the youngest, and we're so exhausted from working all day and climbing all those stairs up to our tiny garret that we're more interested in sleeping than partying."

"Have you made friends with any of your neighbors? Like the Pooles?" asked Carole. "They seem terribly interesting."

"I'm sure they are, but I don't really know them. She asked me to help her with the kitchen redo, but she pretty much had it all figured out, just used me to get access to some European brands that aren't generally available here."

"What's she like?" persisted Carole.

"Very French. Knows what she wants and gets it," said Celerie, with a big sigh. "Very detail-oriented."

"What about the professor?"

Celerie was sitting on the sofa, studying the windows. "He wouldn't let me touch a thing in that apartment except the kitchen, and believe me, it could use some freshening up." She shook her head. "I see him coming and going, sometimes, but all I get is a nod. He's always forgetting something, so he comes and goes a lot. Some mornings it takes him three or four tries before he's out the door."

Carole smiled. "A real absent-minded professor. Somehow I wouldn't have expected him to marry a woman like Angelique. She's much younger, isn't she?"

"Hard to tell; those French women keep their looks." Celerie was jotting something on a pad of paper she'd pulled out of her bag. "They seem quite happy. I mean, I never hear them arguing or anything, and I would if they did. Those walls are not as thick as you'd expect."

"I bet you're glad Hosea's gone," ventured Carole. "He must have been a bit of a wet blanket."

"I can't say I miss him," admitted Celerie. "But we certainly didn't wish him any harm."

"Neither did we," Carole was quick to say. "Frank had nothing to do with..."

"Of course not." Celerie's affirmation of Frank's innocence was a bit too quick and too vehement. "Do you have any color preferences?"

Carole wanted to get the conversation back to Prospect Place. "I couldn't help admiring the curtains in Hosea Browne's apartment, the night we were there," she said.

Celerie raised an eyebrow. "That dark red?"

Carole knew she'd made a mistake. "No, the lining."

"Kind of a pinky beige?"

"Yes!" agreed Carole, who didn't have a clue.

"You certainly do have quite an eye for detail," said Celerie.

"Not really. I couldn't tell you another thing about the room, except that it was old-fashioned."

"Like Hosea himself," agreed Celerie. "A gentleman of the old school, if there ever was one. His brother is quite different."

"Jonathan? Was that his name?" Carole asked, pretending ignorance.

"Yes. He's back from Peru. He was involved in some sort of accident, he said. He's got his leg in a cast, and he's using a crutch. I hear him playing that Peruvian flute music all the time."

"Poor man," said Carole. She knew she ought to be guilt-stricken, but what was done was done, and she was actually pleased, not to mention relieved, that he was out of the hospital and apparently on the road to recovery. "What about the little old lady in the basement?" she asked.

"Millicent Shaw?"

"Yes. What's she like?"

"Sweet. Agreeable. I don't really know, except that I don't like her curtains. They're made from Indian bedspreads, I think, unlined, and they look horrible from the outside. They don't go with the style of the house at all. Kind of sixties hippie chic, if you can believe it."

"Did she and Hosea get along?" asked Carole, persisting in her effort to get some information out of Celerie and hoping she wouldn't become suspicious.

"As well as any of us did," said Celerie, with a shrug. Then she straightened up, as if receiving a sudden inspiration. "I think I have an answer to your problem."

"You do?" Carole was all ears. Did Celerie have a suspect in mind?

"Festoons!"

Carole didn't have a clue. "Festoons?"

"Absolutely. Lush and gorgeous, with plenty of passementerie..."

Carole was even further in the dark. What the hell was passementerie? She was pondering this question when the door opened and Polly let herself in.

"What sort of passementerie?" inquired Polly. "Fringe? Balls?"

Ah, thought Carole, mother to the rescue. It must mean fancy trim, the sort of stuff they put on cushions and curtains.

"All of it," declared Celerie. "This is a big space, and we want to make an impact. I've seen some gorgeous, oversized stuff from a place in Florence. They make it to order, and we'll go for size, because it will be quite high up, and we want to be able to appreciate its bespoke beauty."

While she was talking, Polly had heard Poopsie yip and went to find her. Returning with the dog in her arms, she sat down on the couch. Poopsie seemed perfectly content to remain in her lap, resting her chin on her paws and occasionally giving her a devoted glance. "I think Carole was thinking of some simple linen sheers," said Polly, stroking Poopsie's chin.

"I don't think sheers will have quite the impact we need," said Celerie, making a last-ditch effort to save a sizable commission. "We want to give an impression of luxe, of richness, no?"

"Sometimes less is more," said Polly, as the dog flipped onto her back for belly rubs.

Sheers? Festoons? Carole was confused. "I don't really..."

"Of course not," agreed Celerie. "It's a big decision. Tell you what, I'll work up some sketches and get back to you; how about that? Then you can see how both styles will look."

"Sure," said Carole, relieved to be off the hook.

"Of course, I will need a deposit before I can begin," said Celerie, not quite meeting Carole's eyes. "A thousand is customary, to get started."

Carole hadn't expected this. "Just for a sketch?"

"I draw them myself; I don't use a computer," Celerie was quick to explain. "They're really lovely little water colors that you can frame, if you want. And I'll provide estimates, too. It's quite time-consuming, but any portion of the deposit that isn't used gets credited to your account."

"Of course," sighed Carole, going to fetch her checkbook.

When she returned with the check, Celerie practically snatched it out of her hand. "I'll be in touch," she promised, grabbing her Coach bag and making a quick departure.

When Celerie had gone, Polly released Poopsie, who ran across the floor to the door, sniffing the floor and following the designer's trail. At the door, she stopped and pressed her nose against the crack, determined to sniff up every last trace of Celerie's scent.

"I've never seen her do that," observed Carole.

"She smells her fear," said Polly. "That woman is desperately afraid."

"Of what? Of Frank?"

"No. Not at all. I think she has money problems. Why else would she suggest fancy curtains with fringes and flounces? It's all wrong for this place; elaborate Italian passementerie would look ridiculous with exposed brick walls, Frank's leather chair, that sleek entertainment center. No, there's only one reason she would suggest it, and that's because it's obscenely expensive and she can tack on a nice big markup for herself. That's why. She wants to get as much money out of you as she can. I bet she's down in the lobby, sending an image of that check to her bank. The money will be in her account before she leaves the building." She glanced at Carole's Vuitton bag that was sitting on the console table. "And she had a Coach bag. You can pick them up at Macy's. Or Nordstrom's Rack."

"I think you're right," said Carole, who had just written a check for a thousand dollars and didn't have anything to show for it, which wasn't the way she usually did things. She reached for the phone and called Connie.

"Hi, sweetie, I need you to do something for me."

"Something legal?" said Connie, cautiously.

Carole pretended she didn't hear that. "Find out everything you can about Celerie and Mark Lonsdale; they live over there in Prospect Place."

"Um, I don't think I can do that."

"Why not? Hosea Browne retained your firm, right? You've got all the applications, the deeds, all that stuff for Prospect Place."

"Yeah, Ma, but they don't leave that stuff lying around. I have limited access. I'm the low girl on the totem pole. First-year associates are lower even than the secretaries, than the cleaning crew. We are dirt."

"Didn't they teach you anything in law school?" muttered Carole. "The secretaries have all the information! Make nice with the secretaries!"

"Okay, Ma. I'll try," said Connie. "I've got to go now."

"Hold on," cautioned Carole. "I got somebody here wants to talk to you. Your *grandmere* from Paree!" She handed the phone over to Polly, who had a big grin on her face.

"*Cherie*!" she exclaimed. "You must let me take you to lunch."

While Polly made plans to meet for lunch the next day, Carole wandered over to the window to check out the view. But she wasn't really seeing it. Her thoughts were running round and round in her head, seeking the solution to what seemed an increasingly difficult question: Who killed Hosea Browne?

Chapter Fifteen

Wednesday morning, Carole picked up Mom, and they went together to get Frank-O out of the hospital. He looked much improved and was sitting up, impatient to be released. Carole left Mom to help him get dressed and went downstairs to deal with the paperwork. It was quite simple: all she had to do was essentially sign her life away by promising to pay whatever the health insurance company decided it wouldn't cover. The figures for a three-day stay without surgery were quite staggering, even to her.

"We could have put him up in the Four Seasons for less than this," she told the clerk. "And there the food would actually taste good, and he could've had a massage."

The clerk didn't appreciate the joke, but merely handed Carole a release form that she was supposed to give the nurse at the duty station. In the elevator on the way back up, Carole wondered if she was supposed to tip the nurses, like you had to tip everyone when you checked out of the Four Seasons. She decided against it, suspecting that they considered themselves professionals.

Poor Frank-O wasn't looking as good as he had earlier.

Getting dressed had tired him out, and she was glad for the wheelchair the nurse insisted they use for the trip down to the parking garage. She brought the car right up to the door, and he got in under his own steam, but he was out of breath by the time he'd hauled himself into the SUV and got his seat belt fastened.

"Whew," he sighed. "I guess I'm not as well as I thought."

Carole checked him out in the rearview mirror and discovered his face was quite gray again. "It's always like that," she told him, remembering her two hospital stays when she'd given birth to him and Connie. "You feel great sitting in bed in the hospital, but it's a different ball game when you get home."

Especially with an infant to care for, she thought.

"Don't worry," said Mom, "you're still healing. You'll feel a lot better after we get you home and you have some of Big Frank's garlic soup."

"Yeah, Nonna. Plus I got a whole bunch of prescriptions."

When they got to the house, Big Frank came out and helped him get out of the car and into the house, where they sat him on the sofa, which Mom had covered with a fresh bedsheet and a couple of pillows. Once Frank-O was settled with a cup of soup and the TV remote and covered with a cozy, crocheted throw, Carole went off to CVS to get the prescriptions filled. When she returned with the drugs, she found he'd fallen asleep, and she joined Big Frank and Mom in the kitchen, where they were sitting at the table. Mom was working on a sudoku, and Big Frank was rolling tiny little meatballs.

"For wedding soup," he said. "Nothing better when you're sick. Poor kid, he's gonna need some building up."

"He's got a bunch of pills," said Carole, opening the

bag. "I got one of those plastic things with a box for morning, afternoon, and night, so you can keep them all straight." She peeled off the plastic wrapper on the pill organizer and studied the instructions on each vial, counting out the doses. "I feel like Nurse Nancy," she said, with a little chuckle. "At least it keeps my mind off Frank's troubles."

"That reminds me!" exclaimed Mom, putting down her pencil. "You know, when I was over there on the East Side, getting the boot off Christina Fornisanti's car, something funny happened."

"Yeah?" Carole was working her way through the bottles. One blue to be taken three times a day with food, one small white before bed, one green to be taken two hours after eating; just taking the pills was going to be a full-time job for Frank-O.

"Yeah. I had to wait around quite a while, because they're not as quick to take the darn things off as they are to put them on, and while I was waiting I saw that old lady come back."

"Millicent Shaw?"

"I don't know her name, but she lives in the basement apartment."

"Right, that's Millicent."

"Well, Millicent goes in the apartment, and pretty soon this big Black guy comes walking down the street, and when I say big, I mean big. He must've been at least six six, something like that, with huge shoulders."

"Sounds like some sort of athlete," offered Big Frank.

"Yeah, like that, but he was in regular clothes. Well, sorta regular. One of them workout outfits you see people wear, with a black sweatshirt and a hood. Sunglasses, too. Like he was up to no good and didn't want anybody to recognize him."

"He doesn't sound like the sort of person you generally see on the East Side," said Carole.

"Not at all!" exclaimed Mom. "But he was sauntering along as if he owned the place, and he went right down to Millicent's front door and knocked on it."

"I know she told me she was involved in the civil rights movement, and she's still interested in social justice," said Carole. "Maybe he's a political activist, something like that."

"He didn't seem like a do-gooder to me," snorted Mom. "Unless doing good pays real well. He had to wait a good while before she opened the door, and while he was waiting, he took off the hood, and I could see he was wearing a humungous diamond earring. Really big, so big I could see it from across the street."

"So what happened when she opened the door?" asked Big Frank.

"She hugged him, that's what she did. Gave him a big hug, just like I'd do to Frank-O if he wasn't so weak." Mom picked up her pencil. "And then he went inside, and she closed the door, and that was that."

"How long did he stay?" asked Carole.

"At least a half hour, because it was that long before the parking guy came and took off the boot."

"That's pretty interesting," said Carole, wondering if there was a connection between the Black man and Hosea's murder. Could he be a hit man, hired by Millicent, coming for his payoff? Not likely. You don't hug a hit man, and besides, that kind of thinking was wrong and racist. Just because a guy was Black and wearing a hoodie didn't mean he was a criminal, as Connie would be the first to remind her.

Remembering that Polly was having lunch with Connie

and the apartment would be empty, Carole decided to grab some time for herself. It had been a while, she realized, since she'd had a free moment. So after checking that Frank-O was comfortable and a round of hugs with Big Frank and Mom, she headed home.

"First things first," she told Poopsie, as she made herself a huge peanut-butter-and-jelly sandwich and poured herself a tall glass of whole milk. The dog gave her a look when she sat down at the table with her lunch, but Carole was quick to defend herself.

"I'm splurging," she told the dog. "I'm sick of salad and Pellegrino, and this is what I want to eat, so keep your opinions to yourself."

Chastised, the dog settled down at her feet.

Carole savored every bite of the sandwich and even treated herself to a couple of Double Stuf Oreos, Frank's favorites, before taking Poopsie out for her noontime walk. Then, back at the apartment, she made herself a cup of tea and sat down at Frank's computer. She was no computer whiz, but she had mastered Google, which never failed to find what she needed, whether it was a Korean face mask or an Italian purse. It had also provided interesting information about people, whether she was looking up celebrities or neighbors she'd suspected had complained about Poopsie, so she typed in Stuart Poole's name to see what she could see.

Wow! There were absolutely thousands of references to Stuart Poole, the guy was a road hog on the information highway. She opened up the first listing, and the computer detoured into Adobe, taking its time to load, and when the little hourglass disappeared all of a sudden, the screen was filled with dense text. She began reading; it was all about trade in colonial times and was putting her to sleep, so she hit the little red X with the cursor and got out of there.

She obviously had to be choosier about what files she opened; she'd wasted a good ten minutes on that sucker, so she scrolled down the list of references. As it turned out, most of them were on the same subject, something called the Triangular Trade, which took place hundreds of years ago. The professor was apparently an expert on this subject, which she'd learned in high school involved sailing ships that carried goods like cotton or timber from the American colonies to Europe, where it was traded for guns and liquor. The ships then sailed to Africa, where they traded these goods for captive natives. This human cargo was then brought back to either the American colonies or Caribbean islands, where they were sold as slaves to work on plantations in exchange for sugar and rum. It was awful and disgusting, and she wondered why it held such fascination for Professor Poole. But, she reminded herself, having an interest in bad behavior didn't mean a person would actually do anything bad. She herself enjoyed an occasional romantic novel, for instance, but it didn't mean she'd ever consider being unfaithful to Frank. Not even with that gorgeous and very hot *Bridgerton* duke. No way.

She went back to Google and typed in Angelique's name, but nothing came up. Weird, she thought, unless it was because she'd only recently married Professor Poole. Or maybe she'd kept her family name; a lot of professional women did that these days. Maybe she could find out more if she had that name.

She entered the names of the other Prospect Place residents, and amazingly enough, there was plenty on them all. Facebook and Instagram, X and LinkedIn, tons of citations. Celerie Lonsdale had a website for her interior design business, but although there were plenty of pretty pictures, Carole couldn't find any mention of passementerie. Mark Lonsdale was included in a website for American Dream Mortgage Company as one of the members of Dream Team Providence, "The team to make your dream of home ownership come true." Maybe a bit of hype, thought Carole, thinking of current interest rates. And the site actually offered little information beyond a photo of Mark's smiling face. She stared at the picture a moment or two, wondering if he whitened his teeth, and decided he must before hitting the red X.

Millicent Shaw was mentioned in a report of a fact-finding visit to Guatemala made by the Social Concerns Committee of the First Parish Unitarian Church on Benefit Street, but she was only noted as a member of the group.

She figured that she knew more than she wanted to about Hosea, but she was curious about Jonathan Browne. She discovered that he, like Professor Poole, had thousands of listings. Unfortunately, she couldn't make head nor tail of any of them. They were all obscure references in scientific journals to Section VIII or Substratum XYZ; it was enough to give a girl a migraine. She was clearly in way over her head; she needed help.

She sat for a moment, fingering her phone, when she suddenly remembered hearing somewhere that Betty Strazullo's kid Gary was a private eye. She googled Gary and discovered it was true. Strazullo Investigations had a nice website; they promised confidentiality in all investigations, which included divorce and custody, missing persons, background checks, and surveillance.

Gary himself took the call and declared himself eager to help. "Frank's getting a bum deal," he told her, "I'll do whatever I can to help him." He even said he'd only charge one fifty an hour, instead of his usual two hundred.

Carole found herself thanking him for the privilege of paying him, which she thought was screwy, but you didn't get something for nothing, and she knew she needed help. She decided to surprise Frank and throw something together for dinner, maybe a chicken cacciatore, since they always had chicken breasts in the freezer, and it was nice and easy.

When Polly came home, she took over, pulling an apron out of the drawer and taking the spoon out of Carole's hand. Carole popped the top on a diet soda and sat on one of the stools at the island, and asked how lunch went with Connie.

Polly took a wineglass out of the cabinet, got the chardonnay out of the fridge, emptied the bottle into the glass, and then tossed the empty bottle into the recycling. "She looked very tired," said Polly. "And she was dressed like an old lady in an ugly, navy blue suit."

Carole sipped her soda. "She works sixty-hour weeks, and the law firm has a dress code. I got her some pretty underwear for her birthday."

"Oh, that's right. Saint Joseph's Day, isn't it?"

"Yeah. I'm planning a little do," said Carole.

"And when were you going to tell me?" asked Polly. "I'll need to get something to wear."

"Honestly, it slipped my mind, what with everything that's going on."

"I understand," said Polly, opening a can of San Marzanos and adding them to the cacciatore. "There's the phone."

Carole answered, surprised to hear Gary's voice so soon. "It's just a preliminary report. I haven't gotten to everybody, but I thought you'd like to know. I was doing a routine check of birth certificates, and guess what I found out?"

"I don't know, Gary," said Carole. "Suppose you tell me."

"Well, in 1981, Millicent Shaw gave birth to a male child, seven pounds nine ounces, name of Nelson Mandela Shaw. No father's name is given."

Carole couldn't believe it. "Millicent had an illegitimate child?"

"Sure looks that way, and there's more."

"More?"

"Yeah, the kid was, um, African American."

"How could he be, if she was his mother?"

"Well, you know, obviously the father must be Black."

"Oh, of course," said Carole thinking of what Mom had told her about Millicent's African American visitor. "So that means he'd be forty-something now, right?"

"That sounds about right," said Gary. "Well, I just thought you'd want to know."

"Sure thing, thanks," said Carole. "Keep up the good work."

"I will," promised Gary. "Like I told you, I just got started. I bet there's plenty more. There always is."

Carole's mind was racing as she set the table, putting out the handwoven napkins and place mats she'd bought on Nantucket last summer and the French faience plates with roosters, in honor of the chicken cacciatore.

"Very nice," said Polly, as Carole lit the candles. "A table setting should always have a touch of whimsy."

"I've got more than a touch," said Carole. "I've got a whammo for Frank when he gets home."

When Frank walked in, Carole popped the cork on a bottle of Asti and gave him a big smile.

"So what's the celebration for?" asked Frank, as Carole filled the flutes.

"Well, Frank-O's out of the hospital and on the mend at your folks' house," said Carole, raising her glass. "And we're having a home-cooked dinner..."

"That is cause for celebration," agreed Frank, taking a healthy swallow.

"There's more," said Carole. "I got a big break in the investigation today."

"Yeah?" Frank was all ears.

"You remember the little old lady in the basement apartment..."

"Mildred Something?"

"Millicent, Millicent Shaw. Well, it turns out that she had an illegitimate child back in 1981. A little Black boy."

Frank's eyebrows popped up. "You kiddin' me?"

"No. I got it on good authority from Gary Strazullo, who found the birth certificate."

"And if Gary Strazullo could find it, so could Hosea Browne, is that what you're saying?" asked Frank.

"That's exactly what I'm saying, because if Hosea Browne found out..."

"What is the problem?" asked Polly, refilling her flute from the bottle. "A single woman had a child forty-odd years ago, so what?"

"You didn't know Hosea Browne," said Carole. "He told us he wouldn't tolerate any impropriety in his family home, and I think that to somebody like Hosea, an illegitimate child would definitely qualify as improper."

"Millicent would be out on her ear," said Frank.

"And I think Millicent definitely wants to stay in her apartment," said Carole.

"Which gives her a big motive for killing Hosea."

"Seven pounds nine ounces of motive," said Carole, raising her glass. "Here's to Millicent!"

Chapter Sixteen

By the time they finished dinner, the Asti had gone flat, and so had Frank's spirits. "You know, I'm not so sure that you're right about Millicent," he grumbled, pushing his plate away.

"How come?"

"Well, it's a condo, right? Everybody owns their apartment. Hosea couldn't make her leave."

Carole bit her lip and considered. "Maybe there's a special clause in the deed, like in the hoitsy-toitsy gated community we looked at. You know, no RV parked in the yard, no motorcycles, campers, or clotheslines."

"No bastard babies? I never heard of a clause like that," said Frank.

"There might be something about upholding the moral tone of the place," said Polly. "They wouldn't want some madam setting up shop in the family manse; they've probably got a way to deal with a situation like that."

"Maybe Connie could find out," suggested Carole.

"She hasn't been much help so far," grumbled Frank.

"They work her like a slave at that place," replied Carole, eager to defend her cub.

"So we won't give her more to do," said Frank. "You and Mom can go back there, do your cleaning lady routine again, and see what you can find out."

Carole didn't like the sound of this at all. "Oh, Frank, it's a waste of time..."

"No way. They saw you there before; they're getting to know you, so you'll be able to chat up the residents."

"Celerie did say that Jon Browne is out of the hospital and has taken up residence in his apartment," said Polly, earning an evil look from Carole.

"That settles it then," said Frank. "You and Mom go over there, and you find out about the Black kid, and maybe see if you can do anything for Jon Browne, and while you're at it, just casually ask about deed restrictions."

"Okay," said Carole, in a sarcastic tone, "how exactly do you suggest two down-at-heel cleaning ladies turn the conversation to deed restrictions? Hunh? And don't forget, he might remember me from the accident."

"I hardly recognized you, and I'm your mother," observed Polly.

"See? You'll think of something," said Frank. "So how about some coffee and maybe a biscotti or two?"

Angelique was surprised when she opened the door on Thursday morning and found Mom and Carole standing on the stoop with their cleaning gear for the second time in one week. She didn't hesitate to express her displeasure.

"I thought I made it clear that you would come on Mondays," she said. "And frankly, I have to say that I was not happy with your work. I don't think you even got past the hall."

"Emergenshy," said Mom, nodding furiously. "Het to leeeeve and no finish."

Beside her, Carole joined in the nodding. She overdid it,

and her wig slipped a bit, but Angelique didn't seem to notice.

"All right," said Angelique, with a big sigh. "But I hope you understand that there will be no additional payment for today's work, and in the future, I expect you to keep to the schedule we agreed upon."

"Yesss," hissed Mom. "Unnerstan' goot. Nott pwoblem."

"I think you should consider yourselves on probation," continued Angelique. "If I'm not satisfied with your work today, we will not continue this relationship."

"Ookey-dookey," said Mom.

"I hope I've made myself clear."

"Ver' kleeeer," said Mom.

"All right, then," said Angelique, stepping aside and admitting them to the building. "I think you better start downstairs. Millicent complained that the hallway and stairs down there weren't even touched." She opened the door to the basement stairs and watched as they went down, toting the vacuum cleaner and their buckets of cleaning gear.

When the door closed behind them, Mom whispered to Carole, "Do you think she suspects something?"

"No," said Carole, sticking a finger under the wig and scratching. "Help is hard to find, and she wants to keep us, believe me."

Carole was looking around the hall, a narrow, dark space with one door leading to the outside, another to Millicent's apartment, and a third to what she discovered was a communal storage area used by all the tenants. She made a mental note to give that area a thorough search, but first they needed to get started on the cleaning. She could see why Millicent had complained; the carpet was soiled with leaves and dirt tracked in from outside. She got busy with the vacuum, and Mom manned the duster, whisking cobwebs out of the corners and running it along the moldings and baseboards. They were so absorbed in their work that they didn't notice Millicent until she tapped Carole on her shoulder, making her jump.

"Oh, I didn't mean to startle you," she said, apologizing.

Carole just smiled and nodded, continuing her mute act.

"Isss gooot," said Mom, waving the duster around. "Ookey-dookey, no?"

"Oh, yes. Absolutely. I didn't mean to complain, but the hall was . . . well, now it's just lovely, and I certainly do appreciate your hard work."

"Nein pwobwem," said Mom, smiling and shrugging.

"It's wonderful to have you ladies," said Millicent. "I know Angelique can be a bit exacting. I think it's because she's French."

Mom smiled and nodded.

"Well," continued Millicent, twisting her fingers awkwardly, "I do wonder if you might have some extra time today to give my place a quick once-over. I'm expecting some company, a rather special guest for dinner tonight, and it would mean so much to me . . ."

Mom was on it in a flash. "How mooccch?"

"It's a small apartment, really just a studio," said Millicent. "Fifty dollars?"

"Ookey-dookey," said Mom, holding out her hand.

Millicent scurried back into her apartment and returned a moment later in her coat and hat and carrying her reusable Whole Foods grocery bags on her arm as well as five crisp ten dollar bills in her gloved hand. "Just one thing. Please don't let Tiggles, that's my cat, out. He's a bit of an escape artist."

"No pwobwem," said Mom, snatching the cash and pocketing it. As soon as Millicent was out the door, they were stepping into her apartment, entering carefully lest Tiggles make a break for freedom. The cat, however, took one look at them and scooted under the bed.

As Millicent had said, it was little more than a studio. A large front room served as living, dining, and kitchen, all in one. A curtained alcove contained a twin-size bed, and a tiny bathroom was tucked behind the kitchen area.

"Not what I expected," said Mom, taking in the colorful African dashiki-cloth curtains and vibrant sofa cushions.

Carole was looking at the collection of framed photos that hung on one wall. She recognized many of the faces: Martin Luther King, Rosa Parks, Malcolm X, a young Jesse Jackson, Rev. Al Sharpton. A beautiful young woman with long, flowing hair appeared in some of the photos, too, and Carole realized she must be the young Millicent. "Wow," she said, "it's no wonder she got knocked up."

"Yeah," said Carole. "I wonder why she never married?"

"Maybe it was like Obama's mom, you know, a grad school romance that ended when her boyfriend went back to Africa."

"Or maybe he got killed," said Mom. "Like those cop killings you hear about."

"Like poor George Floyd," said Carole, as grim images from the TV newscasts replayed in her head. She turned to Millicent's desk and flipped through a little stack of bills and letters that were piled under a small wooden sculpture of a very pregnant woman used as a paperweight. "I guess she's got a sense of humor," she observed, holding it up for Mom to see.

"A fertility figure," said Mom, surprising Carole. "I saw an exhibit over at Providence College when I was taking a class in stagecraft."

Carole put it right down, as if it were a hot potato, and went back to the mail. A photo of a fortyish Black man fell out of one letter, and she showed it to Mom. "Is this the guy you saw?"

"Yeah, that's him."

Carole unfolded the letter and read the neat, squarish handwriting. "He is her son, and get this, he says he hopes to meet her; he's been searching for her for years."

"Like one of them stories you see on TV."

"Even better," said Carole, chuckling. "You'll never guess who he is."

"Who?"

"Nellie Shaw!"

"The football player?" Even Mom recognized that name. Nellie Shaw's career started at Brown University, but he was picked up by the Buffalo Bills before graduating. He went on to break records and collect Superbowl rings, ending up with the New England Patriots before retiring. *The Providence Journal* had followed his career closely, considering him a favorite son of the city, and had recently trumpeted his admission to the Football Hall of Fame.

"Yeah, and I bet he's coming to dinner tonight," said Carole. "I wonder what Hosea would think of that?"

"He'd probably be waiting by the door, hoping for an autograph," said Mom.

"I think you're probably right; even the most bigoted people make exceptions for superstars," said Carole, reaching for the Pledge.

"Yeah, they somehow think they're the exception that proves the rule," said Mom, switching on the vacuum.

When they finished cleaning Millicent's place, they decided to start at the top of the house and work their way down, and they began hauling the vacuum and all their cleaning equipment up the stairs. They'd only reached the third floor when they heard a tremendous thumping coming from inside Jon Browne's apartment. Carole dropped the vacuum, and Mom knocked on the door; a deep male voice ordered them to come in.

Stepping inside, they found a slightly younger version of Hosea Browne sitting on a big leather couch, his injured foot elevated on a leather hassock, with a book in one hand and some sort of primitive ceremonial staff in the other. He gave a final thump with the staff and glowered at them. "What the hell are you doing out there?"

"Kleeenink," said Mom.

"You're making a hell of a lot of noise," he grumbled.

Carole had to admit Jonathan Browne wasn't exactly the Indiana Jones type she had expected. He was prematurely bald, and even though it was hard to tell because he was sitting down, he seemed to be quite small and wizened, as if the hot sun of the tropics had shriveled him somehow.

"Shorry," said Mom, with a shrug. "I get you sometink? Drinkk? Sometink to eeeet?"

"Tea," he said, with a wave toward the kitchen.

Getting a nod from Mom, Carole scurried off into the kitchen to make the tea. "Ver dushty," she heard Mom, as she filled the kettle and set it on the stove, which was stained with splashes of spilled liquids. "Veee kleeen?"

"No!" roared Browne. "Don't touch anything."

Peeking through the door, Carole was amused to see Mom tapping her foot, raising a small cloud of dust.

"Okay, okay," said Browne, as if granting her a favor.

"You may vacuum the rugs. But gently, as they're very old and valuable."

Mom got to work giving the assorted Oriental rugs in the living room a quick once-over and continuing on into the next room, which was a study. Carole presented the mug of tea on a small tray she found leaning against the backsplash, along with a sugar bowl, a pitcher of cream from the fridge, and a teaspoon. She even added a napkin, getting a nod of approval from Browne. That job done, she joined Mom in the study, where she found the vacuum running and Mom looking over the papers on his desk. Joining her, she discovered they were mostly academic journals, old Peruvian newspapers, maps, and photographs of holes in the ground. If there was a clue hidden in this junk, she didn't have time to look for it. She picked up the vacuum and continued on into the bedroom, where she found a huge mahogany, four-poster bed with crumpled, unmade sheets. She quickly set the bed to rights, scooted around with the vacuum, and returned to the living room. Mom was carrying the tray back to the kitchen. Browne was reading his book.

When Mom returned, they gathered up their cleaning things and were on their way out the door when he suddenly exploded, throwing the book across the room with a roar.

"Damned fool idiot!" he shouted.

Carole bent down to retrieve the book and discovered it was written by none other than Stuart Poole, PhD. It wasn't a regular book like you'd get at Barnes & Noble, with a colorful dust cover; it was a hefty paperback with a plain paper cover and was titled *Eighteenth-Century Slave Trade in Providence, R.I.*

"Yoooo vant?" she asked, raising one eyebrow.

He was fidgeting with that primitive staff of his. "I guess so," he grumbled. "Better to know your enemies, right?"

"Eh?" she asked, approaching timidly and placing the book on the table beside him.

"Nothing, nothing," he said, flapping his free hand and baring his yellow teeth in something resembling a smile. "All I can say is my poor departed brother, Hosea, must be rolling in his grave—or, more accurately, rattling in his urn." He glanced at the mantel, and Carole followed his gaze, spying a simple bronze container set in the middle, beneath a painting of a clipper ship in full sail. "It's hard to believe a reputable publisher like HarperCollins would even consider trash like this book."

"Funny-looking book, no?" said Carole.

"It's an advance copy," said Jonathan, adding a snort. "Nice of them to let me know what's coming."

"Bye-bye," said Mom, grabbing her arm and dragging her out. "Veee dun noww."

"Did you see what I saw?" asked Carole, as soon as they were back in the hall. "He's got his brother's ashes on the mantel!"

"I tell you, these WASPs don't know how to have a decent burial," said Mom, with a disapproving sniff. "The poor man. I bet there wasn't even a memorial service, let alone a proper Mass. He's probably floating around in limbo, or the other place, wishing they'd get him settled instead of leaving him on the mantel like a vase or something." She shuddered, looking over her shoulder at the door to Jon Browne's apartment, as if expecting the ghost of Hosea Browne to come walking out. "Gives me the creeps. I think we ought to get out of here."

"Me, too," said Carole, starting to haul the vacuum up

the stairs to the attic level, where the Lonsdales had their apartment.

They'd just about finished vacuuming the rather cramped hallway when her cell phone rang. Funny coincidence, she thought, realizing the caller was Celerie herself. It was enough to make you think Mom wasn't so crazy after all, with her fear of ghosts and talk of ESP and atmospheric vibrations.

"I have some samples I'd like to show you," said Celerie. "And I need to measure your windows so I can make a precise estimate. Would it be okay if I came over this afternoon?"

"Shuu . . ." began Carole, catching herself using her cleaning-lady accent. She stood up straight, reminding herself she was Carole Capobianco, the stylish wife of a very wealthy and extremely successful businessman, and assumed her natural voice. "About what time?" she inquired, reminding herself to behave like a demanding client.

"Whatever is convenient for you," said Celerie. "It will only take a few minutes."

"In that case, I suppose it's all right," said Carole, sounding as if it was an imposition, despite her eagerness to have another stab at questioning Celerie. "Let's say three-ish."

"Umm, actually two would be better for me," countered Celerie.

Whatever happened to *whatever is convenient?* Carole wasn't about to surrender; she had an image to uphold. "Two-thirty? That's the earliest I can do."

"Well, if that's the only time . . ."

"Unless you want to do it next week," said Carole, raising the ante.

"No, not at all. Two-thirty will be fine."

"Good," said Carole, mentally toting up one for herself. As if anyone was keeping score, she thought, wrapping up the vacuum cord for the trip down to the second floor. Who was she kidding? She didn't know who she was anymore, or if she was coming or going. She'd done a lot of cleaning, but she hadn't made much progress at all in this so-called investigation, and she had a nagging sense that time was not her friend. The longer it took, she feared, the more time the murderer would have to hide his—or her—tracks.

Chapter Seventeen

Carole was thoughtful as she wrestled Mom's vacuum down the stairs and then trudged up the street to Christina Fornisanti's car. She suddenly remembered the painting in Hosea's apartment of the storm-tossed ship *Orion* and the figures of drowning people. Now that she thought about it, they all seemed to have dark skin, and one falling figure, captured in midair, seemed to have actually been thrown from the ship. Carole had seen a series of stories in the *Journal* about the slave trade in Providence and other Rhode Island towns, and she knew there were instances when African captives destined for slavery in the New World were thrown overboard in the middle of the Atlantic Ocean. Sometimes it was punishment for troublemakers, sometimes it was because of sickness and fear of contagion, and sometimes it was to lighten the load when a ship got in trouble or if it needed to outrun British Navy patrols.

Now that she thought about it, she wondered if that series of stories in the *Journal* had something to do with Stuart Poole's forthcoming book. She knew the name Browne had popped up in some of the items, and she recalled there had been two Browne brothers back in the eighteenth century who had very different attitudes toward slavery, in a way foreshadowing the way the issue tore families apart a century later in the Civil War. One brother had become disillusioned with the slave trade and became an ardent abolitionist, while the other continued to take part in the profitable trade and became very wealthy.

Considering the painting in Hosea's apartment, it seemed likely that he and his brother were descended from those same Brownes. But which line? The slave trader or the abolitionist? The painting could be taken either way: a reminder of a sinful past or an expression of family pride. Maybe not exactly pride in the actual practice of slavery, but in his forebear's entrepreneurial spirit or seamanship. Something along those lines.

And, she thought, hoisting the vacuum into the Corolla's trunk, Jon Browne certainly seemed to think that Hosea wouldn't have appreciated being reminded of this stain on the family's honor. He might well have considered Stuart Poole a viper in his breast or something like that, considering he was living in the Browne family manse. If Hosea had challenged Poole, might the professor have reacted angrily, setting aside his pen and reaching for a blunt object?

"How come you're so quiet all of a sudden?" asked Mom, when they were seated in the car.

"I'm thinking that maybe the professor had a motive for killing Hosea Browne," said Carole.

Mom was incredulous. "That little guy who's always got his nose stuck in a book? He couldn't hurt a flea."

"Don't be so sure," said Carole. "You know that old saw about the pen being mightier than the sword? Well, he's probably been working on that book about the slave trade for years, and it's likely that he's mentioned the Browne family's involvement. His whole reputation is staked on this single book; it's his life's work."

Mom was driving cautiously along Benefit Street, weaving her way past the occasional oncoming car. There wasn't much traffic, which was a good thing, considering that the cobblestones and the parked cars made the narrow road a bit of an obstacle course. "And you think Hosea might've tried to put the kibosh on it, something like that?"

"Yeah. Remember, he had a lot of power as a director of the university."

"But what would be the point? Everybody knows the Brownes were slave traders. It was in the *Journal*."

"Yeah, but now there's talk about reparations—paying money to people whose ancestors were slaves."

"That's crazy. How could anybody document something like that after all these years?"

"I dunno, but that's what professors do, Mom. They dig around in musty old records and find out stuff like that. Who was sold and for how much and what that would be in today's dollars, and who profited and was the money spent or socked away in an investment and what it's worth now. Plus there's the matter of enforced labor; that had a value. And I heard how they've recovered some slave ship down south somewhere, and they're trying to recover DNA from the wreck that could be compared to the DNA of folks living there today who are descended from slaves. Those folks could then sue on behalf of their wronged ancestors."

Mom was chugging slowly up the hill in front of the statehouse; honestly, Christina Fornisanti ought to get a tune-up or something. "So you're saying that, because of the professor's book, Hosea might have had to pay a lot of money to . . . to whom?"

"I don't know. Maybe individuals, maybe a scholarship for African American kids at Brown."

"So what you're saying is that Hosea could've been putting the squeeze on the professor not to publish his book or maybe just to change it, and the professor got mad and bopped him on the head?" asked Mom, as she pulled up and braked in front of the Esplanade.

"Yeah. What do you think?"

"I think you should come home with me and have some of Big Frank's manicot', and spend some time with your son . . ."

Carole felt the familiar sensation of guilt settling on her, like a heavy winter coat. "Oh, Mom, I wish I could, but . . ."

Mom clucked her tongue. "I know. I know. Just keeping up with Frank is a full-time job, and you've got your mother there, too."

"How is Frank-O doing? Is he behaving himself?"

"He's a good boy, and he and Big Frank are getting on like a house afire . . ." she said, suddenly turning bright red. "Oops. I didn't mean that. And he's stronger every day. Looks like himself again."

"He's taking his pills?"

"For sure. He's no trouble at all. You can be proud of that boy, Carole."

Mom patted her hand, and Carole thought it would be nice if her own mother were a little more like Mom. Maybe she was carrying some extra pounds and she wasn't the most fashionable dresser, but she was always ready to help. Most of the time, you didn't even have to ask; she was right on it, giving you whatever you needed before you even knew you needed it.

"Thanks for everything," said Carole, giving the older woman a hug.

Mom squeezed her back. "For what? I'm not doing anything special."

"No, Mom. You're pretty special," said Carole, getting out of the car.

Carole was amused at the look the concierge gave her when she entered the lobby, still in her cleaning-lady disguise. It was Barry, the stickler for the rules. She thought he was going to challenge her and was planning to surprise him by revealing her true identity, but didn't get the chance because he was distracted by another tenant collecting her dry cleaning.

She continued on her way to the elevator, where Joao was busy polishing the stainless-steel doors. He gave her a big smile and asked, "You work for Miz Capobianco?"

Carole decided to play along. "Yes," she said, "I'm here to walk to dog."

"That dog is a little troublemaker," said Joao.

"I got a way with her," said Carole.

"She pays good, hunh? Miz Capobianco?"

Carole nodded. "Pretty good."

"She's a nice lady."

"Her husband's kind of grouchy," said Carole.

"Yeah, well, he's got a lot of problems," said Joao, pushing the fifth-floor button for her before she slipped through the closing doors.

Truer words were never said, she thought, as the elevator carried her up. Frank definitely had some problems.

Poopsie greeted her at the door, jumping excitedly. Polly wasn't home; she'd left a note saying she'd gone over to the Alliance Française for a lecture on French cinema, so Carole grabbed the leash and snapped it on the dog's collar. Once outside, Poopsie didn't want to go up the hill, and she didn't want to go down the hill, so Carole followed her lead and took her around the edges of the parking area, which was against the rules, but who was going to explain that to Poopsie?

Poopsie especially liked exploring the grassy bank at the back of the parking area, and Carole didn't mind; it was sunny and sheltered there, and she figured she might as well absorb some vitamin D; it was supposed to be good for you. She was standing there, basking in the sun, when her cell phone went off. It was Connie.

"Hi, honey," she said, hoping Connie had turned up something.

She had. "I did like you said, Ma, and I started chatting up the girls in the secretarial pool."

"Never underestimate people," advised Carole.

"You said it. They're a great bunch of girls, and they're all worried about this one, Vanessa, who's losing her home."

"All you brainy lawyers there can't do anything to help her?" demanded Carole.

"Well, yeah, one of the partners, actually, is working on it, trying to get it straightened out. But he isn't getting anywhere because the mortgage has been sold, and he's having a hard time figuring out who actually has it."

"The bank, duh."

"No, Ma. It's more complicated now. The banks sell the mortgages to investors; sometimes they're part of mutual funds, and there's a lot of mortgage brokers that aren't banks. It's a mess, and you'll never guess who's right smack in the middle."

"Who?" Poopsie wanted to go up the hill, and Carole was tugging on the leash, trying to restrain her.

"Mark Lonsdale!"

Poopsie heard Connie's voice and was suddenly alert, listening to every word, just like Carole. "How exactly is he involved?"

"Well, he's the one Vanessa got the mortgage from, one

of those interest-only deals from American Dream, which ought to be called American Nightmare, and she's been calling him, trying to refinance, but she never gets him."

"What, like he's hiding?"

"More like he's been fired, Ma. American Dream cut their workforce by fifty percent last week."

"That explains a lot," said Carole, as Poopsie resumed her sniffing progress along the edge of the parking lot.

"I'm glad I could help," said Connie. "I gotta go now."

Carole suddenly remembered that Celerie was coming over and glanced at her watch. Actually, she was probably on her way. She had to get back upstairs and out of her disguise, fast.

Carole was just zipping up her jeans and slipping into her leopard-print Manolos when Celerie arrived, accompanied by Pinky, who was toting an enormous ladder, easily eight feet long. Poopsie most certainly didn't approve of the ladder and started barking, so Carole locked her in the bathroom.

"Sorry about that," apologized Carole, returning and holding the door wide open for them. As Celerie whisked past her, she did a double take and gave Carole a puzzled look, then snapped her fingers at Pinky, who wasn't bringing in the ladder quickly enough for her.

"Where do you want it?" he asked, pausing in the doorway.

"You can just take it over to that window," Celerie said, pointing across the living room.

He carried it carefully past the furniture and set it up, spreading out the legs, then joined them by the door. "You can call me when you're ready to leave," he said.

"Thanks, Pinky." Carole gave him a big smile and slipped him a ten, taking it out of the purse she'd left on the hall table. After he was gone, Carole turned to watch Celerie, who was climbing up, stepping lightly in her heels and pencil skirt. Minutes later, she was unrolling a massive contractor's steel measuring tape, asking Carole to hold the bottom.

"Twelve feet even," she said, snapping the switch and rerolling the tape. Back down, she busied herself measuring the width of the window.

"Can I get you some tea or something?" offered Carole.

"No, thanks," said Celerie, jotting down the measurements.

"Uh, how's your husband?" asked Carole, wishing she'd been able to phrase the question rather more subtly.

"Mark?" Celerie shut her notebook. "He's fine."

"And how's he weathering this mortgage meltdown?" persisted Carole. "I heard American Dream made some big staff cuts lately."

"Well, you know what they say, when one door closes another one opens. Mark got a good severance package, and he's going into consulting."

Carole wasn't fooled; she knew consulting was just another word for unemployed. "Is the consulting business good?"

"As good as can be expected," said Celerie. "It's early days yet." She was descending slowly, carefully negotiating her way down the ladder. "Your husband is involved in the Factory project, isn't that right?"

"Capobianco and Sons has the plumbing contract."

"That's all?" persisted Celerie. "He's not an investor?"

"No, no," said Carole. "Why do you ask?"

"I just wondered if they're soliciting bids for interior decoration. You know, choosing fixtures, carpet, colors, things like that. I've done quite a bit of corporate work."

"Oh," said Carole, as light dawned over Marblehead, Celerie was networking, looking for a referral. "I'm sorry. He doesn't have anything to do with that."

"Just thought I'd ask," said Celerie, struggling to close the legs of the ladder together.

"You don't need to do that; I can call Pinky," said Carole.

"No. It's not heavy. I've got it," she said, hoisting the ladder on her shoulders and carrying it through the living room, stopping to pause at the doorway. "By the way, the design for the windows is more complicated than I thought at first."

Carole thought she'd better make herself clear, before she got stuck with something she didn't want. "I'm worried you may be going in the wrong direction here. I really want something simple."

"I understand," said Celerie. "But sometimes simple is the hardest thing to achieve. You have to get every detail exactly right, or it just looks cheap."

"I suppose so," sighed Carole.

"So I'll need another five hundred dollars."

"Five hundred!" exclaimed Carole. "I already gave you a thousand, and I haven't even seen a sketch."

Celerie gave her an apologetic smile. "Perhaps you don't understand how much custom window treatments cost," she began. "Why, I just finished doing some for a lovely restored colonial home on Hope Street: living room, dining room, and master suite. The total came to nearly sixty thousand dollars."

Something in Celerie's tone took her right back to those miserable days at Mount Holyoke, when everyone knew she was the scholarship girl who couldn't afford nice things. She'd come a long way since then, but it was true;

she had no idea how much custom window treatments cost. The last time she bought curtains was at Walmart, with Mom, who wanted to perk up her living room. They'd splurged on a designer line and bought matching throw pillows, and it all came in under a hundred dollars. "Okay," she said, with a sigh. "I'll get my checkbook."

But after she'd handed over the check and watched Celerie trudge down the hall to the elevator, carrying the ladder, she suspected she'd been had. The woman hadn't wanted help, because then she'd have to tip Pinky. Her husband had lost his job, money was tight, and she needed cash. Fast. Closing the door, she got right on the phone to Gary Strazullo. There had to be a cheaper way to get information about the Lonsdales than spending thousands of dollars on curtains she didn't want.

"I was just going to call you," said Gary. "I've got some information."

"Yeah?"

"Yeah. I found out who Millicent Shaw's kid is, and you'll never believe it."

"Nellie Shaw, the football player," said Carole.

"The great football player," persisted Gary, disappointed that Carole already knew his big news.

"Yeah, she's having him over for dinner," said Carole.

"You seem to be way ahead of me," complained Gary.

"Actually, I'm beginning to wonder what I'm paying you for," grumbled Carole.

"Hold on," said Gary. "I've got something else. You wanted to know about Mark Lonsdale, right?"

"That's right," said Carole. "I heard he lost his job."

"But did you know he's under investigation by the state AG for selling mortgages to people who didn't have a hope in hell of ever making their payments? Did you know that?"

"Not exactly," admitted Carole. "Is it serious? Is he in big trouble?"

"To be honest, I'm not sure. Used to be something that would get you a slap on the wrist, but these days it's a big issue, and the AG wants to make a name for herself as a champion of the little guy. So, yeah, I think he could be looking at some serious time."

Carole's mind was clicking, making connections. "So tell me, Gary, when did the AG's investigation start? Was it before Hosea Browne got killed?"

"Oh, yeah. Subpoenas were issued three weeks ago; the grand jury was scheduled to meet this week, but it was delayed because of Hosea Browne's death."

"Was he in trouble, too?"

"No. He was supposed to be an expert witness on banking."

"So Mark would have had an interest in getting rid of him before the grand jury met?"

"Bingo," said Gary.

Carole was feeling pretty good about her day's work and was celebrating with a late lunch of Polly's reheated cacciatore—two solid leads, thank you, deserved some solid food and even a small glass of vino—when Polly came in.

She could have been coming straight from the grand boulevards of Paris, dressed in her neat black coat with the blue scarf wrapped around her neck and her quilted Chanel bag.

"How was the lecture?" asked Carole, looking up from her meal.

"*Mon Dieu!*" exclaimed Polly, dropping her chin in horror and pointing at Carole. "What have you done to yourself?"

Carole didn't have a clue. She was wearing an oversized white linen shirt, black jeans, and those fabulous Manolos; what was the problem?

"Your hair!"

She'd just had her color done, thought Carole, reaching up to fluff her hair and feeling instead the stiff artificial fibers of the wig. Horrified, she jumped to her feet and ran across the room to the mirror. It was true; she was still wearing the ugly brown wig from her cleaning lady disguise.

"I forgot," she whispered, pulling it off.

"I hope nobody saw you like that," said Polly.

Carole remembered the odd look Celerie had given her when she opened the door. She went back to the table and downed the rest of her wine in one gulp. She might have two solid leads, but she'd blown her cover. Her days as a cleaning lady at Prospect Place were definitely over; she'd have to come up with another way to investigate Hosea's murder.

Chapter Eighteen

Carole dressed carefully for Angelique Poole's pastry class on Saturday morning. Angelique had seen her in her cleaning lady disguise, and she wanted to make sure there was nothing in her appearance to suggest that earlier incarnation. The horrible housedress had been a flowery orange print, so Carole decided to stay as far away from that end of the spectrum as possible and chose a blue cashmere turtleneck, skinny gray jeans, tall, black leather boots with pointed toes, and four-inch heels. It was a bit of a squeeze getting into those new jeans—had she gained a pound or two?—but she was dying to wear them. They were the very same ones that Meghan Markle had been pictured wearing in *People* magazine.

She also took special care with her makeup, going a little heavy on the eyes and choosing a bright, cherry-red lipstick. She had used a shampoo that was supposed to enhance blond hair, whether natural or dyed, and she was pleased with the results because her highlights were brighter than ever. All in all, she decided, taking one last look in the floor-length mirror, Angelique would have to be clairvoyant to identify her as the cleaning lady.

Polly was sticking with what had become her uniform since taking up residence in Paris, a knee-length skirt and low heels, except she'd switched her usual suit jacket for a tailored shirt and scarf. "I didn't want to risk getting flour on the jacket," she told Carole. "Do you think they supply aprons, or should we bring them?"

Carole had a few aprons, and they were nice and clean because she hardly ever cooked and rarely wore them, so she tucked them in a vintage Marc Jacobs tote bag, and off they went to the class. Polly was actually hoping to improve her baking skills, but Carole couldn't care less; there were at least a dozen terrific bakeries in Providence. She was interested in questioning Angelique about her husband's work and what Hosea thought about it.

When they arrived in the kitchen classroom at Johnson and Wales, she was surprised to see Connie among the dozen women assembled for the class. "Connie!" she exclaimed, wrapping her arms around her in a big hug. "What a wonderful surprise!"

"*Grandmere* insisted," said Connie, giving Polly a big smile.

"I thought it would be a nice break for her," explained Polly. "She works so hard."

"*Faites attention, mesdames*," trilled Angelique, clapping her hands briskly, ending their conversation. "Take your places, *s'il vous plait*."

Carole stood at the work station between Polly and Connie and looked around, taking in the gleaming white kitchen and her classmates, most of whom were clad in designer clothes and had expensive coiffures and plenty of bling on their ears and manicured fingers. No wonder, she knew the class didn't come cheap. These well-heeled students were a colorful contrast to Angelique, who was togged out in crisply starched whites and a traditional chef's toque, with the nails on her working hands clipped short and free of rings and polish.

"*Bonjour, mesdames*," began Angelique, silencing the chattering women. "This morning, we are going to make two traditional French desserts: tarte tatin and profiteroles. I have chosen these two classic dishes because they use different pastry techniques: *pâte brisée* for the tarte tatin and *pâte à choux* for the profiteroles." She raised a finger to emphasize a point: "Although they are seemingly quite different, I assure you that, for both, our goal is the same—to produce a pastry that is light, crisp, tender, and buttery."

"Sounds divine," whispered Connie, watching intently as Angelique proceeded to demonstrate the technique for *pâte brisée*. In a matter of moments, she had mixed flour, butter, salt, water, and a pinch of sugar into a compact ball.

"You must work quickly with light movements," she said, demonstrating. "And now, this is the most important step—*fraisage*, in which we push the dough firmly with the heel of our hands to work the butter evenly through the dough."

After the demonstration, the students set to work mixing their pastry, while Angelique went from one to the other, offering advice. When she reached Polly, she gave a little squeal of excitement. "*Absolument parfait*," she declared, admiring Polly's work.

"*Merci, madame*," chirped Polly.

Angelique's eyebrows shot up. "*Êtes-vous française?*" she asked.

"*Americain, mais j'habite à Paris*," explained Polly. Carole knew her mother was trying to help here, but she still found it irritating when she spoke French. Almost as irritating as when she scarfed down all those croissants and pastries without gaining an ounce.

"*Paris me manque,*" sighed Angelique. "We must meet after class, no?"

"*Bien sur,*" agreed Polly, winking at Carole when Angelique moved on to Carole's work station. "*Non, non,*" she said, shaking her head and beginning to gather the crumbled pastry together. "*Comme ca!*" she announced, giving the neat ball of dough a final pat.

Connie looked a bit nervous as Angelique studied her pastry; Carole knew she was a super-achiever who'd never gotten a grade below A and would be devastated if the professor did not approve of her work. "*Tres bien,*" Angelique finally announced, even adding a little smile of approval, and Connie's shoulders dropped in relief. Crazy, thought Carole. It wasn't like this was the bar exam; it was just a ball of dough.

The class was a lot more fun than Carole expected, and she enjoyed seeing Connie finally relax as she concentrated on the challenging task of combining flour and butter to create perfect pastry instead of struggling to decipher the implications of the federal tax code in relation to estate planning. When they all gathered at a long table to taste their creations, Connie didn't just sample her tarte tatin and profiteroles; she scarfed them down like a woman who'd been deprived of sugar and chocolate for far too long. Carole watched with delight as her daughter licked her fork, then felt her spirits plummet as Connie picked up her tote bag and announced she had to get back to the office. She gave her mother and grandmother pecks on the cheek, thanked Angelique for the lesson, and vanished out the door.

Carole's jeans were tighter than ever when she and Polly joined Angelique in the bright coffee bar at the college. Tarte tatin had turned out to be a tremendously rich upside-down cake made with apples and more butter than she normally consumed in a year, and profiteroles weren't so fancy after all; they were nothing more than cream puffs, but they'd filled them with *crème au beurre*—more butter!—and smothered them with an absolutely amazing *sauce au chocolat*. In total, she figured she'd consumed more calories in one morning than she had eaten in the past week, rationalizing that it was stress eating and discovering that she really needed to loosen her waistband.

"Black coffee for me," said Angelique, signaling the waiter. "These weekend classes are fun, but exhausting." She had changed out of her whites and was now dressed in a skirt and blouse similar to Polly's outfit, apparently the French uniform for *les femmes d'un certain age*.

"You prefer the professional students?" asked Polly.

"It's easier because I know what they know; we are all on the same page. But this morning, I had you, Polly, and you know what you're doing, and I also had that little Chinese lady who was treating *pâte brisée* like wonton dough!" Angelique, Carole noticed, was much too polite to include her rather subpar effort in her critique.

The student waiter arrived, and Polly and Angelique ordered coffee, while Carole requested mint tea. They didn't have it, so she had to settle for Earl Grey. Carole didn't say much; she was too busy sipping her tea and concentrating on trying not to feel nauseous from the rich food and her uncomfortably tight jeans, but Polly and Angelique were getting on great. They'd established that their favorite park in Paris was the Luxembourg Garden and the best museum was the Tuileries and the best shopping was at the

Clingancourt flea market. Carole was beginning to feel as if her chance to question Angelique was slipping away. What she really needed, she decided, was a change of venue. The bright lights and minimalist design of the coffee bar simply did not encourage intimacy.

"Isn't that new bar, Bar Bleu, near here?" she asked, rather abruptly. "I've heard so much about it, and I've been dying to try it. Why don't we continue our conversation there and try one of their signature cocktails?"

"Fine with me," agreed Polly, who had never turned down a drink in her life.

There was a moment when Angelique seemed to hesitate, and Carole thought she might have miscalculated, but then she smiled and agreed to the change. After a short, two-block walk, they were all settled in comfortable armchairs in the cozy bar; each had a blue martini to sip, and the confidences were flowing.

Angelique asked Polly how she happened to decide to live in Paris, and Polly told her all about her marriage to Jock Prendergast and how she needed a change after the emotionally devastating but financially rewarding break-up. "Where better than Paris?" she declared. "And why did you ever leave?"

Angelique shrugged. "I met my husband when I was vacationing on Saint Martin; it was very fast, very intense. At first, I thought of it as a fling, a vacation romance, fun, not serious, but he asked me to marry him, and"—she smiled—"I said yes."

"But you left Paris for Providence," said Carole, amazed.

"Providence is very nice. I like it here."

"But it's not Paris," said Carole, pressing the point. After all, it was hard to imagine that any woman would abandon Paris for an old stick like Professor Poole.

Polly leaned forward and squeezed Angelique's hand. "You wanted to get away from a man?" she asked.

Angelique gave a little smile. "Worse than that, a situation. My father was involved in a scandal involving a DNA mix-up that sent an innocent man to jail. It was a very big thing in France, and even though he really wasn't guilty of doing anything wrong, his name, my name, was dragged through the mud."

"What a shame," cooed Polly, as the waiter arrived with fresh drinks. "Carole knows exactly what that's like, don't you?"

"There is a difference," said Carole, bristling and thinking that her mother probably didn't need a second martini. They were supposed to be grilling Angelique, not airing the Capobianco family's dirty laundry. "Here in America you're supposed to be innocent until proven guilty. In France, it's the other way round."

"But everybody thinks Frank killed Hosea Browne," declared Polly.

"Oh, no," protested Angelique, "I don't think that. Not at all."

Carole was on her quicker than a hungry flea on a sleeping dog. "Who do you think killed him?"

"I don't know," said Angelique, going all wide-eyed innocent over her martini glass.

"When we were interviewed about buying into Prospect Place, I got the feeling that Hosea wasn't too popular with the other owners," said Carole. "Is that true?"

"I can only speak for myself," said Angelique. "I found him old-fashioned and reserved. My husband explained that Hosea is, I mean was, a particular sort of New Englander, a traditional Yankee, that's all." She giggled. "He said people like Hosea are an endangered species, so no, I didn't dislike him." Angelique gave her a cool smile and put down her glass. "I see what you're doing. You're looking for the murderer, no? And you think it might have been my husband. Why do you think that?"

"I don't, not at all," protested Carole. "But he did write a book about the slave trade that I don't think Hosea would have liked very much. And Hosea was in a position to scuttle your husband's work."

"That's true, but we are civilized people . . ." Angelique was on her feet, reaching for her coat.

"Did Hosea try to block publication of the book?"

Angelique finished buttoning her coat and was slipping on her gloves. "I don't know. You would have to ask my husband," she said, picking up her purse and sliding it over her arm. She gave Polly a little smile and a nod. "*A bientot*, and thanks for the drinks." Then she turned and trotted across the bar and out the door.

"You were so rude," chided Polly.

"Me? She's the one who stuck us with the tab," said Carole.

"Stuck you," said Polly. "I haven't had a chance to change my money. All I have is euros."

By the time they got the car out of the garage and were headed over to Mom and Big Frank's to check on Frank-O, Carole had regained her good humor. "I'm going on a green tea detox," she declared. "Nothing but green tea for three days."

"*Bonne chance* with that," said Polly, when they opened the kitchen door and were met by the familiar scent of herbs and tomatoes. "What is that delicious aroma?"

"Just gravy," said Mom, dropping her spoon and hugging them in turn. "Big Frank hasn't been cooking much lately; he's been down in the cellar helping Frank-O with his project."

Carole was worried, listening to the clangs and bangs issuing up through the heating vent. "Isn't Frank-O supposed to do it on his own?"

"It's all Frank-O's ideas," said Mom. "Big Frank just helps with the heavy lifting."

"You think he'll mind if I take a look?" asked Carole.

"Why should he mind? Go on! Your mama and I will have a cup of coffee."

"I could use some coffee," admitted Polly, apparently feeling the effects of three blue martinis. She collapsed onto a chair at the kitchen table, which was covered with a plastic cloth and littered with newspapers and sudoku books.

In the cellar, Carole was relieved to see that Frank-O looked much better. His cheeks were rosy from the exertion of working on the sculpture, and his voice and breathing were almost normal. His hair was still bright blue.

"So what exactly is this?" asked Carole, once the hugs and greeting were over. She gestured to the assemblage of copper pipe that was taking up most of the free space in the cellar workshop. "What's with all the copper pipe?"

"Offcuts," said Big Frank. "From the Factory job."

"Yeah, Mom. This whole sculpture is made from recycled pipe that Big Frank salvaged from the trash pile. It all would've been thrown away."

"Really?" asked Carole. "Isn't copper pipe expensive?"

"Yeah," replied Big Frank. "For sure. But this is all little bits, too small to use."

Carole studied the sculpture, which was indeed pieced together from many small lengths of pipe, some measuring only a couple of inches. "I can see that you were able to make a very intricate design," she said. "It's really complicated, like a puzzle."

"Yeah, Mom!" agreed Frank-O, enthusiastically. "It's called *que*, spelled with a q."

"Oh," said Carole, not much the wiser.

"You don't get it, do you?"

"I guess not."

"Well, cu is the scientific notation for the element copper, and *que* is pronounced the same way and is a common word in several languages, including French where *que* is a question. It means *what*."

Carole thought about this. "Q-u-e is the beginning of the word *question*."

"Right, Ma! I didn't think of that."

Carole was beginning to doubt that her son was as smart as she liked to think he was. "So this whole piece is a kind of copper question mark?"

"Wow, Ma. You've got it!" Frank-O was beaming at her. "You're really cool."

"Thanks," she said, heading back upstairs. "I'm starting detox tomorrow," she explained to Mom. "In the meantime, I'd love a glass of chianti."

At the table, Polly pursed her lips and gave her a disapproving glance. "You're driving," she said, "and I'd like to get home alive."

"I guess I better have some Pellegrino," said Carole.

After leaving Mom and Big Frank's, they stopped on Atwells Avenue and picked up some groceries, some nice lemon chicken and pasta salad from Venda Ravioli for supper, and some cannoli for Frank from Scialo's.

Polly wasn't happy about the cannoli. "Why don't you make some profiteroles, like you learned in class?" she asked. "French pastry is so much better than Italian."

"Try telling that to Frank," said Carole, ordering a dozen, assorted.

Then they were back in the car, passing the Factory, on their way home. A big sign had gone up announcing that apartments would soon be available and the rental office was now open.

"Let's stop," said Polly, impulsively. "I'd like to see what it's all about."

"You want to look at apartments?"

"Sure," said Polly.

"How come?"

"Just curious."

"I thought you loved living in Paris." Carole wasn't sure how she felt about her mother moving back to Providence.

"I do love living in Paris, but the dollar doesn't go very far there these days," said Polly.

Carole wasn't sure she liked the sound of this. "So you're really thinking of moving back here?"

"Don't panic," said Polly, chuckling. "I'm just thinking about it. Exploring my options."

"I'm not panicked," Carole was quick to say as she pulled into a parking slot. "I'm just surprised."

Getting out of the car, she noticed that, except for a few pickup trucks belonging to contractors, the partly finished parking lot was empty. People weren't exactly flocking to the rental office. And when they followed the signs that pointed the way to the office, which was located in the lobby, they found the door was locked tight. They cupped their hands around their eyes and peered in, observing a tastefully designed waiting area, but couldn't get inside.

"It looks nice," said Polly. "What's the deal here? Mixed use?"

"Yeah," said Carole, waving her hand. "As you can see, there's a number of buildings. They're rehabbing them for various uses: offices, residences, retail. They're also opening up access to the river and landscaping the grounds. It's going to be real nice."

Polly looked around, as if she was imagining how it would all look when the project was completed. "Where was the fire?" she asked, suddenly, surprising Carole.

"Over there," said Carole, pointing across the parking lot to the blackened brick building.

"I want to see," said Polly, marching across the fresh asphalt. It soon ended, and they had to make their way across raw, rubble-strewn earth to the shell of a building. As they got closer, they could smell the lingering scent of the fire and could see the yellow tape that had been strung across the door. Polly ignored it and ducked under, stepping inside, where she paused. "Poor Frank-O must have been terrified."

"I imagine so," said Carole, whose heart was beating faster as she looked around and imagined the black smoke he had said filled the building. "He was in a hallway; he said he was confused and disoriented. It was a miracle the firemen found him in time. He could've died from smoke inhalation."

"How did the fire start?" asked Polly, stepping farther into the building.

Carole grabbed her by the elbow. "I don't think we should go any farther; the building might be unstable." In the distance, she could hear voices, probably workmen involved in demolishing the damaged sections. "Besides," she added, pointing to a smoke-blackened sign, "this is a hard-hat area."

"Oh," said Polly, looking down at the wooden floor planks, black with soot. "Do they think somebody set the fire?"

"I don't know." What Carole did know was that she

didn't understand her mother's sudden interest in the site of the fire, and she didn't much like poking around in a dangerous, burned-out wreck of a building. Just being there was giving her PTSD. "Let's get out of here."

"Do you feel it, too?" asked Polly. "There's something evil here."

Carole stood still, noticing that the sun had disappeared; the afternoon had turned dark and cloudy, but that's what happened in New England. The weather changed all the time. And there were occasional voices and noises; some workers were obviously on site, and that was to be expected. But evil? She didn't think so. She preferred to think that a guardian angel had been looking out for Frank-O and saved him from a bad situation. "Nobody was killed, you know. Frank-O was the only one who was injured, and he's going to be fine."

Polly wasn't convinced. "Okay, I know you think I'm crazy, but there is definitely a bad vibe here."

Carole took her arm and led her back to the car. "So I guess you won't be getting an apartment here?"

She gave her head a firm little shake. "No way."

They were approaching the Esplanade when Polly admitted her psychic episode might have been the result of all the rich pastry plus the martinis. "Maybe it's like Scrooge in that story when he thinks Marley's ghost is a fragment of undigested beef. I know one thing for sure. I have really got to pee."

"That's a relief. You really had me freaked out there," said Carole, laughing as she turned onto Edith Street. "I can let you out at the door if you want. There's restrooms right off the lobby."

"I want," said Polly.

Carole pulled to a stop, and Polly ran for the door, waving the fob that unlocked it, and dashed inside. Carole continued on down the street and turned into the garage, winding her way up through the levels. Somebody must be holding an event, she thought, observing that the garage was a lot fuller than usual. Her favorite spot was filled, of course, and she was kind of picky about parking the Cayenne. It was big, and she didn't like to squeeze into a tight space where it could get dinged. On the other hand, she didn't want to go up to the very top level because that was uncovered. She finally found a suitable spot on the last covered level and hurried over to the elevator, toting her groceries and discovering she could use a pee, too.

She was tapping her foot impatiently, waiting for the elevator, but it wasn't coming. There was no familiar groan as the mechanism answered the call and began moving, and the little lights above the door were dark. She pushed the button harder, but it didn't light up.

It must be out of order. She was going to have to use the stairs and in these heels, too. It was only a flight or two down to the pedestrian bridge, and she clattered along, hanging on to the metal handrail, going as fast as she dared. She was almost there when a stocky guy in a black hooded sweatshirt passed her, going up. She didn't think anything of it; he was probably one of the college kids living in the building, and she was focused on her need to pee when she was suddenly yanked from behind by her hair and thrown down onto her back as her bags of groceries and her Prada bag went flying.

Adrenalin surged through her body, but before she could scream, the guy was on top of her and pressing a gloved hand over her mouth. "Shut up!" he hissed at her.

She was rigid and wide-eyed with fear, and noise was coming from her mouth; she couldn't seem to help it. His face was inches from hers, but he was wearing a black Covid mask and all she could see were his eyes, dark and glittering as he pressed his arm against her neck. "I said shut up," he said, looming over her.

She managed to stop the noise, struggling to breathe and squirming uncomfortably against the metal-edged concrete steps pressing against her back. She watched him warily. What was she supposed to do? Talk to him and try to make a connection? A human bond, that's what you were supposed to try to create. But what did you say?

"You'll never get away with this," she whispered. "Somebody's sure to come along."

"Shut up and don't move," he said. His voice was muffled by the mask, and she knew she ought to study what she could see of him in order to identify him later. She obediently froze, then gasped in terror, catching a glimpse of something shiny. Metal. A knife? Was he going to cut her? A closer look revealed it wasn't a knife, but scissors. A huge pair of shiny scissors. What was he going to do with them?

Then suddenly, his body weight shifted slightly as he pressed his arm across her chest, pinning her down as he rose slightly, and she felt cold metal against her belly under the waistband of her jeans. "This'll teach you to mind your own business," he growled, starting to work the scissors inside the jeans.

She understood in a flash. He was going to cut her jeans because it took too long to pull tight jeans off a resisting woman. She'd read about this: rapists with scissors. He was going to cut through her nine-hundred-dollar jeans that were identical to Meghan Markle's and rape her!

The hell with that! It wasn't a decision; it was an automatic response, like a reflex. Before she knew what had happened, she had driven her stiletto heel into the back of his leg, causing him to yelp with pain and reach for his wound. She took advantage of this change in position to slip her hand down to his groin, where she grabbed as much as she could and gave it a squeeze, using every bit of strength she had. He rolled off her, curling into a fetal position, moaning and clutching himself. Still on her back, she used the railing to haul herself onto her feet and clattered down the stairs as fast as she could go, screaming all the way. She didn't have time to mess with the fob at the pedestrian bridge; she kept going all the way down and through the door to the safety of the street, with its steady steam of passersby. Then she stopped, leaning against the door, panting and sobbing, gulping the fresh air as warm pee streamed down her legs.

Chapter Nineteen

The first person to approach her was a large Black woman who worked in one of the nearby office buildings. Carole knew her by sight; they always exchanged smiles, but didn't know her name.

"What happened to you?" the woman asked, removing the large pashmina she always wore over her coat and wrapping it around Carole's shaking shoulders.

"He tried to rape me," stammered Carole, through her chattering teeth.

The woman looked up at the stairwell, then gave Carole a reassuring hug. "Are you okay, honey?"

Carole took inventory and discovered she was more frightened than anything, and, of course, she'd wet herself. "I peed my pants," she confessed, horrified. "My new jeans."

The woman gave her another hug. "Never you mind. That'll wash right out," she said, as a couple of other women approached. "Some guy tried to rape her," she told them.

"In the garage?" asked one. "My friend's purse got snatched last week," said another. "Down on Promenade Street."

Soon a group of clucking, cooing women had surrounded her, mostly office workers and a few neighbors. One man she recognized, a young, super-fit guy she often saw jogging when she walked Poopsie, also joined the group and offered to run back upstairs to retrieve her purse and groceries. He was gone before she could warn him to watch out for the guy who assaulted her, and she waited anxiously for his return. He was back in minutes, reporting that the rapist had gone, leaving her things where they'd fallen. When he handed over her Prada bag, she discovered nothing was missing, not even her wallet, which was stuffed with close to a thousand dollars. "Thanks," she told the guy, as he handed her the bag of groceries. "That was really brave of you."

"No big deal. I was hoping he'd still be there. I was gonna give him a—well, never mind." He gave her a wave and jogged off.

Carole discovered that while she was still shaken by the experience—her hands were shaking and she was trembling, struggling to catch her breath—she was also growing increasingly furious. Who did her attacker think she was, to treat her like that? To knock her off her feet, grabbing at her and pawing her. It was outrageous.

"I'm okay," she said, in a quavery voice and pulling out her keys with the entry fob. Then, remembering the pashmina, she shrugged it off and returned it to its owner. "Thank you so much for helping me. I'm Carole, by the way. Carole Capobianco."

"Beverly Robinson," said the woman, introducing herself.

"Well, thank you so much for helping me, Beverly. But now I can take it from here."

One of her neighbors, a gentleman she often met in the elevator but didn't know by name, insisted on taking her elbow and escorting her into the building. "You should report this to the concierge," he said, as Carole headed straight for the elevator.

"Maybe later," said Carole, who suddenly just wanted to get behind the locked door of her apartment and out of her clothes and into the shower.

"Really, it's a security issue," said the man. "It affects all of us."

Carole wasn't so sure. She remembered the way her assailant had warned her to mind her own business. This was no random attack; it was targeted at her, to scare her. But why? Reaching the elevator, she pressed the button. "I'm fine, honest. The less said, the better."

"I understand this was a traumatic experience, but refusing to deal with it is a big mistake," he told her. "I'm a psychologist, and . . ."

The elevator doors opened, and Carole got in. "Thanks again," she said, giving her head a little shake. He got the message and didn't attempt to join her, but stood back as the doors closed. Carole found herself breathing a huge sigh of relief as the elevator carried her upward.

Moments later, she was back in her apartment, her beautiful apartment, and Poopsie was sniffing at her jeans as her mother helped her undress.

"*Mon Dieu!*" exclaimed Polly. "I never should have left you."

"Don't be so sure," said Carole, darkly.

"What do you mean? If there were two of us, he would have gone after somebody else."

Carole studied her mother critically, guessing she maybe weighed a hundred pounds. Maybe. "To be honest, I don't think you'd offer much protection. He could have assaulted us both, then where would you be, with those fragile bird bones of yours?"

"I could have screamed, or beat him with my purse, or something."

Carole shook her head. "I don't think that would have made much difference. This was a warning to me to mind my own business."

"Because you're investigating the murder?"

"Probably," said Carole, peeling off her jeans.

"I'll put those right in the wash," said Polly, grabbing the jeans and underpants and trotting down the hall to the closet containing the washer and dryer.

"Thanks, Mom," called Carole, turning on the shower, and for once, Polly didn't object to her use of the word.

As the glorious and healing hot water streamed over her, Carole wondered who exactly it was who wanted her to mind her own business. Someone who felt threatened enough to hire some goon to send a message. Was it one of the Prospect Place residents? She didn't think so; it wasn't their style. They all had their problems, for sure, but they hardly seemed likely to resort to violence. The Lonsdales needed money, but that was hardly a unique situation. Lots of people were in the same boat these days, and being temporarily strapped was hardly a motive for murdering Hosea Browne. And while Mark was under investigation for selling bad mortgages, Carole was pretty sure he was the low man on the totem pole. Investigators were probably more interested in the information he could give them about his bosses than in indicting him.

As for the Pooles, well, Carole didn't think that much of anything apart from his books and research made the least impression on Stuart. He seemed to live in a world of his own, encased in academic privilege. If push came to shove, she was willing to bet that Stuart's weapon of choice really was the pen rather than the sword. And Angelique? Well, she had seemed pretty angry when she left the bar, but

Carole figured she was one woman who believed revenge was a dish best served cold. Besides, according to Susan Weaver, if Hosea caused her any trouble, all she had to do was bake him a tarte tatin to get back in his good graces. As she knew herself, it was hard to argue with a tarte tatin.

But what about Jon Browne? He stood to inherit Hosea's substantial fortune, minus some generous bequests to the university and hospital, but Carole hadn't gotten the impression that he cared. In her brief encounter with him, she'd been reminded of the hermits of old, those saints who sat on pillars or withdrew to the wilderness in their scratchy hair shirts. He didn't seem to care about creature comforts or material things; all he wanted to do was get back to Peru to dig up bits of bone and shards of pottery.

And then there was Millicent, with her illegitimate son. Carole turned off the water and reached for a towel, beginning to pat herself dry. There was a time, she reminded herself, when giving birth to an illegitimate, mixed-race child would have been scandalous, but those days were long past. And if that child turned out to be a Football Hall of Famer, and a Brown alumnus, even Hosea would have been impressed. Maybe he even would have begged for an autographed football!

No, she thought, smiling to herself as she reached for the blow dryer, she didn't see any of the Prospect Place residents as murderers or rapists, and she couldn't imagine any of them having anything to do with the creep who attacked her in the stairwell. And then there was the matter of timing: the attack came after she had paid a visit to the Factory.

She paused, boar-bristle brush in one hand and dryer in the other, staring at her astonished face in the mirror. The attack probably didn't have anything to do with Hosea, she realized; it was all about the fire. Somebody didn't want her snooping around the Factory.

In that context, the guy in the hoodie, the guy who wasn't interested in her money and probably wasn't really interested in raping her, made sense. It was all about the warning, the warning to stay away from the Factory.

When Carole emerged from the bathroom in her terry-cloth robe and slippers, her mother had a glass of port waiting for her. She settled herself on the couch, and Poopsie jumped up beside her, resting her head in her lap. Carole sipped the delicious port, stroked the dog's soft coat, and suddenly felt that maybe everything wasn't quite right with the world, but she was going to be okay. And then there was a knock at the door.

Polly went to answer, discovering the picky concierge Barry, accompanied by a uniformed patrol officer. "Just a moment," she said, holding up a finger before quickly closing the door and dashing to the couch, where she scooped up Poopsie. "There's a cop," she told Carole, carefully shutting the dog into the master bedroom before hurrying back to the door.

"We got a report of an assault in the garage," began Barry, clearly miffed at the delay and speaking in a disapproving tone, rather as if it was Carole's fault and she'd somehow invited the attack. "Management policy in that situation is to contact the police immediately."

What the hell, thought Carole. No apologies, no expression of concern for her well-being? Where were the flowers, the cards? No promise to install video cameras, no assurance that nothing like this would ever happen again?

"That's right, ma'am," said the cop, who seemed just

about old enough to have graduated from kindergarten. "I'm here to escort you to the hospital..."

For a rape exam, thought Carole, leaping to the obvious conclusion. "I wasn't raped," she said. "I fought him off."

"We can still collect DNA evidence from your skin and clothing," he told her, blushing furiously.

Carole couldn't believe it. It was bad enough that she was attacked in the first place, but now they wanted her to submit to an intrusive exam and no doubt waste a lot of time answering stupid questions. No way. "I took a shower and my clothes are all in the washer."

"That was very irresponsible," scolded the cop. "We can't nail this guy without evidence."

"That's right," added Barry, with a little sniff. "And now everybody's in danger."

Carole made a time-out signal with her hands. "I think we're forgetting who's the victim here."

"Exactly," said the cop. "And I am here as part of the department's Victim Assistance Program."

"Well," said Carole, "you're a day late and a dollar short. I could've used you an hour ago, but now I'd appreciate some privacy."

"That's right," said Polly, opening the door and giving a clear signal that it was time for them to leave.

"Here's my card," said the cop, pulling a black leather case out of his pocket. "In case you reconsider." Carole didn't reach for it, so he placed it on the coffee table.

"Management will be getting in touch with you," said Barry, sounding like a teacher warning about a visit to the principal or a call to the parents.

Not getting any response from Carole, the two turned and made their way to the door. There they paused, and the cop turned and, cap in hand, said, "Have a nice day."

Carole's jaw dropped, thinking it was rather inappropriate advice, considering the circumstances.

Polly shut the door behind them. "America has gotten very strange," she said, and for once, Carole had to agree with her mother.

They had the lemon chicken for dinner; it hadn't been damaged and neither had the pasta salad or, thank heaven, the cannoli. Carole made Frank drink a double Dewar's before she told him about the attack, and it had the desired effect. He declared he was going to bust some heads and find out who was behind the attack, but agreed to wait until after he'd eaten. By then, he was a lot calmer, and she told him her idea that maybe the attack, and even Hosea's murder, had something to do with the Factory job.

"After all," she reminded him. "He was killed at the Factory, not at Prospect Place. Something's going on there, I'm sure of it. First there was the fire, and now this attack on me. They're both warnings."

Frank helped himself to a second cannoli, pistachio dipped in chocolate, his favorite, and Carole refilled his coffee cup. "I don't think so," he said, before biting off half the cannoli. "Everything was fair and square with that job. Old Hosea, you gotta give him credit, he was a stickler for doing everything according to the book. The bids were sealed; there were no kickbacks, nothing like that. The low bidders got the jobs, and as it worked out, just about everybody got a piece of the pie. Nobody had any cause to complain."

"But some pieces of the pie were bigger than others, no?" asked Polly.

"Yeah," said Carole. "And no offense here, but you know

that honest and aboveboard is a concept that a lot of people don't agree with. Maybe that's why Hosea was killed."

"For being honest?"

Carole and Polly nodded.

"Now you're making me lose my faith in humanity," said Frank, pushing his chair back from the table. Carole expected him to settle down on the recliner to watch the sports network, but instead he went into the den. She followed him, surprised to see him seat himself at the desk and open a folder.

"Everything okay?" she asked, worried that there was a new development in the case against him. "Did the DA come up with new evidence or something?"

"Nah." He smiled at her. "Don't worry, Vince is on the job. No, this is about the fire; the insurance adjuster has some questions about the value we're claiming for lost material."

"Lost material?"

"Yeah. Pipe and stuff that got damaged in the fire. He says what we're claiming is too high based on the recovered debris, something like that."

Carole thought guiltily of Big Frank's offcuts and decided some things were better left unsaid. "That's what insurance companies do, right?"

Frank chuckled. "Yeah, babe. That's what they do. They like to collect the premiums, but they sure don't like to pay the claims."

Carole left Frank with his paperwork, and she and Polly cleared the table and loaded the dishwasher; the buzzer on the dryer sounded, and Polly went to unload and fold the clothes. Left to her own devices, Carole wandered over to her favorite window and looked out at the view. The Coca-Cola sign was a swirl of red neon; the river gleamed in the dark, reflecting the glow of the streetlamps; the houses and restaurants on Federal Hill were all alight. And just beyond the bridge, in the shadows, lay the Factory.

As she looked out, something Mitch Chase had said that day at the hospital popped into her mind. Something about there being plenty of misery to go around. At the time, she'd just thought he was referring to the inevitable delays caused by Hosea's death and the fire. But what if he'd meant something else? And now the insurance company was questioning their claims. What if the company demanded an investigation of their accounts. Was everything as aboveboard as Frank claimed?

Come to think of it, she didn't like the way Frank had dismissed her suspicions about the Factory. He'd been awfully quick to tell her she was on the wrong track, but how did he know? What did he know? What was he keeping from her? She could see his reflection in the window, sitting there at his desk. He wasn't studying the paperwork; he was just sitting there, staring at nothing. That wasn't like him; his attitude was all wrong. He wasn't the kind of guy who sat around doing nothing; something was bugging him, and she didn't think it was the insurance company. Was it because of the attack? Did he think she was lying about not being raped; did he think she was spoiled goods?

No, she decided, she was being paranoid. Frank knew she'd be a lot more upset if that creep had succeeded in raping her. And then he surprised her, the old fox, by suddenly heaving himself out of his chair and coming to her, slipping his arms around her waist and nuzzling her neck. "Are you really okay?"

"Yeah," she said, placing her hands over his. "It was scary, but he got the worst of it. Even the cannoli were okay."

"You gotta take care of yourself; you gotta do it for me. I don't know what I'd do without you."

This wasn't like Frank, not at all, and Carole was touched. She felt tears stinging her eyes, and she gave his hands a squeeze.

"Well," he said, releasing her, "I guess I'll take the dog out."

Talk about out of character, thought Carole, who couldn't remember a single time when Frank had volunteered to walk the dog.

While he was gone, Carole gave Gary Strazullo a call. "Do me a favor," she said, "and check out Chase and Mooney. I think they may be up to something over at the Factory."

"No problem," he said.

Maybe no problem, thought Carole, maybe otherwise. "And Gary," she added, "be real careful, okay?"

When Frank came back with Poopsie, they all three settled on the sofa to watch a Netflix movie; Polly had withdrawn to her room to write notes and make calls to some of her friends in France. Carole wasn't looking forward to going to bed; she was afraid she'd have trouble sleeping, so she stayed up after Frank yawned a few times and declared he was turning in. She watched *The Late Show*, made it through the monologue, but the guest was Rachel Maddow and she couldn't take that woman, so she gave up and brushed her teeth, took a few Tylenol PMs, and headed to bed.

It was no good; every time she closed her eyes, she replayed the frightening attack. The way the guy grabbed her from behind, catching her by surprise, and the way he'd pushed her down on the stairs. She remembered the look in his eyes and the way his weight pressed down on her, on her neck, and the overwhelming sense of fear that had flooded every cell in her body. It wasn't just in her mind, either; she felt her breaths coming in short pants and her stomach contracting and her legs itching to move. She checked the clock; it was one in the morning, so she got up and peed and took a couple more tablets, even did some yoga stretches. That seemed to work, and she drifted off for a few hours, but at four o'clock she was awake again, and she knew she'd never get back to sleep. She went out to the living room and curled up on the couch with a couple of pillows, an afghan, and one of Polly's French magazines. A few minutes later, Poopsie appeared, stretching and yawning and shaking her collar.

Why not, thought Carole. At least walking would relieve the cramps and tingly sensations in her legs. So she slipped back through the bedroom and into her California Closets walk-in, where she got into her track suit and clunky, dog-walking boots. Back in the living room, she went to the door, where she clipped the leash onto Poopsie's collar.

Outside, the air was fresh and cool. It was a clear night; the sky had lightened from black to deep azure, dotted with stars and a silver sliver of moon. Maybe she was crazy to be out alone, but she wasn't going to live in fear, not her. Not when it felt so darn good to move and breathe the fresh, clean, early-morning air. She loped up the hill and turned onto Smith Street. Nobody was out this early; there was only an occasional car, probably somebody coming off the night shift or heading in for an early-morning job. The lights were on at Dunkin' Donuts, so Carole walked that way and ducked inside with Poopsie to get a coffee. The guy behind the counter, still groggy himself, didn't seem to mind about the dog. Then, coffee in hand, she continued along Smith Street and down Caverly, past Frank-O's apartment building. He ought to be coming home soon, she thought, sending up a heartfelt prayer of gratitude. For Frank-O and for herself. It could have been so much worse.

Then she was down by the river, and the sky was brightening, blue giving way to gray, and Poopsie was in hunting mode, nose to the ground and tail straight back, on the prowl for fowl. Carole smiled at her little joke; it felt good to be strong and alive, keeping pace with the dog. For once, she wasn't pulling and yanking at the leash; they were moving together in the same groove, covering ground as the sky gradually took on a rosy tint and Carole found herself, once again, at the Factory.

Chapter Twenty

Carole wasn't about to go wandering through the fenced construction site, even though the chain-link gate was wide open. It was still pretty dark, for one thing, and as a contractor's wife, she knew such places could be dangerous. As numerous signs advised, it was a hard-hat area, meaning that an individual could fall into an open sewer or get hit on the head by a falling timber. Accidents happened; workers occasionally got hurt when unstable scaffolding collapsed, ditches caved in, or heavy machinery toppled over.

She stood for a moment with Poopsie, surveying the site, which had a stark beauty in the early-morning light. The rosy sky was reflected in the new windows of the apartment building, and the black, twisted branches of the leafless trees were a dramatic contrast to the lightening sky. But the empty shell of the burned building was an unpleasant reminder of the fire that sent shivers down her spine.

"C'mon, let's go home," she urged Poopsie, giving the leash a little tug.

Poopsie planted her legs and pulled against the leash, straining to go through the gate.

"Come!" ordered Carole, in her best obedience-class voice.

As usual, it made absolutely no impression on Poopsie. She was pulling against the leash as hard as she could, looking for all the world like a ridiculously undersized sled dog.

"Breakfast!" said Carole, employing one of Poopsie's favorite words. "I've got bacon for you."

Poopsie wasn't the least bit interested in bacon; she was interested in something on the construction site and was bound and determined to check it out. She gave one last heroic tug, and the plastic catch on her rhinestone collar snapped, throwing Carole off balance and right onto her bottom. Poopsie was a white blur, racing through the construction site with her nose to the ground and her tail up.

Carole was furious and frustrated. "Poopsie!" she yelled, stamping her foot, but she might as well have called the wind or tried to halt the tide. Poopsie had a mind of her own, and she wasn't going to give up the chase when every microscopic fiber of DNA, carefully refined through decades of selective breeding, was telling her to follow that alluring, irresistible scent, whatever it was.

Carole sighed and looked down at the broken collar and leash. The dog trainer had warned her about this, recounting horror stories of dogs that broke free and ran across train tracks and superhighways with predictable results, and even dogs that ran until they got themselves lost or dropped from exhaustion. Fortunately for her, the site was fenced, but it was enormous, covering acres of riverside property. The only way she had any chance of recovering Poopsie was to follow her. And now, she could see much better since the sun was rising, and, with luck, she wouldn't stumble into an open drainage ditch or step on any live wires.

She picked her way carefully, stepping over rocks and scrap wood and broken bottles, the wind-tossed discarded snack bags and dead leaves here and there. The air still smelled sharp and sooty from the fire. She was headed in the direction she'd last seen the dog taking, running past the burned-out building and the almost finished apartment building, deep into the heart of the complex. Carole scanned the area, looking through the neat rows of coiled tubing and pallets of brick and shingles, hoping for a glimpse of white tail. She called the dog's name a few times, but soon gave that up, realizing she was yelling into the wind, which carried her voice in the wrong direction.

She was down by the river now; she could see a little flock of ducks paddling along. Just the sort of thing Poopsie loved, but she was nowhere to be seen in the trees and undergrowth that lined the banks. Carole turned around, unsure whether she should continue into unfamiliar terrain or just retrace her steps, when she heard a single, sharp bark. Poopsie!

The sound seemed to come from one of the little temporary structures Frank was using as storage sheds, so she trotted toward it; as she drew closer, she noticed a Chase and Mooney stake truck with its engine running. Odd, she thought, so early in the morning. Very odd. She could see the CAPOBIANCO sign clear as day over the door of the shed, which she now realized was wide open.

Frank would never, ever leave a storage shed unlocked; that was something she had no doubt about. Plumbing fittings were expensive. In addition to the copper pipe, there were dozens of fancy Bye-Bye Toilets, each worth over a thousand dollars. There was no way he would leave such valuable material in an open shed, available for any scavenger who happened by. Or for a rival contractor like Chase and Mooney, who could cut costs by stealing from the Capobiancos. Deeply suspicious, Carole ducked down behind a pallet of bricks and waited, watching to see what was going on.

She didn't have to wait long before Mitch Chase and another man—a man in a black hoodie who looked a lot like the guy who attacked her in the stairwell and who happened to be limping—appeared in the doorway, carrying a bundle of pipe between them that they heaved into the truck. It landed with a tremendous racket; they weren't at all concerned about making a lot of noise. Carole's jaw dropped; she could hardly believe what she was seeing. How low could people go? Mitch Chase was supposed to be a friend—a business rival, sure, but somebody who grew up in Providence, just like Frank, and went to the same schools, starting with kindergarten. They both played on the same high school football team, for God's sake. And even though Frank had made sure he'd gotten a contract for a big part of the project, the HVAC, here he was, stealing Frank's copper pipe, and she gasped in shock, watching as the two carefully heaved a boxed Bye-Bye Toilet onto the truck.

She was reaching for her cell phone to call Frank and alert him to what was happening when Poopsie suddenly appeared, coming around the corner of the building. Tony and his accomplice didn't notice the dog; they were heading back inside the shed to pilfer more stuff, so Carole peeked out from behind the bricks and tried to catch the dog's attention by whispering and waving.

Poopsie saw her—she stopped in her tracks and looked directly at Carole—but decided to ignore her whispers and frantic gestures. Instead of coming like a good dog, she continued around to the rear of the stake truck and jumped onto the tailgate. Carole sent up a quick little prayer for heavenly protection and dashed toward the truck, intending to grab Poopsie and get the hell out of there before Mitch and his accomplice came back.

She wasn't fast enough. She'd just reached the truck when they appeared in the doorway. "Hey!" yelled Mitch, dropping his end of the bundle of pipe, making a huge clatter.

Carole figured her best option was to play dumb blonde. "My dog ran away; she's in your truck!" she exclaimed, holding up the leash. "Her collar broke, and she got away from me."

"Oh, yeah?" said Mitch. He sounded suspicious and was coming closer.

"Wow, Mitch! I'm so glad to see you," said Carole, her heart thudding like a runaway train. "Can you help me get the dog?"

"Sure," said Mitch, taking the leash.

"You could just loop it around her neck," suggested Carole, keeping her eyes on Mitch and ignoring the other guy. She didn't want him to get the idea that she recognized him.

The good part about all this was that Poopsie was really cornered. Carole and Mitch were both standing at the back of the truck, and she was watching them warily.

"You sure start work early," said Carole, keeping up the fiction that Mitch wasn't doing anything wrong in the hope of reassuring him that she was so dumb she hadn't realized that he was up to no good.

"Yeah, early bird and all that," said Mitch, hoisting himself up onto the truck with a grunt, leash in hand.

Seeing him coming, Poopsie began digging frantically under a tarp.

"What the hell!" he muttered, as she produced a rusty old rag, then nimbly dashed through his legs and leaped off the back of the truck. Tail wagging, she dropped her prize at Carole's feet and sat, giving Carole a big, doggy grin. Carole picked up the rag, intending to give it to Mitch. It was stiff, like a cleaning rag that was soaked in liquid and then left to dry, and she realized with horror that the reddish-brown stains she had assumed were rust weren't rust at all, but dried blood.

Next thing she knew, Mitch and the other guy had grabbed her by the elbows and were dragging her back to the shed. She was screaming as loud as she could and trying to dig her heels into the ground. Poopsie was barking frantically, circling around them, and Carole was twisting this way and that, trying to break free. She managed to get one arm free and was pulling away, but Mitch yanked her back, catching her around her neck and clamping his hand over her mouth. Poopsie didn't like this; she decided she'd played nice long enough and lunged at his heel, biting down on his Achilles tendon.

Mitch screamed with pain and released his hold on Carole, trying to kick the dog away, but Poopsie hung on, just like her wild canine cousins did when they brought down a deer. The other guy still had Carole and was dragging her toward the shed, using a move similar to the cross-chest carry Carole had learned in a Red Cross lifesaving class, which she was pretty sure was not his goal. She was kicking and screaming her head off; she was trying to bite his arm or claw his eyes, and she finally managed to grab his hair and was yanking it as hard as she could. "You're not getting away this time," he growled, and next thing she knew, they were hit by an enormous force that threw them both to the ground. Stunned, Carole shook her head and made out a huge, enormous animal that had attached itself to her attacker's arm. He was writhing and screaming in pain as she got to her feet, staring in disbelief to find he was struggling with a massive pit bull.

Carole was scrambling about, looking for a weapon she could use to protect herself, when a voice yelled, "Hold!"

The pit bull obeyed, keeping his victim's arm firmly clenched in his powerful jaws and planting his enormous paws on his chest. That guy wasn't going anywhere.

Poopsie, on the other hand, had let go of Mitch's leg but was keeping him at bay, prancing around him and growling, lunging at his ankles whenever he tried to move. Carole reached again for her cell phone, but she could already hear sirens in the distance.

"I called the cops," said the pit bull's owner, and Carole turned to face him, recognizing the kid who worked at the Esplanade.

"Joao!" she exclaimed, as a couple of cruisers screamed through the gate, blue lights flashing. "I think you saved my life. I owe you big-time."

He gave the dog a look, checking that it was maintaining its hold on the guy, then smiled at Carole. "You got any more of that lasagna?"

This time, it was different in the courtroom. The prosecutor, the judge, even the reporters and photographers were all smiles. All charges were dropped against Frank, and he left a hero, a shining example of how the justice system worked to spare the innocent and convict the guilty. Carole didn't quite buy it, and she doubted the others did, either, but maybe that's why they were all so happy. It didn't happen often, but for one shining moment, truth and justice had really triumphed.

Poopsie wasn't there, of course, but Carole considered her the real hero. Of course, she had to share some credit with Joao and his pit bull, Murphy, but Poopsie was the one who found the blood-soaked rag that linked Mitch Chase to Hosea's murder. The prosecutor had outlined the case against him at the arraignment, alleging that Mitch became angry when Hosea demanded that he replace some substandard ductwork at the Factory. Fueled by rage, he'd grabbed a pipe and bludgeoned Hosea to death.

"But what I don't understand," said Polly, when the whole family—even Connie, who'd managed to get away from the law office and Joao from the Esplanade—gathered for a celebratory lunch at Café Nuovo, "is why they thought Frank did it."

"It was Mitch," said Connie. "Mitch threw a whole lot of suspicion on Pop when the police interviewed him. He claimed that Pop really had it out for Hosea; he said the two of them were always at odds. He basically substituted Pop's name for his own, recounting various arguments he himself had had with Hosea. My friend who's in the prosecutor's office told me all about it."

"Who is this friend?" asked Polly, curious. Was this a possible lover?

"Jenny Fornisanti."

"Christina's daughter?" asked Mom.

"Yeah. She's a secretary there."

"Didn't I tell you? Talk to the secretaries?" said Carole.

"Right, Ma. And it was good advice." Connie took a sip of water. "But to get back to what Jenny told me, the case against Pop got stronger when they interviewed Hosea's neighbors at Prospect Place. They all remembered how angry Pop had been when Hosea rejected his offer and how Pop said he wanted to kill him."

"People say that all the time," said Frank-O, adding a shrug.

"It was just an expression," said Frank, consulting the wine list.

"They now think that Mitch was hoping that, by setting up Pop, he'd not only get away with murder, but he'd pick up the plumbing contract, too," continued Connie.

"Fat chance of that," said Paulie. "He's got a lousy reputation."

"Yeah, it was thanks to Frank that he got the HVAC, and then he couldn't even get that right," added Big Frank.

"But then the whole job was put on hold," said Frank. "I guess that's when he got the not-so-bright idea of stealing our pipe."

"What about the other guy?" asked Joao. "The guy Murphy took down."

"Yeah, the guy who attacked me in the parking garage," recalled Carole, with a shudder.

"Vlad something, something Russian," said Connie. "Romanov maybe."

"Like the czar?" asked Polly.

"Maybe not," admitted Connie. "I'm bad with Russian names. Anyway, Jenny said he tried to cut a deal and was quick to say he was just doing what Mitch told him to do, but they've got him on aiding and abetting . . ."

"That's all?" Carole was disappointed.

"But he was on parole, which he violated, so it looks like they're both going to be spending some serious time in the slammer."

"*Incroyable*," said Polly, shaking her head. "*Quel cauchemar.*"

"What a nightmare," said Carole, translating, wondering how much longer Polly planned to stay with them.

"Very true, but all's well that ends well," said Ma, who was taking a Shakespeare class at the senior center.

"I think this calls for champagne," said Frank, signaling the sommelier. "I want to make a toast to my beautiful, smart wife, who saved my ass."

"And don't forget our little dog, too," said Carole, smiling at her husband.

Frank, busy beckoning the sommelier, didn't answer.